SLEIGHT OF HAND (VIGILANTE JUSTICE SERIES)

Bristol Kelley Book One

V F STREETS

Page Turner Books

For Matt,
Thank you for being patient with me as I walk this path

GET the prequel to Sleight of Hand FREE

Simply by signing up to for the (no-spam) newsletter, I'll send you a free prequel to Sleight of Hand - and an extra little bonus -

Find out more at the end of the book.

Chapter 1

BRISTOL STUDIED the man lying at her feet. His tweed jacket had patches on the elbows, and he was wearing boat shoes. All that was missing was a bow tie.

He looked fit and may have been attractive, but it was hard to tell with part of his face missing.

Bristol shook her head and scoffed. She had no trouble remaining unemotional at work, but seeing someone with his face blown off was repulsive. You can almost taste a shot like that, in the face at close range. It has a tang, similar to the metallic smell of blood that now filled the small space. Bristol could imagine a smug expression on his face before it was removed.

She reached into her back pocket and grabbed out a pair of latex gloves, stretching them onto her steady hands as she gave the man another scan. His hair stuck out at a strange angle, stiff with blood or pomade; it was hard to tell in the low light.

The man's right arm was tucked behind his back. Bristol leaned over, pulled the arm out, then ran her thumb across his knuckles. She yanked back his sleeve and examined the watch on his wrist. She checked the time against her own. 11:43 p.m. She was meticulous about keeping the right time and apparently so was he.

Bristol stepped around the man and lifted his other hand. A large green stone gleamed against a fat gold band on his ring finger.

She dropped the hand and reached into her pocket to pull out her phone, then lifted it above her head, over the man. After the phone made its faux camera click, she checked the picture to make sure she had the angle right then looked up at the girl standing farther back into the cabin of the yacht, near the helm. She was shifting from one foot to the other, her arms crossed against the cool air creeping into the cabin.

The girl was around nineteen with what appeared to be a two-hour makeup routine. Her nails were manicured and most likely fake, and judging by the pushup bra that peeked out from her shirt, her original intention was to either impress or seduce the dead man at her feet.

The girl snapped her gum a couple times. "Is this gonna take long?"

Bristol nodded at the Smith and Wesson laying on the couch. "Can you grab your gun and just hold it up for a sec?"

"Why?"

"So I can do my job."

The girl snapped her gum again but obeyed. Things ran much smoother when people did what Bristol asked instead of arguing.

Standing in a Charlie's Angels pose, the girl pouted

her lips. That would work just fine for Bristol. She held up her phone and took another picture.

"Wait, can I see?" the girl said.

Bristol held the girl's gaze long enough to make her annoyance clear, then checked the picture. She selected the two photos and hit send.

"If you're going to put that up on social media, I want to see it first."

"It's not going on social media." This girl had never had to suffer the consequences of her actions, and here Bristol was preserving that tradition.

The girl clicked her tongue and tossed the gun back onto the white leather couch. "I don't know why my dad called you. Can't we just put the gun in his hand and call it suicide?"

"If you wanted to do that, you should have planned it better."

"Hey, I didn't plan this." The girl jammed her hands on her hips and looked at the dead man but then made a face and averted her eyes.

Bristol tucked the phone back in her pocket and moved into the galley, running a gloved finger across the marble countertop. A pair of onyx salt and pepper shakers, in the shape of cats, were the only occupants of the counter. She wasn't a fan of cats, or small dogs for that matter.

"Do you have a small dog?" she asked the girl without looking at her.

"Yeah, why?"

Bristol nodded. "Just confirming a theory." She pulled open the door under the sink and spotted what she was looking for — a bottle of oil. She read the label, not because it mattered but because she couldn't help herself. Ultra Premium Extra Virgin Olive Oil. Expensive. She had baby oil in her bag, but cooking oil would be better if forensics found it. It could be explained away more easily.

She walked back with the oil and crouched next to the man. "Can I ask why you shot your professor?"

"How'd you know he was my professor?"

Bristol sighed and dipped her head. If this job didn't involve people who were alive, she'd like it a lot better. Instead of explaining, she lied. "Lucky guess. So, what, he didn't give you an A in history class?" She flattened the man's left hand. It was just beginning to stiffen.

"Close." The girl shifted on her feet. "I was shagging him for an A. He told me tonight I was only worth a C. Hey, how'd you know he was my hist — "

" — Lucky guess." If she didn't need the money, she would have walked out right then. She had standards.

The girl started chewing on one of her fake nails. "What's with all the questions?"

Bristol poured oil onto her hand then rubbed it onto the man's finger. "Call it professional curiosity." She had never tested oils of different price points for suitability to the job at hand and made a mental note to experiment later.

The girl took a step closer, leaning forward to get a better view of what Bristol was doing. "So, you gonna tell me why we can't make it look like a suicide?"

Bristol paused and looked up. "What's with all the questions?"

The girl curled her lip. "Call it *professional curiosity.*"

Bristol bit the inside of her cheek then pointed across the man. "He's lefthanded."

The girl's eyes lit up, and Bristol knew what she would say before she said it.

"But you just pointed at his right hand." Her voice held the delight of a student correcting her teacher.

Bristol took a deep breath. "His watch is on the right."

"So?"

"People wear their watch on the hand opposite the one they write with."

The girl looked at her wrists then held up a gold watch on her left arm and smiled triumphantly. "That's pretty cool. But what does *that* have to do with suicide?"

"If it *were* suicide, he wouldn't have shot himself on the right side." She worked the ring off the finger and smiled. Expensive or not, the oil did its job.

The girl was now eyeing her. "My dad is paying you, ya know. You don't have to steal stuff." Bristol ignored her, but the girl crossed her arms and continued. "But I still don't understand. Why couldn't he have shot himself with his right hand?"

Bristol stood and put the ring on her middle finger, stone facing inward, pressing her fingers together to hold it in place. "Let me show you." She glanced down at the girl's watch, then walked over and slapped her hard across the right side of the face.

The girl spun and fell onto the couch.

"Bitch!" She grabbed at her face with her right hand and reached for the gun with the other.

She lifted it awkwardly toward Bristol, who reached out and spun her hand around the girl's wrist, taking the gun from her easily. "See how important the dominant hand is when handling a gun?"

The girl's dad came stomping through the door at Bristol's back. "What the hell is going on in here?" He had been waiting on the dock; Bristol had told him not to disturb her.

"Look what she did!" the girl shrieked, pulling her hand away from her face for a second.

"Suggest to your daughter that she lower her voice," Bristol said as she moved back into the galley where she could monitor the two of them. She held the gun at her side and kept her finger near the trigger.

The dad jammed his hands on his hips the same way the daughter had. Bristol bit her lip to keep from smiling.

He jutted his chin forward, "Wha'd you do that for?"

"Do you want your daughter to go to prison?"

His eyes flicked to the gun then back to Bristol's face. "What does hitting her have to do with it?" he said, keeping his voice low.

"If we're going to convince the DA that this was self-defense, it needs to *look* like it." She had enjoyed it a little too.

The girl's dad looked from his daughter to Bristol and then back to his daughter, who stood with her mouth gaping, blood beginning to leak between her fingers. He fidgeted with the bottom of his shirt, then went back out the door.

Bristol tucked the gun into the back of her pants then grabbed her bag from where she had left it next to the door. Pulling out a tissue, she cleaned the excess oil off the man's hand and the ring. She slipped the ring back in place, twisting it around toward his palm, careful not to remove the new blood and flesh on it.

She took a couple of steps back over to the girl, who flinched at her approach but didn't move back. Stupid, but at least she showed some guts.

Bristol punched her in the stomach.

The girl doubled over, unable to breathe. A few seconds later, she managed a shallow wheeze. Bristol waited until she could take a full breath before shoving her hard against the table, hopefully severely bruising a rib. She didn't always get her force right. Something else worth experimenting with.

She bent over to help the girl, who had turned a sickening shade of gray. Maybe the force had been a bit much.

"At least now you had a reason to shoot him, right?"

She slipped her arm around the girl, who looked at her with frightened eyes. Bristol was personally familiar with that look.

"It's okay. I'm done now." She helped the girl maneuver around the dead man and directed her out the door, where her dad was waiting, facing the other way. He turned when he heard them emerge and rushed over, wrapping a protective arm around his daughter, probably for the first time in a long time. He looked at Bristol with narrowed eyes. "I'm not paying the full rate.

Bashing my daughter didn't need to be part of the plan."

Bristol pulled her gloves off. "You called me because you had a problem and I fix problems. You want people to be on her side? She has to look like a victim. Besides, I've got photos that will be sent to the appropriate authorities if I either don't return home or don't receive my full fee. Oh — " She retrieved her bag from inside and pulled out a business card. "Here's a good lawyer you should hire. She'll coach your daughter on what to say and how to act."

"We have a lawyer," the dad said, his teeth set.

She thrust the card toward him but softened her voice. "Take it. She specializes in these cases."

He looked at the card but didn't move. "She understands the situation in full?"

"In full."

He stared at it for two long seconds then lifted his hand and took the card, sliding it into the pocket of his trousers.

The sound of a boat traveling down the canal rose from the left. Bristol leaned down as it advanced, pulling a cloth from her bag, then turned back as it moved past. She grabbed the gun from the back of her pants with the cloth and held it out to the girl, the cloth wrapped around the muzzle. The girl took it and dropped her arm back to her side, her other arm wrapped around her middle, the gash on her cheek forgotten. She looked like she was going to throw up, and her breathing was erratic.

"Probably be a good idea to get her to hospital now.

Have a nice evening." Bristol shouldered her bag and stepped up onto the side of the boat, then dropped down to the dock that led back up to the house.

The boat that had passed was mooring at a dock on the other side of the water, a few houses down. Bristol stepped back into the thick shadows. She saw a man half dragging a woman or a kid, she couldn't tell from this distance, toward the house. Two more large men were walking at the back. If she were a police officer, she would find the scene suspicious enough to investigate. Everything about that formation said trouble. But she wasn't a cop. She also didn't move.

Her phone dinged, and she pulled it out, still watching over the water as the group entered the house. Then she looked down to read the text that had just come in. Her breath hitched, and she turned and bolted for her car.

Chapter 2

BRISTOL BIT her lip as she ran another red light. It was late enough that the traffic was sparse, but she didn't have the time to deal with police. She rolled through the last stop sign and pulled up outside her apartment building.

Pushing her shoulder into the car door, she tumbled out and only just pulled her bag clear as she slammed the door shut behind her and sprinted across the courtyard.

The key jammed in the main door lock for her complex, and she came close to breaking it in two but finally got it open and bolted up the three flights of stairs, arriving at the apartment next to hers.

She knocked rapidly then tried the knob. It was unlocked. As she eased the door open, she peeked her head around. "Mrs. D?"

She caught sight of the eighty-two-year-old woman hanging half out the window on the other side of the living room. Bristol ran over, putting a hand on either side of her waist.

"Oh!" The woman jumped.

"What are you doing? Come back in here." Bristol said, pulling gently. The woman smelled of medicated cream and fifty-year-old perfume.

"Oh, Bristol," Her voice was frail but even at her age, the woman could still get around, which wasn't always a good thing. "I'm so glad you came."

"Is everything all right? I thought you were hurt."

Mrs. Deacon put a hand across her heart and shook her head. "Yes, well, my cat's stuck out on the ledge." She shook her head again and swallowed. "If anything happened to Sheba, I don't know what I'd do."

Bristol's shoulders dropped, and she pinched her lips together.

A couple months ago, she had come home and heard whimpering coming from the apartment. The poor woman had fallen and was stuck for several hours with no family or friends to call. Bristol had asked why she hadn't called 911. Mrs. Deacon had responded, "Oh, they're very busy. I don't want to bother them" and waved away Bristol's concern.

Bristol normally kept people at a distance, but she couldn't stand the thought of Mrs. D being in pain and on her own again, so she gave her her cell number and made her promise to get in touch if there was ever another emergency. She didn't consider cats an emergency.

"Here," she said, taking Mrs. Deacon's arm and directing her to the couch.

The apartment was identical to Bristol's but backwards, with an open-plan kitchen, enough space for a small dining table, and a living area with the bedroom and bathroom next to that. Mrs. Deacon had skipped the dining table and instead set her couch facing the kitchen, with a TV on the countertop and a coffee table in the middle.

"You sit down here and wrap this blanket around you." The air had continued to cool. Winter was arriving early in LA this year.

"But what about Sheba?" The woman said in protest, trying to rise.

"Cats *do* have nine lives you know. I've seen the videos. They can fall from much higher than the third floor and be fine." As soon as the words had emerged from her lips, she regretted it. Mrs. Deacon's face slackened, and her eyes went wide. Bristol put her hands up in surrender. "I'll get your cat."

She tried to keep the annoyance out of her voice but failed. Fortunately, Mrs. Deacon seemed only relieved. She picked at the fuzz on the blanket and started humming.

Bristol went to the window and leaned out. The cat sat about five feet away, licking her paw like a queen. Bristol held out her hand and rubbed her index finger and thumb together, then added kissing noises. The cat stopped and looked at her, then continued its grooming.

Bristol gripped the windowsill and breathed out. "This cannot be how my night ends," she mumbled.

"What's that dear?"

"Have you ever thought of getting a ground-floor

apartment? Then you wouldn't have to worry about your cat being up so high."

"Sheba and I like the view," she said as Bristol turned in from the window. The woman's face changed, and a strange smile crossed her face. "You know, you are a very lovely young lady. Are there any special men in your life?"

"Uh, you don't have any cat food around here by any chance?"

"Oh, yes, yes, under the sink."

Bristol gratefully turned away from Mrs. Deacon and headed for the kitchen.

She pulled open the door and found a box of dry cat food, a generic brand. She didn't know much about cats, but she had a feeling that the Queen of Sheba would not be impressed with her offering.

A fishy smell puffed out from the box as she grabbed a handful.

Tucking her fist around behind her, she went back to the window. When she held her hand out, the cat looked at her hand and walked forward but stayed out of reach, poking her nose out for a sniff before turning and brushing her tail across Bristol's fingertips. The cat then turned again and looked at her.

Bristol threw the food at Sheba who flattened her ears but then stretched forward and ate a piece that had landed in front of her.

Bristol would have yelled but didn't want to give her the satisfaction. Instead, she turned back into the room, drumming her fingers on the windowsill. *I can save a girl from a murder charge, but I can't get a goddamn cat inside.* "Do you have any tuna or anything?"

"I've got canned salmon, but that's for my breakfast tomorrow."

"You eat salmon for breakfast? How about *I* make you breakfast tomorrow."

"Oh, that would be lovely dear, but I've smelled your cooking. I think I'll look after myself if you don't mind."

"You are a very wise woman."

Bristol spotted a woven basket with a pile of yarn and a pair of knitting needles sticking out the top. "I don't suppose that yarn is free?"

"Oh no, that's a sweater I'm making for a friend."

"Right. I think I might have something at my place. I'll be back in a minute."

When Bristol opened the door to her apartment, the weariness from the night hit her hard. She tossed her bag to the side and shut the door so she could have a minute before tackling the cat problem again. She rubbed her face hard as she moved to the kitchen. If she remembered correctly, there was a pile of canned food she had bought when she moved into the apartment a few years ago to avoid grocery shopping for a while. It was possible she had bought tuna, and it was most likely still there. Eating out was more her style these days.

She pushed boxes and cans around in the cupboard and found three that looked promising. One was tiny corn cobs, but the other two were tuna. She tossed one in the air and caught it against her chest as she turned.

Movement at the bottom of the door caught her eye.

A slip of paper was being pushed under the door. She wasn't a fan of surprises or secret notes.

Tossing the cans onto the couch, she dove for the door, yanking it open. No one was there, but she caught sight of a bulky figure down the hall. She resisted the urge to yell out. If he didn't know he was being pursued, he might slow down. If he had something to say, he could say it to her face.

She took off down the hall and grabbed hold of the corner of the wall, using her momentum to swing herself around, and almost crashed into the man who had waited for her and was swinging for her face. She had just enough time to lift her arms in defense as the punch smashed into her. Her legs slipped from underneath her, and she crashed to the floor. Pulling her legs back, ready to kick, she prepared herself for the onslaught, but no attack came. She sprang back up and took off again. By the time she reached the final turn and got out the door, the man had jumped into a white van and was gone. She ran out to the street to get a glimpse of the license plate, but there wasn't one.

Breathing hard, she kicked a pebble and headed back to the building. That wouldn't be a love note waiting for her. Whoever it was knew enough to expect her to pursue them and was ready with a punch to her face. She wasn't thrilled that that person knew her address.

She pulled on the main door. Locked. Things were not going well. She banged her head lightly on the door a couple times then buzzed Mrs. Deacon and waited, picturing the woman asleep on the couch. She had just buzzed again when a pear-shaped woman with big teeth came out the door.

"Hiya," the woman, somewhere in her forties, said. "Forget your key?"

"Ah, yeah."

"It's a good thing I'm headed out so late. I have a friend who's in a bad way right now."

Bristol gave her an obligatory smile, the closed lips kind. The woman blinked a couple times when she didn't respond with more, so Bristol felt compelled to say something. "Well, it's a good thing you're such a great friend, otherwise I could have been stuck out here all night." That got a big smile from the woman, turning her face into a wall of teeth. She patted Bristol on her arm as she walked past.

I really don't understand people.

When she got back to her neighbor's door, Bristol could hear *Jeopardy* emanating from Mrs. Deacon's TV. She'd be fine for a bit longer.

Back in her apartment, Bristol picked up the white envelope. *Why bother to use an envelope?* It wasn't sealed and contained half a piece of paper that had been ripped off a pad. It was cheap and flimsy. She unfolded it and read: *Meet me at Alfonso's Cafe at 9am tomorrow. I've got a job for you.*

She caught a whiff of cigar from the paper, but it didn't give her any further clues.

The note read harmlessly enough, but its appearance under the door was a warning: *we know where you live.* She didn't appreciate being threatened, especially by someone who wasn't man enough to meet her face to face.

She'd turn up all right, but not because she wanted the job.

She tossed the note on the table and grabbed the cans of tuna. She had a cat to save.

When Bristol opened the door to Mrs. D's place, the old woman lifted her chin to acknowledge Bristol as she walked in but kept her eyes on the TV. "What is … Berlin?" She said to the TV. The contestant on the TV echoed, "What is Berlin."

Bristol was impressed. "Not bad Mrs. D. You know your stuff."

The woman laughed. "Just don't tell anyone this is a rerun."

"Wait, are you cheating?"

"Shh," Mrs. Deacon said, her hands gripping the blanket, "I'll take Animal Talk for 500, Alex."

Heading for the window, Bristol couldn't hold back a smile. She leaned out and saw that the cat was continuing to groom herself. Bristol cracked the can and swore as the juice spilled all over her hands. She flicked her wet hand at the cat, who was licking its white bibbed chest.

"I don't know what anyone sees in this stuff," she said to the cat.

Bristol tapped the bottom of the can on the ledge, and the cat moved closer, sniffing as it came, and finally moved within reach. Bristol grabbed it by the scruff of the neck and pulled it in. The cat scratched up her arm, hissing all the way, and Bristol had to maintain a high level of self-control to keep from throwing it. She let it go with an abrupt toss that didn't hurt the cat but made Bristol feel better then shut the window.

"Maybe next time your cat climbs out on the ledge, instead of saying you need help urgently, you could let me know your cat got out again and I'll come without breaking any laws."

Mrs. Deacon just smiled at her cat as it curled up in her lap.

"Right. Well, good night Mrs. D." Bristol said as she patted her shoulder.

The cat hissed, and Mrs. Deacon looked at her. "Well, would you listen to that? I don't think Sheba likes you very much."

"That's okay." Bristol lowered her voice. "I don't like her much either."

"What was that?"

"I said I hope you have a good night."

"Thank you, dear. You too. I'll let you know if I have any more trouble with my cat."

"Great."

○○

With the night finally over, Bristol went straight for a shower. She stood in front of the full-length mirror and noticed a bruise on her thigh she hadn't seen before but wasn't surprised. At five-foot-eight, she wasn't short, but her slight frame often caused people to underestimate her. After the guys at the gym where she trained realized her ability, it wasn't long before they stopped pulling punches.

She raked her long dark hair from a topknot, pulling at the tangles. Her thoughts drifted back to what she had seen at the dock, across the inlet.

Something was wrong, and it wasn't just that a person had been dragged into the house. It made little sense why they would do that when there were houses all along there whose residents could see what was happening. Unless they wanted someone to see. Either way, it wasn't her problem. She spent all her time making things appear different than they were, and sometimes it felt like everyone was doing it too. She looked down at her scratched-up arm. The bleeding had stopped, but when she flexed her forearm, one scratch opened up again. She couldn't go helping everywhere she was needed. That's how people got hurt.

Pushing the concerned curiosity away, she got in the shower and let the steaming water pour in rivulets down her body. The whoosh of water over her ears drowned out any further thoughts.

The shower relaxed her, but the note under her door was prodding the back of her mind like something caught, and she didn't know how to shake it loose.

Wrapped up in an enormous fluffy bathrobe, Bristol pulled her hair around her shoulder, braiding it as she padded into the kitchen to pour herself half a glass of pinot. She never had more than half a glass. She liked to be in control, and she wasn't in control if she couldn't think straight. She sat in the armchair that faced the window and stretched her legs across the space to rest her feet on the coffee table.

Leaving the wine on the table to her side, her fingers found the ridges in the fabric of the arm of the chair and she leaned her head back as she ran her fingernails along the trough. Her arm was still stinging from the scratches but not enough to keep her from drifting off into asleep.

Chapter 3

COLE GULPED the last of his coffee and leaned back on the park bench, crossing his legs with his ankle resting on his knee. He stretched an arm along the top of the bench. He had a long reach that didn't leave much room for anyone else.

A stiff wind was blowing across the park, and he tugged at the collar of his leather jacket. He had pulled it out of the closet as soon as the air hinted at a cool change. It was a gift from his dad. He expected the thought to bring a pang, but it didn't. His dad had made the appearance of an effort with the gift when he left for college. And now, after more than ten years, it was finally perfect.

He loved this time of year. Living in the consistently warm climate of LA didn't afford him enough opportunity to dress the way he preferred. Not for a guy who grew up in Chicago.

He breathed deeply and then regretted it. His face screwing up as he tossed the empty coffee cup into the garbage next to him. He slid down the bench a little farther.

Across the street stood Lincoln Tower. It wasn't as tall as the Wilshire Grand, but it was shinier. Even on this cloudy day, the building's angles seemed to reflect rays of light that were previously invisible to the naked eye.

It held offices mostly, but one floor was being renovated.

He absentmindedly rested his hand on the round metal lunch container that sat beside him. The polished steel gleamed nearly as bright as the building he would shortly enter. He pulled his sleeve back and looked at his Rolex, a gift from himself. 9:00 on the dot. He stood and stretched, then grabbed the container and sauntered across the street. He loved days when he got out of the office, even if it meant going into someone else's.

Just before the doors opened for him, he got a glimpse of himself in the brown leather and grinned. Yeah, winter was a good time of year. He ran his fingers through his sandy hair then waved lightly at the guard on the door. The guy smiled and lifted a finger then let his eyes glaze back over and returned his attention back to nothing in particular.

If they aren't trained properly, they think if you're nice to them, you're not a threat.

He figured the guard to be about twenty-five. A lean frame but filling out at the waist. Cole guessed he had been in the job a few years. He probably thought security would provide a bit of excitement, only to be disappointed, but not motivated to make a change. He could do with better posture. Cole stretched his own shoulders back in response to his assessment.

He didn't bother glancing up at the three security cameras high on the walls. He already knew they were there.

Straight ahead was the guard at the front counter, a long termer. He was nearing sixty-five and had a shock of white hair and startling icy blue eyes.

Cole's shoes squeaked on the marble floors. The natural timber panels behind the counter softened the coldness of the floor and the chandelier lights that dripped from the ceiling added a soothing effect.

The building was designed and built by a company owned by Silas Lincoln. Cole had met him once at a fundraising dinner. He was different from most filthy rich people Cole had met over the years. He stood quite aloof but seemed to be aware of every particle of air that surrounded him. He had an edge about him that said he owned everything and everyone. Cole didn't like him much, but Robert Carlson, the one whose business inhabited the Lincoln Tower, was more overtly slimy. He was a man who liked power and money and made sure everyone knew it. He had government contracts and other rumored alliances that were top secret, or so the rumor went. More than likely the guy exaggerated his importance. That's not to say there weren't valuables in the building that needed protecting.

The guard at the desk spotted him and gave him a nod then tilted his head to the right. Cole nodded, lifted the container, and angled to the right in response.

One of the most important things Cole had ever

learned is that routine is your enemy. Especially if you have enemies. Preparation was one thing, but routine can be used against you.

Cole had been coming into the building regularly over the past couple weeks with his lunch container. It was all routine for these guys now, and that's how most of them are taught. You follow the system. The manual is king.

Cole's face spread into a wide grin as he approached the metal detectors. The majority of his success was based on the fact that people forget how to think for themselves.

He got in line behind two other people who were ushered through.

A guard in the same gray uniform as the rest of them, the least fit of the lot with a belly hanging over his belt, sat in front of a screen.

"How's it going, Ron? I've got another delivery for breakfast," Cole said in an overly bright tone, because he knew it would annoy the man.

Ron grunted. "Nice pail." This had become Ron's routine response every time Cole had come through on earlier occasions. Cole responded with his part: "With expensive breakfast comes an expensive container."

He tipped it toward Ron as though they were toasting.

"You're the best dressed delivery boy I've ever met," Ron grumbled. He obviously didn't like his job.

"They pay me well. Do you want me to put a word in? I think you'd like it." Cole kept his tone bright. It was a delicate balance, getting under people's skin. You had to annoy them enough to keep them from asking too many questions but not so much that they would go out of their way to get back at you.

The first time he came, he prepared by getting the number of one of the offices and calling up to let the lucky employee know he was randomly selected to receive a free breakfast from the best breakfast place in town. He only had to call three different numbers before someone believed him and he could legitimately bring in a fancy breakfast. That first time, the guard at the desk had called up to confirm, and Ron had put the container through the X-ray. Now the boys just removed the lid and had a look, but even that was only because they wanted to know what could be fancy enough to warrant such extravagant packaging. Cole slid the container to the side of the metal detector and over to another guard, Kyle, who he knew was thirty-two because last week he had told him about his birthday party and the girl he took home.

Kyle pulled the lid off the container and took a deep breath in. "Might have to confiscate this one," Kyle said, also routine.

Thinking of the surprise Kyle would get if he did, Cole laughed and walked through the arch to take back possession of his food.

"When are you going to bring extras for the rest of us?" Kyle asked, but Cole didn't waste time moving toward the elevators.

Like taking candy from a baby.

"If I were the boss, I would," he said as a woman in

a flattering red dress stepped off the elevators. He smiled at her. She smiled back. They always did.

He turned and watched Kyle and Ron straighten themselves. Kyle was fit, but he sucked in his gut nonetheless.

Cole stepped into the elevator with a handful of other people. All of them he had seen before.

Last week he had had a conversation with the tall skinny guy in the corner. They had been the only two on the elevator that morning, which was unusual.

Cole smiled at him as he turned and took his place. Gary was his name, if Cole remembered correctly. Gary's wife had gone out of town, and he was stuck carting the kids around to their various after-school activities. Cole had nodded and grunted his assent at the difficult things "we parents have to do for our kids." It was so easy getting people on your side. He even told the guy he had a son who also played soccer, and that his son's coach was just as frustrating. If they had stayed on the elevator long enough, the guy would have laid bare his whole life story.

Cole, on the other hand, had no plans for marriage or kids on the horizon. He wasn't against the idea, but his own parents hadn't made it and the drama it had caused was enough to put him off. So unless someone interesting enough came along to convince him otherwise, especially after fake conversations with guys like Gary, he was happy to keep things the way they were.

Cole leaned forward and pressed the button for the 45th floor, the last of the main offices. Floor 46 was being renovated, although Cole had found out from one of his contacts that work had stopped because of some decorating issue. And only people with a keycard could go above floor 46.

Everyone with him in the elevator worked below the 40th.

"Wife back yet?" Cole turned slightly, directing his question to Gary.

"Yeah, thank goodness. Everything's gone pretty much back to normal."

"Glad to hear it."

"Yeah, my son scored a goal on the weekend, too."

Cole pretended that it was the best news he'd heard all morning. "That's great!"

"Yeah." Gary was beaming. Everyone else stood uncomfortably silent.

Cole bopped his head to the cheesy music emanating from the ceiling, drumming his fingers on his leg. People are funny when they're in public places that press them up against one another. Society dictates that you pretend you're the only one there. Cole got a kick out of breaking through that haze now and then. But more importantly, it meant people are trying so hard to ignore you, they remember your odd behavior more than your appearance.

Everyone filed off floor by floor, and Cole lifted his finger to wave off the last passenger, although the man didn't make eye contact. Once Cole was alone, he pushed the button for floor 46.

Chapter 4

BRISTOL WOKE WITH A START, bolting upright in bed. She hadn't slept well.

Several times she had awoken to the same dream. She knew it was rooted in her past, so even when she woke, it stuck to her.

The glow from the clock showed it was 5 a.m. She shivered slightly but kicked the blankets off. Sleeping was highly overrated.

Unease hung at the back of her neck, and she rubbed it hard to no effect. She needed to be ready for her 9 a.m. appointment. There could be no fear in her eyes when she met whoever wrote the note.

She jerked open her closet door and pulled out a navy button-down blouse and a beige pencil skirt that fit her like a glove, then left them on the bed and went to the kitchen to turn on the kettle to make herself a cup of tea.

While she waited, she started twisting a piece of string that hung from her shirt tightly around her finger until it was lumpy. She looked at it, then slammed her other hand against the wall and let out a huff. This wasn't going to do. She went for a shower to remove some tension.

Squeezing her eyes shut as the water poured over her head, the shadows moved back in. She was huddled in a corner in the dark and a hand reached for her. She turned up the heat, breathing in the steam as her skin reddened, but the dark vacuum at her center didn't retreat. There was one other thing that helped. She rarely went to the gym early on a Friday, but if she wanted to be ready for her meeting, she would have to punch the stuffing out of something first.

She poured tea into a travel mug and dressed quickly in her usual gym attire: joggers, a mint green jersey, and her favorite well-used sneakers. She remembered the cool from the night and grabbed her sweatshirt as well, as she headed out the door.

Twenty minutes later she stood before the barn door-style entrance to a nondescript shed. There was no sign. Eli didn't want random gym junkies turning up to use his equipment. You only came here if you were invited, and the only reason Bristol was invited was because a long time ago Eli had made a promise to her mother. And she made sure she was worthy of the honor by training hard when she was there. Kickboxing was her weapon of choice, and it had served her well over the years.

The door was locked, so she banged on it with an open hand and waited.

The sky was just beginning to leak light, turning everything pasty. The pale light made the air colder. The heat from the shower had sapped out of her skin, and she pulled on the sweatshirt while she waited. Normally she'd bang again, but Eli wasn't a man to be rushed, so instead she tapped her fingers against her leg.

Finally, the door rattled and opened. A wall of a man, like a mahogany in both stature and color, stood at the door. Even at sixty-two years old, Eli was an intimidating sight. At six-foot-four, with more muscle than fat, he was a man you wouldn't mess with, and Bristol was glad to have him on her side.

"I knew it was you without even looking," Eli said, frowning at her. Then he grabbed her around the shoulders and pulled her into a hug. "Bad night?"

"You know me too well, Bear," she said as she squeezed him back, then moved past him into the gym.

Most people called him Bear, although they misunderstood where the nickname had come from. Bristol was one of only a few who called him by his proper name and one of even fewer who knew the origin of his nickname.

Most people admired him for his muscle, but it was Eli Baker's mind that fascinated Bristol the most. He had a PhD, and it was during his time at med school that he got the nickname. He was playing the part of a man with a mental condition that was presenting at the hospital, and the other students needed to assess him. Another classmate dared him to strip naked as part of his symptoms. Never one to back down, he was awarded the nickname "Bare" for his effort. But because everyone at the gym assumes it relates to his size, the name changed to "Bear" over time.

He knew everything there was to know about the human body. He could have had a job in any medical facility he wanted, but in the end he came back to the gym.

She shivered and tossed her bag down on a bench. "Geez, it's colder in here than out there."

Running in place, she scanned the room to decide where to start.

The building was a big open room with a boxing ring in the middle and bags, weights, and other machines scattered around the outside.

Eli stood with his arms crossed watching her. "You want to tell me about it?"

"Tell you about what?"

He tipped his head down and looked at her under his course brow. He was like the father she never had, but that didn't mean she would allow herself to be more vulnerable than necessary.

She let her body sag in exaggeration.

Eli ignored it. "You'll feel better if you talk about whatever brought you here this early."

"I'll feel better if I blow off some steam."

"Mmhm."

"Actually," she said, happily changing the subject. "I *did* have a question for you."

"Shoot."

"I want you to teach me about the force it takes to break bones."

Eli laughed his low bellowing laugh that seemed to start at his knees. "I don't ask and you don't tell, right? I wouldn't expect you would have any trouble breaking bones."

"It's not the breaking of bones I want to understand. I like to be efficient and not break things unnecessarily."

"Is this a question you are asking after the fact?"

"Not sure. I mean, I got the job done, but you know how I like things to be precise."

"Mmm. Well, when looking at the force it takes to break bones, there are a lot of considerations. Are you more likely to cause compressive or tensile stress?" He had a doughy look on his face. He was holding it slack, making fun of her.

Bristol rolled her eyes. He always started teaching her this way, asking questions he knew she wouldn't be able to answer. "You're the one with the degree. I'm just a lowly high school graduate," she said as she walked over to a punching bag to warm up.

Eli stood behind it. "So which is it?" She punched the bag in response. "You don't want gloves?" He asked.

"I haven't got time for gloves." She punched it again and started bouncing on her feet. "And besides, a few scrapes on my knuckles will go well with the attire."

Eli smiled. "I'll assume tensile. But still that's not an easy question to answer."

"Make it easy."

"Okay, about 4,000 newtons of force." Bristol pushed full force into the bag. Eli didn't move. "I can teach you to apply enough force to break the bone, but as we already discussed, you've got that one covered. If you want to stop short, it's tricky. It depends on a lot of factors: the angle of the force, the size of the bone. You never bring me easy questions."

"Well, what else do you do with a PhD besides answer difficult questions with that giant brain of yours."

"Are you sweet talkin' me?"

"Of course. It's one of my best tactics for getting what I want." She push-kicked into the bag.

"Yes, kicks will always be the best way to break bones."

"Which kick has the most force?" Bristol asked, delivering a roundhouse.

"Which one do you think?"

Bristol was bouncing on her feet again and shook her head. "Always the teacher."

"Didn't you ask so you could learn? So which one? Show me."

Bristol switched her stance, pushing her front foot to the back, then inflicted the roundhouse from that position.

"Not bad." Eli nodded appreciatively.

"How about pushing someone into a table?"

"What?"

"Never mind. This isn't exactly helping me to avoid breaking bones, though."

"You want to know the best way to avoid breaking bones."

"Isn't that what I've been asking?"

"Don't get into fights."

Bristol dropped her arms to her side. "You're hopeless."

"That's what they tell me." His smile was wide.

"Will you go a round with me in the ring? I've got some aggression to get rid of before a meeting." She was warm enough now to ditch the sweatshirt.

"I pity whoever's meeting up with you today."

"I pity them more if I didn't come here first."

Eli grabbed a couple mitts from the cupboard and met Bristol on the mat, tossing her a pair of light gloves.

She started out with several jab crosses and then threw in an uppercut before adding a front kick. She was pushing hard, and it didn't take long before she was breathing hard too.

She cleared her mind, focusing on her body, feeling the muscles tense as she prepared for her next move. Sweat slid down her face but the room evaporated around her as she went into fighting mode where all that mattered was how her body contacted the target.

But as her mind stilled, she found herself back in the dark room, huddled in the corner, and as Eli reached forward with the mitt, she saw the hand reach for her in the darkness. She let out a roar and sprang for his hand, batting it away and pushing out punch after punch.

Eli let her go full tilt until she started to get sloppy.

"Whoa, whoa, whoa." He said as he stepped back and dropped the mitts. Bristol was halfway through a kick. He batted her leg away, setting her off balance. She ended up flat on the mat.

"I think that's enough for now," Eli said, reaching

down a hand to pull her up. She batted it away and jumped to her feet ready to keep going, but Eli kept his hands by his side. She was still bouncing and jabbed at him a couple times, but he didn't move. She finally stopped and gave him a dirty look.

"Why'd we stop?"

"What time's your meeting?"

"Not till nine. I've got plenty of time."

"Plenty of time to have a shower, cool off, and go get changed." She glared at him. He had a bad habit of looking out for her. Sometimes she wanted the freedom to self-destruct.

He reached out a hand and popped her lightly in the shoulder. "Still don't want to tell me about it?"

The fight drained from her and she slouched. "It doesn't matter. It's nothing," she said and climbed out of the ring.

Eli stood with his giant hands on his hips looking at her. "You have any friends outside of here?"

Bristol groaned. "Please don't start playing dad. I love you Eli, but I don't need a pep talk."

"You know I worry about you."

"Yeah." She took a swig of water. She didn't like people caring about her. People got hurt that way. It was too messy. She didn't have a choice with Eli. He'd been there so long it was just the way it was, so she put up with it. But at least she could dodge him. The rest of the people in her life she did a good job of keeping at arm's length.

She grabbed her bag. "Time to go."

"You know I'm here whenever you need me."

"Yeah."

He sighed. "Go kick some ass."

"I plan on it."

"And look after yourself."

"I always do."

"Liar," he called out as she pulled the door shut behind her.

Chapter 5

COLE STEPPED out of the elevator into a familiar large space that consisted of a few stud walls and a large frosted glass panel wrapped around to the side. It was an odd shape that left one side unusable, a possible reason they had stopped the renovation.

It was dark by the elevator, so he moved past the walls and hanging plastic that he had cut down previously and made his way to a bank of windows where light was pouring in. A paint bucket rested by the window where he sat on previous occasions to eat his fancy breakfast and take in the view. There was something satisfying about not being rushed in the middle of a job like this. He preferred days like today when he got to see his plan through, but he tried to make the most of the preparation days too.

Looking through the windows downtown, he frowned. It was an expensive view, but there was too much concrete for his taste. His condo in Malibu had views of the ocean, but he had in his mind to get a place with more space one day. The older he got, the more crowded it felt. He had enough money put aside and business was good. If he could find it in him, he might retire early. Although inaction was not his strong suit. He was never very good at sitting still. And yet…

He shook his head. No point getting all philosophical now, he had work to do. He looked down at the food container he had set on the floor in front of him and pulled the lid off. The toast and eggs he cooked up this morning were topped with wilting parsley. The fancy packaging made people think this was a breakfast worthy of praise, but inside it was his own handiwork. He was a good cook, but the eggs were cold now, and because he had no intention of eating it this morning, he hadn't added any salt. He didn't like to eat before strenuous activity. Today he simply pulled out a piece of the soggy bread and used the harder side of the crust to push the egg aside until he could see the bag hidden underneath. He cleared away enough to make a tear and pulled out his gun. Hefting it in his hand, he smiled. The easy part was over. Now came the fun part.

He stood and stretched, then jogged in place for a minute to get the blood flowing.

Moving back to the elevator, he dropped the container on the floor but kept the lid, and after pushing the button for the elevator, he decided to leave his jacket behind as well. No point getting it dirty.

He spun the lid around in his hand and found a latch. Yanking it to one side, a hidden arm popped out. This handy little transformer was one of his own designs. It was lightweight and well concealed, but strong.

He hooked it onto his belt and stretched his arms and shoulders again while he waited for the elevator.

When the doors opened, he stepped in and pushed the buttons for the three floors below, then stepped back onto the 46th floor and held out the lid as the doors closed on it. As soon as the elevator began moving, he ratcheted the doors open again, then released his tool and reset it.

He had tried this the week before. Not all elevators allowed brute force to reopen them. With a guy like Robert in control he expected better, but the guy was more show than substance if his security was anything to go by. When Cole had first seen the guards in the place, he was sure it would be a tougher case, but it hadn't taken long to find the cracks in the system. It had saved him much harder work and meant he'd got the job done faster than anticipated.

He jumped lightly onto the top of the elevator as it dropped below the floor and free climbed up the cables to the door at floor 47.

This is where things got tricky.

The toe of his shoe grabbed at the ledge as he dropped one hand off the cable to release the tool from his belt. He held it in his teeth as he got a firmer grip on the cable, then got hold of the lid again, but his other hand slipped on the cable and he had to drop the tool to keep from falling. The tool clattered on the roof of the elevator below.

It had been too easy. Why not add a little spice?

He tipped his head back in frustration and shimmied down, picking up the lid again as the elevator moved down another floor. He should have pressed a few more buttons for more floors and would have if he hand't thought it would draw attention.

Sometimes he was too precise in his calculations and maybe a little too cocky if he was being honest.

He listened as the doors of the elevator below him closed, then clipped the lid back onto his belt and climbed up three floors as the elevator moved again.

He pulled the lid back out and pushed the tool between the two doors and began moving it back and forth. The doors peeled open an inch as the elevator moved again. He let go of the lid that now held its place and climbed up again.

His arms were shaking. He had been lazy on training lately. It was his own fault and might be his undoing. This was his last chance on the door.

He reached the door again and kept ratcheting, making another inch. The elevator vibrated and started its decent as Cole swung a leg up and his head dropped lower. He reached out to the door, pulling himself toward it. A dark chasm opened up below him, but he ignored it. Heights never bothered him much. Falling, on the other hand…

He kept ratcheting until he could squeeze through, then let the release go and clipped the lid back on his belt. He shook his arms out before reaching for his gun. Even though he didn't expect to see anyone here, in his line of work, you always had to be prepared.

He held the Glock pointing at the floor as he moved.

His intel said that this floor was just a hall with paintings on the walls. Artwork in an office wasn't anything unusual, but now that he was here it wasn't what he expected.

Most of the paintings were bizarre, but there was one nice-looking picture of a girl, around twelve years old, with sparkling green eyes. She wasn't smiling, like in old paintings, but this was contemporary. Only a guy like Robert Carlson would have a floor of paintings no one saw, probably just so he could say he did.

He kept moving down the hall. At the end was another elevator. This one was more personal. It was white and cozy and it didn't need any special keys or passes because no one that would have access to this point would need them. He stepped in and rode up to the next floor.

The doors opened to a plush reception area. A leather couch that would have cost more than all of his furniture combined lined one wall. And there were more paintings. But he wasn't here for those.

An elegant woman with long limbs sat behind a large desk. She had been typing but stopped, still with her fingers on the keys. Her eyebrows were as pursed as her lips. She knew he didn't belong there, but he was, in fact, there, in his jeans and black polo. He smiled at her with one side of his mouth, his eyes low. She didn't blush, but her lips parted so he knew she was unsettled. He walked through like he owned the place, and she reached for her phone. It didn't matter. She was too late.

Chapter 6

BRISTOL WAS fifteen minutes early and had driven past the café once already to get a feel for the place. It was a busy street with lots of foot traffic.

She found a bench half a block down on the other side of the street and waited there, watching everyone who walked into the café to try and get a head start on whoever she was meeting.

A heavyset man with a shaved head and wearing a trench coat entered the café and Bristol looked at her watch — 8:58. She bet herself ten bucks it was him, until another man in a gray suit walked up to the door two minutes later. He took a quick look around and then went inside.

Bristol stood and tugged lightly at the tight skirt that just brushed past her knees.

She breathed deeply as she waited for the red light, then crossed the road. When she reached the café entrance, she took another deep breath and let it out as she pushed open the door. There was a *ding* when the door hit its mark. She hated those little bells over doors, preferring to remain unnoticed. A man behind the counter gave her a long head-to-toe look, but she was used to that. While she would prefer to be the sort of woman no one noticed, she took the cards she was dealt and used sex appeal to her own advantage. The clothes she was wearing shouted business, but the tight skirt could be a distraction, and distraction was one of her best tools. Make them look one way while you hit them from the other.

She pushed her hair back, letting it carve its way down her spine as she looked around the room. The man in the trench coat sat at the counter and the gray suit guy had a booth. Trench coat turned slightly, presumably, to catch her in his peripheral vision, and when she looked at the suit, his eyes glanced to the man in the coat.

They were both there for her.

It was tempting to sit next to trench, just to be difficult and make sure they understood she wasn't impressed, but she decided to keep that knowledge to herself for now, in case it became useful.

She walked to the booth and slid in, angling herself out so she could keep the counter in view. The man in the suit had black hair and a mustache. She hated mustaches more than she hated cats.

He had a strong jaw that jutted out at the sides and gave the appearance that he was permanently clenching his teeth. His nose had been broken a few times. It was straight, but lumpy. His hands were resting flat on the table. They were strong enough to open a jar she couldn't, which were very few, or wrap around her neck, which was the look he had on his face right now, in a sadistic he'd-enjoy-it sort of way.

If she was honest, she was intimidated, but when she felt that way, she was never honest. Instead, she pulled the note from her bag and placed it on the table, pushing it over to him like she was dealing him a card.

"Was that really necessary? I do have a phone, you know."

He grinned. "If you're as good as they say you are, you know why it was necessary."

"Mailing it would have shown you knew where I lived too and wouldn't have been as irritating."

He shrugged. "Message received then?"

"What do you want?"

"Exactly what the note said — your services."

"Not interested." She started to scoot out but caught trench guy's movement and stopped to look back at suit. "You going to sic your dog on me now?"

Suit looked at the man and lifted his hand to signal him to stop. "Will you at least listen to my proposition? You might find it more appealing than you think."

"I doubt it."

"It would put a wife beater behind bars."

She hated the child inside of her that couldn't forget the past. Heat rose to her face, and she pushed back into the seat against every other instinct she had.

"I thought that might get your attention."

"Why did you think that?" Warning flares were rocketing off inside her head. It was time to walk out, but she refused to give in to fear.

"I know a lot about you Bristol Kelley."

She swallowed hard. "And I don't even know your name," she said, her voice smooth even as her insides trembled. Her conversation with Eli this morning about breaking bones popped into her head, and she would have enjoyed inflicting that kick about now. The skirt would have made it difficult, but she had managed more difficult attire in the past.

She rested her scraped knuckles on the table just so he understood she wasn't afraid of a fight.

"Detective Tanner," he said, reaching across to shake her hand. She let out a huff instead, ignoring his hand. How did she miss he was a cop? She must be distracted this morning. Maybe another session at the gym was in order.

"So what's the job?"

"Well, we have a problem and need you to fix it."

She nodded and waited for more information.

"There's been an internal investigation into a drug smuggling issue within the ranks and they are getting close to breaking it wide open."

She rested her forehead into her hand and let out a cynical laugh. "And you want me to frame the wife beater," she said, as she stared down at the table still shielding her face. When she looked up, Tanner was smiling triumphantly.

"I gotta say," he said, shaking his finger at her, "I wasn't convinced about you at the start, but you're beginning to impress me."

"And I assume you're the one getting off the hook?"

He put his hands up in defense. "All I'm saying is

that there is a man, other than myself, who has gotten away with many abuses for a long time because he's on the force. And this is an opportunity to make sure he pays for that … one way or another."

"And how do I know he is what you say he is?"

"You don't want to take my word for it?" She didn't respond. "Fine."

Tanner pulled out a folder and handed it across the table. She opened it and sifted through a bunch of grainy photos. They showed a man, first holding a woman's wrist, then slapping her across the face. The last showed him with his arms wrapped around her from the back, holding her tight as she was obviously scream-ing. She studied the photos but stopped seeing them for a moment. Instead, she saw her mom's boyfriend.

She closed the folder and looked up. "What informa-tion do you have for me to plant on him."

"We've got phone numbers, conversations, and oh — " He reached into his coat and pulled out a package the size of an old cassette tape. He wiggled it in his hand. She nodded, and he slid it across the table to her, but she didn't take it.

"What kind?"

"Good ol' fashioned smack."

"I don't know that 'good' is the right adjective to use here."

"Call it what you like, just plant it on him. I'll also give you an address for an old drug lab if you want to plant some of his stuff there."

He slid a large yellow envelope across the table. "Everything you need is in here."

"Why can't you do all this yourself?"

He held his hands up and waggled his fingers. "Gotta keep the hands clean."

"You say that like they're clean now. And what do I get out of the deal besides putting a guy who deserves it behind bars?"

"That's not enough?" She didn't respond again. "You have no sense of humor, did you know that?"

"That's what they tell me."

Tanner let out a low cynical laugh and pointed at the yellow envelope. "There's a check in there for you." She opened it and found a check for more money than she'd made all month. "That's half. You get the other half once the guy's in prison."

"Is this a joke?"

"What, isn't it enough?"

"Do you think I'm an amateur?"

Tanner grinned. "It was worth a shot."

"You really thought I'd take a check." She ripped the paper in two and set it in front of Tanner.

"Okay, so I'll get you the cash. Half now, half later."

"Can I think about it?"

"Nope."

"And what if I say no?"

"Don't."

She bit the inside of her lip and processed the things she'd need to accomplish and how long it would take. It was a straightforward assignment and should be quick.

"This drug money?"

He shook his head. "I have a wealthy benefactor. He looks after me. He's the one who wanted to hire you."

She would have asked *who*, but she knew he'd never say. She tapped a finger on the table.

He leaned forward. "Just remember the information I have on you is not just your address. We could make life difficult for your friends as well."

"If you knew me as well as you say you do, you'd know I don't have any friends." She crossed her arms casually. The corner of Tanner's mouth rose.

He could have been bluffing, but she didn't want to hear the names of the people she cared about coming out of his mouth. She pushed all her misgivings away and focused on the fact that she could put a wife beater behind bars. The back of her brain itched, but she ignored it. With her past and the work she did now, her brain was always itching.

"Okay. Do you know where he'll be tonight?"

"You're fast," he snickered. She knew he was only saying it to rile her up. There was something in his eyes. She recognized it but couldn't place it, but she knew she wasn't his type.

"I don't like to waste time. Once I get a hold of his phone, it will be smooth sailing. I shouldn't need to be in contact with him after that."

"There's a bar in Burbank he frequents after work on Fridays. I'll text you the directions."

"Fine, now how do I get in touch with you."

He wrote a number on the back of a napkin. "This is a burner number that I'll only have for this job. Do your best to use it as little as possible. Oh, and when you get his phone, wipe out any photos he might have on there. We don't want him to have anything we didn't give him."

She made a mental note and nodded. Taking the napkin with his number, she used it to pick up the drugs and put them in her bag.

"Are we done?" she said, appearing bored, which is not how she felt.

"Unfortunately. My friend at the bar will be disappointed that you didn't run."

She looked at the man and then back. "He doesn't look like he can run very fast."

"He doesn't have to." Tanner wasn't smiling, and Bristol had had enough.

"I've got work to do," she said, and moved out of the booth.

"Well, that's good, because I have a golf swing to work on."

"Where, *Golf N Stuff*?"

"Funny. I prefer to play with the big boys at the Los Angeles Country Club."

It surprised her he felt the need to show off. That was an easy thing to use against someone.

"Figures," she said, and turned on her heel. She brushed past Tanner's *guard dog*, just touching his back as she walked by.

Chapter 7

COLE WALKED FORWARD past the secretary as she lifted the phone to her ear. A door was positioned to the left of the desk, and Cole didn't hesitate to open it.

Inside, a man in his early fifties sat behind the desk. Robert Carlson. Cole lifted his gun and pointed it at the man who quickly stood.

Robert wore middle age exceptionally well. He had a head full of thick black hair, and his custom-made suit showed that he was an active man.

His fingertips pressed into the top of his desk. Cole made note of the man's manicured hands, while his own were greasy after his foray in the elevator shaft. He couldn't imagine how much effort it would take him to have hands like that.

Robert leaned forward, his fingertips white from the pressure. "So how'd you do it," Robert said, his eyes hungry.

. . .

Less than a month ago, Cole received a phone call from Robert's personal assistant, probably the woman outside the door, who said Robert insisted that Cole get to work immediately and would pay for his urgency. She said Robert wanted to ensure that Cole understood Silas Lincoln was emphatic that they use Cole's services. Cole wasn't sure whether to be flattered that Silas knew who he was and what he did or disappointed that Robert felt he needed to drop a name in order to secure his employment. Either way, he had just finished a job and the price was right.

Robert now stepped around his desk and gestured to the other side of the room that held a seating area with more expensive couches. It had dark wood paneling similar to the lobby downstairs, but in this room it was much more imposing.

Cole took Robert's lead and made his way to one couch while Robert sat opposite, leaning forward with his arms resting on his knees and his hands tightly clasped.

Cole laid his gun on the glass coffee table and leaned back as he had on the park bench. He wanted Robert to understand he wasn't intimidated by his surroundings.

The man's gray eyes were sharp. He looked like a man who always had his muscles taught, ready for whatever came before him in business.

Cole usually got one of two reactions from his clients. Some were disappointed by his success. They thought they didn't need his services, even though they paid for them. Those guys often found fault with Cole's methods and made any excuse to explain away their security flaws. Their excuses were followed by anger until they resigned themselves to the changes that were needed.

Then there were those like Robert who were fascinated by his process, eager to live vicariously through the physical adventure. Cole generally had a sense which one they would be by the type of business. He knew this man would be the second type because he was a man who took risks in business and didn't mind taking someone down in the process. Always looking for new ways to do things, he tended to be slippery. Cole had to watch out for this type, because despite their appreciation for his ability, they often learned what they could from his initial break in and applied their own change in security. He always got paid for this part, and it was his favorite, but the real money was in implementing the security fixes using his trusted subcontractors.

Cole linked his fingers together on his lap. "Mr. Carlson, we have a lot of work to do."

"Call me Robert, and I was afraid of that, but — " He put his arms up in gesture, " — that's why I brought you in." He leaned forward eagerly. "So, how'd you do it?"

"It involved climbing up the elevator shaft."

"Seems a bit old-fashioned?"

"The good stuff never gets old. It's the loopholes that offer the most opportunity to those who wish you harm. The areas no one is looking at."

"Was it at least a challenge for you?"

"I've been in more difficult situations." Cole saw a flash in the other man's eyes.

Robert leaned forward and picked up the gun. He looked it over then pointed it straight at Cole's face. "I've got metal detectors."

Cole lifted an eyebrow. "Do you mind? I'm partial to this," he said, circling his face with his finger. Robert's head cocked sideways like a dog pissing on a tree, marking his territory. No matter how confident Robert appeared, Cole had found weak spots, and that made Robert uneasy, even if he tried not to show it.

Robert took his time laying the gun back on the table.

"The gun never went through the metal detectors, but I'll put all that together in a report for you."

Robert leaned back and watched Cole, tapping a rhythm on his leg with his fingers.

"Can you give me an idea of what you have in mind to fix my problems?"

"It really depends on the value of the assets you are trying to protect. I didn't have too much trouble getting in here, but it all took time to put together and it depends on whether it's worth the effort to someone who wishes you harm or wants to steal from you."

Robert leaned forward and grabbed a mint out of a crystal bowl in the middle of the table. He took his time unwrapping it. Cole waited patiently. No one likes to be told they might not be as valuable as they think they are.

Robert leaned back and sucked on the candy, waiting for Cole to continue.

Cole let the silence hang for a second then said,

"Obviously the government contracts you have may be worth something to someone. But it shouldn't be more than retraining your staff and adding a few more safety measures."

"Sounds like I don't need much from you then?" Robert moved the mint from one cheek to the other.

"That's up to you, but I've got the best people for the job. If you don't want the best that's your choice." Cole knew how to play this game. He'd been around the rich and powerful enough in his life.

"Fine. Write up your report. I am eager to see what you've been up to these past few weeks. When will it be ready?"

"Week or two, but I don't like my time wasted."

Robert shook his head. "Do you play tennis?"

"I'm more of a baseball guy."

"Come over to my place tomorrow and we'll play a match, and then you can give me the informal version of your report. I'll make it worth your while."

"Can you do Monday?"

"I've got a special event on Monday and I'm not a man who likes to wait."

"I'm not surprised."

"Make sure you have some solutions for me."

Cole frowned. Robert was playing games. He'd give Robert some of what he wanted but keep some to himself as collateral.

Cole stood and reached out his hand. Robert matched him and the two men shook on it. Robert's hands felt as soft as they looked. A man who let others do his dirty work. Cole made a mental note to make sure he wasn't deceived into being one of them.

"You can take the elevator all the way down if you don't want to bother climbing this time."

"I appreciate it."

As Cole walked toward the door, he remembered the out-of-place painting downstairs. He turned. "That painting, in your hall downstairs. It doesn't fit with the others. Is that your daughter or a relative?"

Robert's eye twitched. "Yes, it is."

"She's stunning."

"Hmm, yes, beautiful." Robert stared past Cole at the wall for a moment as though contemplating an image of the painting in his mind. His eyes were full of longing, and Cole wondered if she was a daughter he never got to see. As far as Cole knew, Robert wasn't married.

Robert took a deep breath and continued to escort Cole from the room. He stood outside the elevator with his hands clasped in front of him. "I look forward to our meeting tomorrow."

Cole looked around Robert and nodded to the woman still at her desk. The corner of her mouth turned up.

On his way back through the hallway, Cole stopped to look at the girl with the green eyes. His hands were twitching at his side and he realized for the first time how unsettled he felt. He turned back to look down the hall before calling the main elevator. He wasn't surprised a guy like Robert could turn his stomach, but he couldn't place where his discomfort stemmed from.

He thought back through the meeting, but nothing stood out. It wasn't having a gun pointed at his face. That had happened before, and he knew he wasn't intimidated by that. There was no point. If Robert had fired, then that would have been the end, and he wouldn't have known the difference. There was no way to stop it, so why bother being worried about it. But there was something. He had learned over the years not to ignore these cues. Maybe it would come to him as he wrote up his report. He groaned at the thought of the report. They were the worst part of the job, but they cleared up any uncertainties, and the writing process helped him identify concerns that he hadn't fully considered at the time of action.

The elevator doors opened, and Cole stopped on level 46 to get his jacket and container, then headed the rest of the way down.

He saluted the guards as he passed them on his way out.

"That took a while," Ron said from his chair.

"I met a nice girl," Cole said over his shoulder.

As he passed through the main doors, his phone rang. He looked at the number but didn't recognize it.

"Cole here."

"Cole, it's Andrew."

Cole didn't respond as he ran the name through his head, trying to make a connection. The guy seemed to know him.

Andrew laughed quietly then said, "Andrew Turough."

"Andrew! It's been a while."

"It certainly has. How've you been?"

"Can't complain. Business has been good."

"That's great."

"How's Jenny?"

"Thirty-four weeks pregnant."

Cole whistled. "Wow, man. I'm so happy for you."

"Yeah, I was late getting to it, but we're pretty excited."

Andrew went silent, so Cole filled the space. "So is there something I can do for you, or is this a social call?"

Andrew sighed heavily into the phone and Cole recalled he used to do that a lot, not turning his head away when he coughed or anything. "I need your help," he finally said. "I've found something. I don't know. I need your eyes on it."

Cole stopped walking. Andrew had been Cole's partner during his short stint at the LAPD and was one of those solid types of people who never seemed to let anything rattle them. Cole sensed that Andrew was rattled.

"Can I ask what this is about?"

"It's just this case I'm working on. I've hit a dead end but something's not right. I thought getting a fresh pair of eyes on it might spark something."

Cole looked at his watch. "I can meet you at the regular place tonight at seven."

"Yeah, that works for me. And thanks."

"Happy to help. And it will be good to see you again."

"Yeah, you too. See you then. And thanks, really.

You know I wouldn't call you for something like this if it wasn't important."

"Don't worry about it. You were always a good friend to me. I don't mind helping you out."

"See you then."

Cole hung up the phone and then ran his hand across his mouth. When he left the force, it was under a cloud. He'd been asked to leave, though he already had one foot out the door. Andrew was there for the long haul. Cole wasn't sure if he wanted to get mixed up in a case, but then, maybe it would feel good to do something worthwhile for a change.

____

Chapter 8

____

BRISTOL DIDN'T MAKE it back to the gym. Instead, she went to see her friend Deb. Bristol was the only one who called her that, and only because they had known each other since they were kids. On the door to her office, a sign read Deborah VanHousen - Attorney. Deb pronounced it "Deb-*or*-ah" but Bristol refused to call her that.

The woman was five-foot-four and always wore stilettos and power suits. She was rounded in the middle and had a mass of curly hair that accentuated her crazy personality. She was like a burger with the works. Sweet, salty, and sour all at the same time.

Bristol pushed through the door and found her friend speaking into a recorder. She saw Bristol straight away and held up a finger while she continued to speak. "New attire, something with a high neck. Can she cry on cue? Natural makeup. Maybe throw in a hiccup at the end if it can be arranged."

She put the recorder down and stood up, prancing

around the desk to give Bristol a big hug. "If it isn't my favorite person," she said in her singsong voice. When Deb wasn't working, she was bubbly to the point of obnoxious, but when she put on her game face in court, she turned into a bulldog.

"That," she said, indicating to the machine she was speaking into, "is a job you sent my way. They rang first thing this morning. Filled me in on all the gory details. You have the coolest job ever." Her voice was fever high.

"It wouldn't work so well if not for efficient lawyers such as yourself, though, would it?"

"Oh, but you make my job so easy. This is money for jam, a job like this. I'm going to present her as a girl taken advantage of by one who should have been her protector. The press will eat it up like the ravenous beasts they are. This girl is going to be a hero before I'm through with her. Although I'll have to see how good of an actress she is first."

"I don't know. She seemed pretty cold to me," Bristol said, sitting in a standard office guest chair.

"They're usually the best kind. They don't mind putting on a show."

"Glad I could help."

"Sit, sit," Deb said, even though Bristol already was. "Margaret!" She yelled through the partly open door as she leaned back onto her desk.

"Don't you have an intercom?" Bristol said, rubbing her ear.

Deb shrugged and Margaret poked her head through the door. She had a haggard look on her face.

"Coffee for me and…" She pointed at Bristol.

"Nothing, I'm fine."

"You sure?"

"Yes."

"*Wait!*" she yelled, as Margaret pulled her head through the door. It reminded Bristol of those arcade games where a creature pops up out of a hole and you hit it with a mallet.

Deb reached behind her and picked up her recorder, tossing it across the room. Margaret fumbled it but got control before it hit the ground. "Type that up for me." Margaret waited for more. "Okay, you can go." Deb waved her hand. Margaret retreated. "Close the door!" The door closed gently.

"You quit smoking again?" Bristol said. She was exhausted already.

"Yes, why?"

"No reason."

Deb shook her head. "No, you need to share. You're spooky the way you do that. How'd you know?"

"It's not that impressive. You don't smell like smoke, and you're more highly strung than usual."

"You're right, it's not that impressive. But what you did with this girl, now that's impressive. You are a genius."

Deb waved her hands in the air and moved back around her desk to sit in her massive leather chair. She leaned back, resting her feet on her desk. "So, to what do I owe the honor of this most prestigious visit, Miss Kelley?"

"I need some information."

"Well, you've come to the right place. You scratch

my back and I…" She made a scratching motion with her blood-red nails in the air. Bristol smiled like she was watching a root canal and trying to make the person feel better.

"There's a police officer in, I believe, the LAPD and I need some info on him."

"Oh good, I can call my honey." Deb's boyfriend was a clerk in the police department, which Bristol found odd. But perhaps Deb needed someone low key to temper her. "What's his name?"

"Andrew Turough."

Tanner was not a man Bristol trusted, and while she preferred to know her subjects as little as possible, sometimes extra data was called for. She wanted to know how bad Andrew really was. She knew from experience how easy it is to make things appear different from the truth. That's why she stayed away from social media.

Deb picked up her cell phone and spoke at it, "Siri, call Loverboy." Deb smiled at Bristol and lifted her shoulders up to ears then dropped them again and pressed the phone to one ear.

"Hey! … Awww, I missed you too … No, I did … "

This continued for a minute. Bristol lifted her arm and tapped on her wrist.

Deb bit her lip. "I need something from you, Snooky."

Bristol sucked her cheeks in and bit down hard. This would give her nightmares. The woman was like Jekyll and Hyde.

"Give me everything you know about an Andrew Turough. He probably works in your building." She put her hand over the phone with it still up to her ear and said to Bristol, "He's looking it up."

Bristol gave her two thumbs up with a big open-mouthed smile making sure her sarcasm was clear. It seemed appropriate under the circumstances.

Deb clicked her nails on the desktop while she waited. "No, really?" Deb gasped. Bristol sat up in her seat, eager to hear the news. "I can't believe it." Deb was shaking her head. She put her hand on the phone again and addressed Bristol. "He said his neighbor's dog has had puppies." Bristol stared for a minute and then shook her head and leaned back in the chair.

"Bingo!" her friend yelled, and Bristol shot up again. Covering the phone again Deb said, "He's in the LAPD."

Bristol lifted her eyebrows and mouthed "and?". Even though she'd known Deb most of her life, she never got used to the woman.

"Thanks so much, Sweetie… Oh!" She hung up abruptly. Bristol was relieved at the quick goodbye. She had been sure it would take longer than the hello.

"His superior had just walked into the room, so we had to cut it short, but he's sending me a screenshot of what he found once he's free again."

Bristol nodded. "I'm headed to Burbank tonight to get in contact with this guy but wanted a background check first."

"Sounds fascinating," Deb said, resting her face on her hand and staring at her friend intently.

Margaret walked in with a coffee for Deb, who

barely acknowledged her. Deb's PAs had a short life span, even when she *was* smoking.

"Tell me more," she said, sipping her coffee.

"There isn't much to tell. It should be a pretty straightforward job. Just need to frame this guy for drug smuggling."

Deb laughed. "Leave it to you to make framing a guy sound like any other job. I take it he deserves it, otherwise you wouldn't take the job?"

"Wife beater."

"Perfect."

Bristol felt sick. "Well, I've gotta get going, but can you forward that info to me when it comes through?"

"Sure thing. Just make sure you delete it when you're done."

Bristol gave her another thumbs up as she walked through the door. She passed Margaret, who was furiously typing.

"Hey," Bristol said, and Margaret jumped. "You're doing a great job."

Margaret smiled wearily and went back to her typing.

Chapter 9

BRISTOL THUMBED through the contents of the envelope that she found at her door when she got home. The
hundred-dollar bills were crisp. She tucked them under
her mattress and went to her closet. Digging through her
clothes, she found a sweater with a deep V. It was a dark
green color that made her eyes pop, and she couldn't
remember why it had ended up in her giveaway pile.
She added a pair of skinny jeans and wedges. She
wanted to look good, but not obvious.

Her plan was simple. Chat up Turough when he
came into the bar. If he didn't respect his wife, then he
wouldn't mind flirting with her. Then she'd get a few
drinks into him and pocket his phone. After she added
the info she needed, she could turn it in at the police
department. Shouldn't be too hard.

As she was driving, the sweater started itching, and
she remembered why it had ended up at the back of her
closet.

She pulled into a parking spot at the bar, and a text

came in from Deb with Andrew Turough's name at the top. She scanned it. Not one mark against his record. She blew out a deep breath and threw her head back against the seat.

"Why does it matter?" she yelled at the roof of the car. After she got his phone she'd know more, but it was looking possible that she'd end up taking matters into her own hands. Her job was already risky, but she had a habit of making it worse. If she could get rid of her pesky morals, her job would be much simpler.

The only thing to do now was to move forward with the plan. She had arrived early to prepare and walked into what was a typical bar with an old-fashioned Irish feel to it. The music in the background wasn't too loud and had a nice folky sound. A good place to unwind after work — or get drunk and go home to beat your wife. She wound her way over to the bar, scanning each patron to make sure her mark wasn't already there. He wasn't.

She sat at the bar, where she had a decent view of the front door to her right. The bartender wasted no time approaching. "What can I get for you?"

"Gin and tonic, thanks." He paused and raised his eyebrows before going to get her order. Most people made opinions of others by their drinks, especially when they're looking to pick up a girl. A sweet mixed drink says, 'I'm here to flirt, come and get me.' If she had a wine, they would think she thought herself classy and wanted men to approach her with style. If she had a whiskey, they'd think she was looking to play rough. Gin and tonic sent mixed signals. She had actually spent months testing out her theory at different bars. This was the drink that got her the least interactions.

The bartender set the drink in front of her. She handed him a twenty and looked around as she waited for her change. She caught the eye of one or two but glared them off. Then she just nursed her drink, or more accurately, wrapped her hands around the glass and didn't drink. She had never actually tasted a gin and tonic, only used it as a prop.

So far, she hadn't been approached, but she knew it was only a matter of time. She kept on her best don't-talk-to-me face and looked to her left just in case anyone was still wondering. Then she felt the air change on the other side. Someone had sat down. A light scent of cologne, a good one, drifted under her nose.

Not a woman. She sighed. She had hoped to avoid talking to anyone else before Andrew came in.

She looked down at her watch, 6:53, then took in the peripheral of a worn brown leather jacket. His feet were perched on the footrest. Jeans and expensive shoes. An unusual patron in a bar like this, same as her. She tried to steal a glance at him in the bar's mirror panels behind the booze, but he was looking right at her. She held his gaze. A couple days' growth — looked like it was on purpose. Looked good on him. His hair was styled in a messy way that worked with the rest of his attire.

Then the bartender walked up to the man, blocking the reflection. "What can I get for you?"

The man turned to Bristol. "What are you drinking?"

"Gin and tonic," she said, without looking at him. He turned back to the bartender. "I'll have a Coke."

"Not drinking tonight?" she said, finally glancing at him. She wasn't the only one working tonight.

"Doesn't look like you are either," he said, indicating to her drink with his eyes.

"Making it last."

"I'm Cole," he said, putting his hand out to shake hers. She looked at it then reached out and shook. "Bristol."

"Come here often, Bristol?"

She turned herself fully toward him tilting her head to the side to see his reaction. He kept his elbows on the bar and his head turned toward her. He was very good looking, and he knew it.

"*That's* your pickup line?"

One corner of his mouth quirked up. "Who says it's a pickup line? I'm asking a genuine question. A woman like you would have access to any bar in this city. So why come here?"

"I like anonymity."

He leaned toward her. "I bet you find that hard."

She matched his lean. "I do."

"Well, I'm sorry to say, you stand out here like a sore thumb," he said, leaning back. It irked her he now thought he got something from her in getting her to lean into him. Maybe she could use that to her advantage. "No, not like a sore thumb, let me rephrase that," he said, putting his finger up. "Like a flower in a weed bed."

She clicked her tongue and squinted her eyes. "That's very poetic." She turned back toward the bar.

He laughed, then said, "So, aside from being hot, what do you do for a living?"

"I thought you weren't doing pickup lines."

He feigned offense. "I'm not. I was merely stating an observation followed by a question. And judging by that sweater, you have some idea of how incredibly attractive you are. But I'm sorry I am really not interested so if you could just lay off."

She turned back toward him. "You really think a girl like me is going to be impressed by your boyish charm?"

"Honestly?"

"Please."

"Yes." He added a grin at the end that said he was joking. She let herself smile a little in return, let him think she was on his side.

He moved his hand across and touched her arm. "But I have to ask, did it hurt?"

"What?"

"When you fell from heaven." She just looked at him. He was playing her, but she didn't know why. He laughed and dropped his head. "The look on your face. I'm sorry, I couldn't help myself." She let herself laugh. Her stomach fluttered a bit, which was annoying, but she could control that. "Okay, all kidding aside, I would genuinely like to know what you do for a living," he said, leaning toward her again.

She licked her lips. He was trying to get under her skin. She needed to get under his. Plenty of other women would have fallen for it. Good thing she wasn't other women. She knew now he wasn't here for no reason.

"You first." She cocked her head to the side and smiled. She saw his eyes change. Her smile held steady, but she saw that he knew what she was doing. That surprised her, but she knew what *he* was doing so they were at an impasse.

"I work in the security business," he said, "you?"

"I'm in the makeover business."

His eyes squinted. "Interesting. So if you were going to make me over, where would you start?"

"Your pickup lines," she said, without hesitation.

"If I didn't know you better, I'd say you were flirting with me."

"You don't know me better."

"But I wish I did."

"Well, if I didn't know *you* better, I'd say you were the kind of guy who flirts to get what he wants."

"I could say the same about you. So what is it you want?"

"To know what you're really doing here."

"Having a drink, same as you." He took a sip of his Coke. "Or are you here for a different reason?"

"Nope." She wasn't smiling anymore, and neither was he, but she could see in his eyes he was enjoying himself. Unfortunately, she was too.

The door opened behind his shoulder and her eyes flitted to the man who walked in. It was only for a second, but the short stocky guy who entered was definitely her man. He had on a sweatshirt and jeans with a baseball cap and he looked around the bar like he was trying to find someone. Her eyes moved back to Cole. He was still watching her, but his face had gone dark.

She took a sip of her drink and was surprised to find she liked it. She used that to change the subject. "This is actually not bad." She needed to get rid of this guy.

Cole nodded, then pulled a wad of cash out of his pocket. She looked at it then back at him. "I've already paid for my drink."

He smiled again, but it didn't spread to the rest of his face. He kept his eyes on her but put his hand up to call the bartender. Leaning across the bar, he spoke quietly to the employee, putting the cash in his hand. The bartender glanced at Bristol but then nodded to Cole.

Cole stood and shouted, "Hey, can I have your attention? The lady here is paying a round for every-one." There was a cheer and those around her crowded in grabbing at her and slapping her on the shoulders. Her face went blank. Cole reached out to her and ran his thumb and index finger along her chin. "Sorry, sweetheart. If only we had more time." As the crowd closed in on her, he turned and moved through to Andrew, leading him out the door.

She jumped up, trying to push her way through, when a large wall of a man stood in front of her and put a sweaty hand on each side of her face then kissed her fair on the mouth. She kneed him in the crotch and shoved him back, which opened up the way for her to push past the crowd, but by the time she made it through the door, Cole and Andrew were gone.

She looked up and down the street, waiting for inspiration. None came.

"Dammit!" she yelled at the night.

There was a couple making out against the wall. They looked at her then walked off around the corner.

Why was he there for her guy? And how could she let him throw her off like that? She thought she had been in control. She shook her head, furious with herself. There were other ways to get to Andrew, but this guy, Cole, being involved might complicate things.

A dark red mustang came around the corner and pulled up next to her. The window buzzed down, and Bristol could see Andrew was in the car. Cole was grinning at her.

"Asshole," she said, and moved closer to the car so Andrew couldn't see her face. Cole's eyebrows shot up at her approach. "Don't flatter yourself."

"Whatever they're paying you, I'll tell you right now, it's not worth it sweetheart."

"I think I can make up my own mind on that." She hated the way he was looking at her. They both knew he won this round. Instead of moaning about it, she began reformulating her plan.

He lifted his phone and, before she realized what he was doing, the flash went off.

"You have a good evening, Bristol. It was an absolute pleasure meeting you. We should do it again sometime."

Bristol flipped him off. His smile widened as he buzzed up his window and drove off. Bristol stepped out into the road and pulled out her own phone, taking a picture and sending a text to Deb: *I need you to look up a license plate for me and give me all you've got on the owner.*

Chapter 10

"WHO WAS THAT?" Andrew asked, laughing as they sped off. Cole made a couple of quick turns out of habit. He knew no one was following but couldn't help himself.

"That, my friend, was Bristol."

"She seemed pretty taken with you," Andrew chuckled.

Cole's face spread into a wide grin. "She was something else. Unfortunately, it wasn't me she was interested in, it was you."

"Hey, I'm a happily married man."

"I know, but with those rugged good looks the ladies just can't stay away."

"Yeah, well, I didn't get a close look, but it seemed to me her attention was squarely on you."

"Only because I got in her way."

"By the look on your face, I'd say you didn't mind the position."

"You know me, I never mind being in that position."

Andrew looked at his friend. His face serious. "You talk a big talk, but we both know it's all show."

"Don't tell anyone."

Andrew laughed but then went serious again. "I haven't seen that look on your face in a long time. This girl's different."

"What's that supposed to mean? You haven't even seen my face in ages." Cole was trying to keep it light, but Andrew wasn't biting.

"It may have been a couple years, but I still know you, Cole."

"You're only saying that because you're happily married and want everyone else to be as well."

"It's true, what can I say? I know when Elly left, it messed you up."

"She did me a favor. We never would have worked out." He glanced at Andrew, who didn't look convinced. "Well, either way, I'm well and truly over her. That was a long time ago."

A diner called Freddy's came up on the corner, and Cole pulled in.

"But Cole, it does come at a cost."

"I know, and that's why I don't pursue any of the lovely ladies."

"That's not the reason."

Cole put the car into park. "Then please enlighten me."

"No one has ever been interesting enough."

"You're probably right."

"So tell me about Bristol."

Cole threw his head back, exasperated. "There's nothing to tell. I only met her. Besides, I'm not meeting with you to get advice on my love life, you called *me* remember? So you'd better show me what you've got."

Cole ordered a mineral water, and Andrew ordered a coffee. "Jenny's had trouble getting to sleep at night," Andrew said to Cole's raised eyebrows, "so I expect to be up late tonight." He pulled out a file from his briefcase.

"At least she doesn't have long to go," Cole said.

"Don't say that to *her*. You'll get your teeth smashed in. She moans every time she rolls over in bed, gets cramps in her legs in the middle of the night which, seriously man, she kicks out hard enough to break some-thin', and gets up to pee every half hour. Surely having the kid out has got to be easier than things are now."

"I wouldn't know," Cole said, taking the file and laying it open in front of him.

Inside was a black-and-white photo of a girl, dead, sprawled out on the pavement. She looked to be in her early teens. He flipped through the pictures and stopped on a closeup of her face. "Pretty girl." He squinted. There was something about her that seemed familiar, but he couldn't pick it. "Overdose?"

"What makes you say that?"

"I don't see strangle marks or a gunshot wound. She doesn't look like she's gotten hit by a car. Not a lot of other reasons you'd find a girl dead on the side of the road."

Andrew nodded. "Found her over a month ago."

Cole moved to another photo, this one of her arm. She wasn't brand new to drugs.

"So what's this got to do with me?" Cole nearly added "and Bristol" but didn't want any extra commentary from Andrew.

"I haven't been able to get anywhere on it."

"Unfortunate, but not all that uncommon."

"Actually, I hadn't thought of you in ages, no offense, then Tanner — "

" — Tanner?"

"I know, Tanner of all people, struts into the place making some joke about your time here. I don't know what brought you to his mind."

"Probably my good looks."

Andrew huffed out a laugh and shook his head. "Whatever it was, it got me thinking that I should call you. That you might be just the person I need."

"I'm still not sure how I can help."

"Well, there's this." Andrew pulled a picture from inside the pile. It showed a photo of the back of the girl's shoulder with two circles, linked.

Cole pinched his bottom lip between his fingers. "A lot of people have tattoos."

Andrew looked around the diner like someone was listening in and then leaned forward, speaking low, "Yeah, but as soon as I started looking into that tattoo, I started to get push back."

Cole crossed his arms. "You think it's an inside job.

That right there tells me I'm not the right person to be looking into this."

"You're the best."

"Nice that you think so, but don't you think there will be an issue if I start poking my nose in, trying to find the bad blood?"

Andrew shrugged. "You're the best. And besides, no one will even know." Cole was staring at the table, so Andrew continued. "Cole, leaving the force was the best thing for you. You were never good at following protocol and it worked for you, but if *I* don't follow procedure, the guilty walk free."

Andrew glanced behind Cole and quickly flipped the photos over as the waitress dropped off their drinks. She was chewing gum and frowned at Andrew, glancing from the photos then back up to his face, but blushed when she looked at Cole. "Anything else?"

"No thanks," Cole said warmly, and smiled. Her blush deepened and she dipped her head and walked off.

Andrew watched her for a second and shook his head. "I don't know how you do that."

"It's a gift. But I was trying to be polite and distract her from the photos. She probably assumes we're looking at porn or something." Cole lifted the tattoo photo again and studied it. "So when your manuals can't give you an answer, you come to me to break the rules."

"Yeah, well, you're not the only one who broke the rules. But you're the one who did it to get justice. There are guys who are still in there breaking the rules to line their own pockets. I can't play their game, but you can."

"I don't know, Andrew. I left all that behind me."

Andrew leaned in, speaking quietly, "Cole, I wouldn't normally give a damn about getting pushed around at work, but I've got a wife and a baby to think about."

Cole nodded. "The cost." He sighed.

"After the baby's born, the pressure will come off a bit." Andrew dropped his head. "Honestly, I feel like I'm getting too old for this."

"You're telling me, you think once your baby is born things will get easier?"

"I don't know." Andrew ran his hands over his face. "I've never felt so tired. I need a bit of help to get through this patch."

Cole studied his friend who had gone pale and, with the bags under his eyes, aged a decade in a second. "So what's the story. You believe this girl was murdered?"

"Internal Affairs is investigating an inside job with drug trafficking. They had a recent seizure where the packaging on one was stamped with two rings linked. I tried to show them the match with the girl, but they weren't convinced."

"So maybe the girl threatened to talk, and they had to deal with her. Or they're just covering their tracks."

Andrew made a face. "In all my experience, this — " he tapped the photos, " — is not how they deal with those sorts of problems. If she turned up washed ashore somewhere or was found buried in a pile of garbage, sure, but this? Come on, Cole. You think they're going to dump her on the street?"

"Possibly, if they wanted it to *look* like she OD'd. Do you have a shot of the mark on the drugs?"

Andrew pulled his phone out and brought the photo up, then handed it to Cole.

Cole squinted then zoomed in on the photo. The circles were faded and could have been made by anything. "If I'm honest with you, I can see where IA is coming from. It's a bit of a long shot." Cole flipped through to the next photo looking for a better view. "What are these?" He said swiping from one picture to the next.

"Oh, that. Not sure. I got a tip about the drugs last week, but when I turned up at the warehouse, all I found were these paintings."

"All of young girls? How many were there?"

"Around a dozen."

"So a guy has a bunch of classically painted portraits. The frames?"

"No frames. Maybe they smuggled the drugs in that way, but if they did, I couldn't find any evidence. Might not be related at all. I got a swipe and sent it off to be tested but it came back negative. I had to let it go."

"Do you have an artist?"

"Guy named Edward Drake. A bit weird. Doesn't normally do portraits."

"Sounds fishy."

"Maybe, but I didn't get anywhere. I don't even know why I've kept the paintings on there. Oh, and there's another thing…" He grabbed the photos and found the one he was looking for, laying it before Cole, who sat forward again.

He lifted the picture of the dead girl's wrists and looked closely. "She's been restrained."

"I just need a little help."

"And I've got nothing to lose."

"I didn't say that."

"Doesn't matter, it's true. You know I'd do anything for you. I'll see what I can dig up. Is this all the info you can give me?" Cole thumbed through the notes. "Doesn't look like you got far on witnesses."

"They don't like cops down there."

Cole grinned. "Sounds like my kind of place."

"Actually, it is exactly your kind of place. Look at the address."

Cole bit back a smile. "I pretty sure I can get you a statement."

"See? I told you you were the best."

"You keep saying that, and one day I might actually believe you."

Andrew reached across the table and grabbed Cole's wrists. "Thanks for doing this."

"Well, it's about time I do something worthwhile, I suppose. There are only so many high paying clients I can run through before I need to earn a little good will."

"You're a better man than most."

Cole snorted. "Generous of you to say."

Andrew tipped back the rest of his coffee as Cole gathered the photos.

"You should look up that girl, Bristol. Find out more about her. For your own sake."

"I might just do that."

Andrew patted Cole on the back as they left the diner.

Whatever part Bristol had to play in all of this, it was clear to Cole that they were on opposite sides. He'd find out about her, but it had nothing to do with his love life.

Chapter 11

IT HAD BEEN a long time since Bristol was caught at her own game, and the outcome wasn't pretty. She wouldn't let it happen again.

She tapped her fingers on the steering wheel. It appeared Andrew wasn't as clean as she thought. Whoever Cole was, she now understood the game he played. Not to mention, he had underestimated her, and his need to show off meant she could find out who he was.

Pushing the button on the phone beside her on the passenger seat, she checked her texts, knowing there wasn't one there. She couldn't expect Deb to get back to her tonight.

With time to kill, she had driven home to change but was now parked down the street from Andrew's house. He arrived home shortly after, and now she was waiting for everyone to go to sleep. She rarely did breaking and entering, but she was eager to get this job over and done with. The lock-picking kit she kept in her glove box was now resting on the passenger seat. She was always prepared for everything. Except Cole. She scrunched up her face.

Movement at the house caught Bristol's attention, and she sank down farther in her seat with her eyes on the front door as Andrew walked out backward pulling his jacket on. He faced his wife, who was very pregnant. Bristol's head cocked sideways. The woman had dark hair like the one in the photos, but she looked different. Maybe it was the pregnancy. Maybe not.

She kissed her husband on the cheek, a wide smile on her face. A smiling wife didn't mean her husband didn't beat her, but the itch at the back of Bristol's brain hadn't gone away. She pulled the photos Tanner had given her out of the glove box and looked closely with a small flashlight. Andrew was hurting *someone* in the photo. When she glanced back up, he drove away. His wife kept putting her arm out to him, and as he drove off, she blew him a few kisses.

Change of plan.

Bristol started her own car as soon as the wife closed the door. She thought back to the exemplary record she got from Deb earlier. He had commendations and no marks against him, which, again, didn't necessarily mean anything. But there were always signs, and so far she wasn't seeing any. She had to admit to herself that she wanted the job to disappear and was willing to believe whatever Tanner said to soothe her misgivings, not to mention that she was ticked at Cole and would love nothing more than to rub Andrew's guilt it in his face.

She followed Andrew several miles until he stopped at Ralphs.

"Grocery shopping in the middle of the night?" Bristol said out loud to herself.

She parked at the back of the lot, then followed him in. He knew where he was going and walked with purpose down the front of the aisles. Bristol grabbed a basket and stayed out of sight. She scanned the other shoppers trying to pick out who it might be he was meeting. It never occurred to her to meet someone in secret at a grocery store in the middle of the night. It was a good rendezvous point. She'd keep that one in mind for later.

The outfit she changed into gave her the appearance of a woman who had been up late at night and needed a snack. With her favorite silky sweatpants, a tank top, and an oversized cardigan thrown over to keep warm in the chill night air, she wouldn't stand out. Even if Andrew recognized her, Cole couldn't have told him much about her. She belonged there as much as he did. For all he knew, Burbank was her hometown too. He headed right, so she went left and circled around the rows of food, half jogging when no one could see her to keep one step behind him from the far end of the aisle.

He stopped at the ice cream section. She moved to the middle of the aisle and crept closer, focusing on the products on the shelf each step she took. When she reached the end of the row, he was only six feet from her. She kept her back to him but kept an eye out for who his contact might be, but all Andrew did was dig through the ice cream. Maybe it was time to bump into him.

She approached, scanning the ice cream. When he slammed his hand on the freezer door and sighed, she turned and moved toward him with her back, crashing into him.

"Oh!"

"Oops! I'm so sorry," she said, purposely dropping the basket. When they made eye contact, there was recognition in his eyes, but he hadn't connected to where yet.

"Do I—?" he said.

She had better be on the front foot. "Yeah?" she said, a question in her voice. "I believe we have a mutual friend, Cole. Yeah, I recognize you from his car."

He froze for a second, unsure. "He said he didn't meet you until tonight."

"Well yes, I only met him tonight, but we had a nice little chat. I thought … " She laughed. "Does he have a need to make his life exciting or something?"

It wasn't her best act, but Andrew was half smiling now. "Sounds about right. I know you made an impression on him."

"I bet," she laughed. It was time to change the subject. "So you must live around here?"

"Yeah," he said, looking back at the ice cream. She scanned his jacket and reached out, tapping the pocket she could reach. No phone. "Wife's pregnant and has these cravings late at night. So here I am."

"That's very nice of you," she said, moving to his other side as though trying to help him decide.

"Well, it's our first baby, so I'm trying to start things out right. Damn!" He said the last part just as she touched his other pocket and felt the phone. She jumped.

"Sorry," he said, misinterpreting her reaction. "She is set on the fudge ripple and they're all out. I can't believe it."

"Well, that won't do." Bristol spun around and spotted a clerk down a nearby row. The guy looked to be in his seventies. "Excuse me," she said, walking toward him. He didn't look up until she almost reached him.

"Oh, hi there, sweetheart. What can I do for you this evening?"

"You wouldn't have any fudge ripple lying around the back, would you? My friend's pregnant wife is desperate."

"Oh! Sure thing, young lady," he said, tipping a nonexistent hat.

"Thanks," Andrew said from halfway down the aisle, but then turned back toward the ice cream. "But I better see what else I can find just in case."

She walked back to him and pointed at a pint. "Mint chocolate chip is my favorite."

"*She* might not mind it, but it's my least favorite, and I'd like to enjoy the spoils of this trip. You have kids?"

She looked at him, her eyes wide. "Me? No, no, no, no. I'm not a very good *kid* person."

"Well, you sure went out of your way for me. I appreciate it."

The old man came back holding up the ice cream container like it was the Olympic torch.

"Hey!" Andrew said. Bristol used the opportunity. She pushed up against him like she was congratulating him. As he took possession of the fudge ripple, she took possession of his phone.

"Well, my job here is done. I guess I should get on with my own shopping." She turned to the old man. "Thank you so much sir," she said, bowing a little to the clerk. He tipped his pretend hat again and returned to stock the shelves.

"Thanks again," Andrew said. "And hey, if Cole gets in touch? He's a great guy. It would be worth your while giving him the time of day."

She smiled and waved him off, saving the shocked expression for once she had moved into the closest aisle. Whatever Cole had said to Andrew, he hadn't mentioned that she was a problem. He must have had a reason for keeping it to himself, but she didn't know what it was, and she didn't like not knowing. He played with different rules than hers. He had outsmarted her once, and she wouldn't let him do it again.

She grabbed a box of Little Debbie snack cakes, biding her time till Andrew was out of the shop. It was late, and she deserved a little something for a job well done. She imagined calling up Cole to gloat but didn't like the flutter it brought on.

Once Andrew left the store, she pulled his phone out of her pocket. Bringing up the home screen there was, of course, a pin code, which would be no trouble for her friend Mick. Bristol stared at the photo of Andrew and his wife on the lock screen. Appearances were deceiving, and Bristol was a master at that deceit. But she had a feeling about Andrew and a feeling about Tanner, and right now she trusted Andrew more. Once the phone was unlocked, maybe she'd have some questions answered. But it could wait till morning.

Cole's phone rang, ripping him from a dream. It had been a good dream.

"This had better be important," he mumbled. "Hello?" He wiped at his eyes.

"Cole, sorry, did I wake you? Of course I woke you. Sorry."

Cole sat straight up in bed.

"Andrew, what's wrong?"

"My phone, Cole. She took my phone."

"What? Who?"

"Why didn't you tell me? I didn't know they had taken it this far. This is crazy. If they…"

"Wait, Andrew, slow down."

" … They've gone too far, Cole. Sending someone to follow me in the middle of the night to steal my phone? What is that?"

"What's happened? Who took your phone?"

"That girl … umm … Bristol! From the bar. Why didn't you tell me who she weas? You acted like she was no big deal, but she is, isn't she? Why didn't you tell me? I didn't know."

"Calm down Andrew and tell me what happened."

"She must have followed me to the grocery store."

"Followed you from where? I made sure there was no one following you when I left you at your car."

"I don't know, my house? Oh my god, she must have been at my house."

Cole heard a thump. "Andrew?" There was a rustling. "Andrew."

"Sorry, I was checking if she was out there now. I can't see anything. Do you know what car she drives?"

"Back up a minute. Why were you at the grocery store?"

Andrew breathed heavily into the phone. "Because I've got a pregnant wife. Now are you going to let me finish?"

"Sorry, go." Cole was still trying to rub the sleep out of his eyes.

"She was there, at the grocery store, but she had on sweatpants. I thought she must be a local, and that's why she was at the bar too. She got the employee to go find me the fudge ripple, and she must have gotten close enough to get my phone from my pocket."

"She got the fudge ripple for you?"

"I hope you're taking this seriously. I've got a clean record. I've got a wife and a kid, and I can't go to jail, or worse. I can't. You've done great out there. I wouldn't do so well. This is my life."

"Okay, I'm sorry. But you're sure it was her? You're sure you had the phone on you?"

"Yes!"

"Okay, sorry. Sorry," Cole laughed.

"You're laughing at me."

"No, not you, me, or rather, Bristol. I thought she was there for another reason."

"What?"

"So she could hit on you and someone could get photos to threaten you with. Geez." Cole leaned back against the bedhead and ran his hand through his hair. "I knew she was too clever for that," he said, more to himself than to Andrew.

"What?"

"Sorry, I should have listened to my instincts, but don't worry. I'll get it back. I think I know what she's doing with it anyway, so don't stress. It would have been worse if you never noticed it was gone and then found it thinking you had lost it."

"Why?"

"Trust me. I'll get it back, okay? Don't stress. I thought they were just trying to discredit you. Look, you just stay out of it from here on out. I'll take it from here. And I'll handle Bristol. Get yourself transferred to another case, and they'll get off your back. Let them think you're scared."

"It wouldn't be that far from the truth."

"Good, that should be easy then. I'll make sure they come after me instead."

"That's not a positive outcome either, but I'll take it."

"You go give your wife a hug from me, okay?"

"Okay."

Cole ran a hand down his face. That's what he gets for being cocky. He should know better. He could tell she was smart. Clever. Not just some girl they slipped a few bucks to play a role.

He found her picture on his phone. The smile that spread across his face vanished as quickly as it had come.

"I'm gonna find out who you are, and you're going to wish you never took that job," he said to her picture. It was a good lesson to learn. He'd let himself go soft. At the end of his time with the police, he had to watch his back constantly. But these days, no one suspected him. Breaking into places to help fix security issues was different. It was straightforward. You didn't need to figure out what was going on in everyone else's head, knowing they were trying to figure out what was going on in yours. He'd forgotten to watch his back, but that was all fixed now. He put the phone down and considered who she might be working for. Someone on the inside, certainly, but how far up was the question.

Cole threw back the sheets and headed for the bathroom. The moon shot though the living room window, cutting a path across the room.

He splashed water on his face and rubbed hard. He had to get himself back in the game.

Chapter 12

BRISTOL WALKED UP to the red brick apartment complex and paused, took a deep breath, and pushed the buzzer. A voice made its way through the static of the speaker. "Yeah?"

"It's Bristol."

"I don't want what you're sellin'."

"Shut up and unlock the door, bonehead."

The door buzzed and Bristol pushed through.

On the second floor, the apartment door at the end of the hall was ajar. Little fingers gripped the lower part of the door. Bristol squatted down and tickled the fingers. A six-year-old girl with orange-red hair jumped out at her, pigtails flailing. Bristol scooped her up and swung her around, kicking the door shut behind her when she walked into the apartment.

"Bishy, I missed you. Why did it take you so long to come visit?"

"Sweetheart, I have been very busy, but nothing would keep me from you for very long." She put the girl down and swatted her on the bum as she moved around the corner. The room opened up in front of her. It had the feel of a warehouse but in a small space. A brick wall was painted white in the living area with a large, comfortable-looking leather couch. An open kitchen was to the left, and to her right she found her friend standing behind a desk, bent over and typing. He pushed the glasses up his slim nose, stood up straight, and tipped his head to the side in annoyance. "You always show up at the most inopportune times," he said, moving around the desk to give her a hug.

"I know, Mick, and I only come when I want something," she said, hugging him tightly. He was shorter than her with a boyish face, so even though he was eight years older than her she thought of him like a little brother.

"I've always loved this place," she said, surveying the room and moving toward a wall covered in photos. She straightened one.

"You just put these up?"

"A few months ago."

"Has it been that long since I've been here?"

"Longer. You're lucky Lila recognizes you." There was a smile on his face, but Bristol knew she was also meant to take it seriously.

She looked back at the photos and reached up to touch the face of the red-headed woman with a bulging stomach standing next to Mick.

"Even after five years I still miss her," Bristol said. Mick said nothing, just pulled his glasses off and sat on the edge of the desk.

He sighed, and she knew he wanted to tell her to let go. Instead he said, "What have you got for me."

"Straight to it then?"

"You're not one for socializing when you've got work to do."

She shrugged and pulled Andrew's phone out of her bag. "I need to know what's on this."

"Bishy, look at this," Lila said, tugging on Bristol's jacket and holding up a mostly colored-in rabbit in a forest.

"Should you be in school, Lila?"

Lila scrunched up her nose. "It's Saturday."

"Oh, of course. Silly me."

Bristol took the picture as if it were priceless. "Did you steal this from an art museum?"

Lila laughed. "No, *I* made it."

"Don't be silly. This was done by a professional."

Lila shook her head hard, beaming. "Nope, it was *me.*"

"Well, you had better keep it safe because that will be worth squillions someday."

"I want you to have it." Lila's straight white teeth shown from her freckled face.

Bristol's eyes widened. "For me? Really?"

"Really."

"I will keep it safe for you then. And I've got the perfect place on my fridge for it, front and center."

"Wanna see my dolls?"

"Sweets, I'd love to, but I have a little bit of work to do with your dad, and then I've got another meeting to get to. But next time I come over, I promise."

"Okay," Lila said, now sulking.

"Lila," Mick said, his voice stern. Lila flopped onto the couch.

"So Bristol, what is it you need me to do once I get in here."

Bristol put a folder on his desk. "I might need you to put this stuff on it. A few numbers and messages. But you can wait till I say, because I am currently undecided about how I will work this assignment." She reached into her bag and pulled out another phone she had bought on her way over and laid it next to the other. "Keep this one handy. It's my 'just in case' phone."

Mick's eyebrows went up. "Okay, so if I'm not adding stuff to the first one, what do you want me to do with it?"

"I want to know what's on it first."

"Shouldn't take me too long. I'll get in touch once it's open."

"Thanks, Mick." Bristol headed toward the door.

"Hey," Mick said, moving quickly toward her.

"You don't have to be a stranger around here, you know."

Bristol nodded. "It's just hard," she breathed, and glanced over at Lila playing pretend with her dolls. She wiggled one, speaking under her breath to the other, who she then wiggled in response. She was lost in her world of pretend, and Bristol was slightly envious and also happy for Lila's innocence. Something she never got much of in her own childhood.

"You think it's easy for me?"

Bristol's head dropped. "I'm sorry, I didn't—"

"—No, I know. It's just that Lila adores you, and she doesn't have another female around."

"I don't think that I'm the best role-model, Mick."

"You don't have to teach her your trade, just be her friend. I miss your friendship too. You weren't just my wife's friend."

"I know," she said, putting her hand on his shoulder. She kissed his cheek. "I'll make an effort to come around more, but right now, I've got work to do."

But all Bristol could think about as she walked out of the building was how easy it was to lie to her friends, and it hurt.

Bristol's phone buzzed, and she pulled it out of her bag, sliding her finger across the screen when she saw who it was.

"Deb, what do you have for me?"

"Oooh, girl, he is *fine*."

Bristol looked up at the sky and dropped her mouth open. "Are you calling me to extol the positive aspects of your boyfriend?"

"No, not him," she said, her laugh deep. "I don't know why you're after this guy, but I hope it's for all the right reasons."

Bristol caught on. "The license plate," she said blandly.

"It belongs to one Cole Sullivan. He's six-foot-two, sandy blond hair, blue eyes, thirty-four. He owns a business that has something to do with security. He has an address on Coastline Drive in Malibu, so he must be loaded. I'll text that through to you after we say goodbye. But finally and most importantly, he is drop-dead gorgeous."

"Yeah, he's not bad looking, but what I want to know is why he is interfering with the subject."

"The subject? Listen to you, always the expert at keeping yourself devoid of all feeling."

"When it comes to my work, yes."

"Honey, I hate to break it to you, but you're pretty good at that on all fronts."

"Thanks for the deep and meaningful but I've got to go."

"You might be interested in one other teeny-weeny fact."

Bristol was already pulling the phone from her ear but put it back. "And what's that."

"He used to be a police officer. I'm not able to give you the specifics of why he isn't anymore, but according to my main squeeze, I can tell you it wasn't a pleasant parting."

"Thanks for your help, Deb."

"Happy to help. I think you should go find this guy and give him a stern talking to. Enemies always do make the best lov—."

Bristol quickly hung up.

She took a deep breath when she got in the car, then looked over at the apartment building. There was work to do, and she needed to remove the sentimentality that had settled in her stomach. Gritting her teeth, she sat up straight and turned the key. It was time to play a spot of golf.

◯◯

Bristol pulled into the manicured driveway of the Los Angeles Country Club, slowing down when she spotted the guard at his post. She smoothed her hand along the slacks she had changed into and tucked in her blouse. She had taken the extra precaution of borrowing Deb's car. The red Corvette fit in around here better than her aging sedan, and she took the scenic route which included driving forty-five minutes out of her way just to enjoy the ride.

She didn't expect to find Tanner, but people here wouldn't be as tight-lipped as those at the LAPD. Asking questions here wouldn't raise the same alarm.

She pulled to a stop as the guard signaled to her. He was in his forties with brown hair and a clean-shaven face. He walked deliberately to her car, like a guy who took his job seriously. For a moment she pictured pulling a gun out on him, just to give him a little excitement. Instead, she smiled softly as he rested his hand on her window.

"I'm here to meet a friend for lunch," she said, looking at him from under her eyelashes.

He smiled. It was neutral, but she saw a muscle tighten in his jaw.

"Are you a member?"

"No sir. I'm meeting with a Detective Tanner." She winced. She should have had his full name ready.

"Is this police business?"

She grinned and lifted her shoulders. "In a manner of speaking."

He noted her licensed plate then indicated forward. "Go ahead through, miss. Just make sure you stop in at reception first."

She wiggled her fingers at him as she drove past but made a face as soon as she was clear.

She pulled into a parking spot toward the back so she could keep everything within view and climbed out of the car, pulling her salmon coat from the seat behind her. The sun had been behind clouds all day, but it was out in full now. She dropped her coat over her arm and lifted her head, breathing in the heat that touched her face. A chilled breeze swept across her, bringing her back to her present task.

When the sun disappeared again, she slipped on her coat and tied the belt in a knot at her waist, then pushed her shoulders back to get ready to do business.

After taking only three steps, she saw Tanner walk out the front door, pulling on a long coat. Two other guys followed him.

"Huh," she said to no one but herself. "Today must be my lucky day." She enjoyed the game of eliciting information out of unsuspecting patrons and was looking forward to it, but that would have to wait. And ultimately this would save a lot of time.

She made her way toward him, squinting against the sun that had reappeared. He pulled some fancy looking leather gloves from his pocket but then stuffed them back in when the sun started peaking out again.

"Tanner," she said when she was about ten feet away. He hadn't previously noticed her. His face puckered as though he had sucked on a lemon, but he said, "What a pleasant surprise."

She smiled politely as he looked her up and down. His two companions didn't look like golfers, and she wondered if he always had an entourage to feel important. "How'd you find me here?"

"You told me yourself."

He looked down at the ground for a moment thinking then nodded. "What do you want?"

"Things aren't exactly going to plan."

"Didn't you get your money?"

"That's not what I'm talking about."

He clicked his tongue. "Why don't we talk somewhere a little more private?" he said, walking toward a small alcove at the side of the building.

"I'm not sure what you're afraid of," she said, following him.

"Huh," he said, turning and crossing his arms. "I thought I made it clear I wanted minimal contact with you."

The other two guys had hung back as she followed, and now they stood close behind her.

She glanced at the two guys like she was bored, then looked at Tanner. "Andrew's got help. Why is that?"

From the flicker in Tanner's eye, she could tell that was news to him. "What help?"

"A gentleman by the name of Cole Sullivan."

Tanner's expression barely changed, but it was

enough to see that this new information had riled him. He rubbed a finger on his temple.

"Sullivan." He spat against the wall. She was sure if the security guard saw that, there would be trouble. "Don't worry about Sullivan. I'll take care of him."

"I'm not worried about Cole. What I'm worried about is why you lied to me about Andrew."

Tanner's eyes flashed. He grabbed her arm and the two other men moved in. "I wouldn't worry about that either if I were you." He let go of her arm and pushed her up against the wall with a hand on each shoulder and pushed his body into hers. "It was suggested to me to go about things the easy way, 'more flies with honey' and all that, but it's not my usual manner of getting what I want. You've got a job to do, and you better do it."

She kept her eyes on his, making sure he understood she wasn't afraid of him. She tried to get a knee in, but with his body weight, she couldn't get enough room to strike. A scratch to the face might have been possible, but she came up with a better idea.

One of Tanner's goons made a move, jutting his chin out to the side, and Tanner backed off. Someone had come into the parking lot.

"So what's it gonna be? Easy way or hard way?"

She swallowed her pride for the bigger picture. Even let a bit of fear enter her eyes. "Easy."

"I'm glad we have an understanding. Now if you'll excuse me, I have better things to do." He started to walk away but then turned back to her. "And if you ever turn up here again or contact me in any way other than that phone number I gave you, you're dead."

She dropped her head and leaned back onto her hands against the wall.

Tanner was strutting to his car with the two guys trailing behind him. He kept an eye on her as he got into his car, and she even saw a little grin form in the corner of his mouth.

After Tanner drove away, she pulled her hands out from behind her and slapped the leather gloves she had stolen out of his pocket against her palm. The truth was, she liked the hard way better. It didn't always pay as well, but some things were better than cash.

Chapter 13

COLE ARRIVED at Robert's mansion and was ushered in by a gentleman in his mid-sixties with a comb-over. They walked through the vaulted entry and past the opulence of a dual staircase. He didn't bother glancing around. The house reminded him of the one he grew up in. It didn't offer much besides a lot of show. He could picture the wine cellar in the basement and more bath-rooms than bedrooms. There would be a pool house and maybe even a bowling alley, although Robert didn't strike him as the bowling type. No pun intended.

The tennis court was out past the pool. Cole hadn't dressed for it. He wasn't sure whether Robert was serious in his suggestion of a game of tennis, and Cole wasn't interested in wasting time playing games. He'd had enough of those this week.

When they reached the court, Robert was playing against a machine, practicing his swing. Cole went to the batting cages sometimes, to burn off steam, but for some reason a tennis ball seemed pointless. He wondered what people got out of the game. Perhaps if he bothered to learn the rules, he'd have a greater appreciation of it. Besides "game, set, match" he knew nothing except don't miss the ball. He stepped onto the side of the court in his blue jeans and a light blue button-down. It was warm enough to roll the sleeves up.

Robert was kitted out. He was as fit as Cole expected. A man with that much money generally goes one of two ways.

"You're not playing?" Robert asked, keeping his eye on the ball.

"You'll have more fun playing against that machine," Cole said, leaning against the fence. After a few more swings, Robert motioned to the man on the machine and walked over to a chair, wiping his face with a towel.

"Don't knock it till you've tried it," Robert said, reading Cole like a book.

"Was I making a face?"

"No one has ever turned down an offer to play here." He said this matter-of-factly and started to walk back to the house, so Cole followed. There was a man waiting by the back door who Robert called over with the flick of a wrist.

"Would you like anything? Coffee? Something stronger?"

"No, thanks. I'm fine."

He waved the man away and motioned for Cole to sit at a small table in the shade at the side of the large patio.

"I take it you'd like to get down to business."

Cole laid a folder on the table and Robert began perusing it. His eyes lifted to Cole and his eyebrows followed. "My staff were not trained to behave this way."

"No, I'm certain they weren't, but over time, people get into habits. And there are ways of getting people to respond the way you want them to. You can distract them while you slip something else past them. There are a few different price points in there. You never told me what you were trying to keep secure, so how much money you want to spend will decide which option you'll want to choose."

"And your company can do all of these options."

"Like I said, I contract the best to get the job done."

"But you oversee the operation."

"Absolutely."

"I've got a question for you."

"Shoot."

Robert smiled dryly. "Why did you leave the police force?"

"You've been checking up on me."

"I never let anyone work for me if I don't know their history. You didn't think I would let just anyone break into my building, did you?"

"Not even at Silas's recommendation?" Robert just smiled. "You're a man with access to a lot of information. Why haven't you found out for yourself?"

"You can't believe everything you read. And while they may have asked you to leave, I think you weren't too disappointed."

"How'd you work that one out?"

"You didn't put up a fight. You seem like the kind of guy who doesn't go quietly. So perhaps the correct question for you is, why were you so willing to leave?"

Cole tapped his finger on the armrest. "I like to get the job done, and I don't enjoy being restricted by policy to do it."

"And that's what makes you so good at your job now."

"Precisely. But I would imagine you know more about me than my police record."

"I know enough to understand you're well trained for your business."

"And always learning."

"I'll read through your report and get back to you," Robert said, rising.

"Can I ask you a question?"

Robert sat back in his chair while Cole pulled his phone out of his pocket.

"Seeing as you are so good at getting information, I don't suppose you could try to find out about someone for me?" He handed his phone to Robert. "I need to know who that is. So far all I have is a first name. I think."

Robert's mouth spread into a wide smile and his head tipped sideways.

"Interesting. I don't know her, but I might be able to find some information. Out of curiosity, who is she?"

"Does it matter?"

"Yes."

"She's interfering with another job I have."

"I should think, in your line of work, you'd be good at dealing with obstacles."

"I am, and this is how I'm dealing with it. My guys haven't found her yet, and I like to know who my adversaries are."

Robert rubbed his chin with his long soft fingers. "Text me the photo and I'll see what I can find out."

Cole stood up and held his hand out to shake Robert's. "I've got a busy day, so we can leave it there. Look over my proposals and get in touch if you have any questions."

Robert stood and shook Cole's hand.

Cole walked out, uncomfortable knowing he had given Robert information to find Bristol, but she wasn't his friend and he owed her nothing.

Chapter 14

BRISTOL PARKED ON COASTLINE DRIVE, two houses down on the opposite side of the road from Cole's place. She hadn't planned on staying long. This was about seeing where Cole lived and getting a feel for it, and she wanted to stretch out her time in the Corvette. Deb was more than happy for Bristol to keep the car when she told her where she was going.

She had spent most of the rest of the day trying to decide whether or not to confront Cole. Tanner was obviously no friend of Cole's, which gave him a bit more credit. But the questions were piling up higher than the answers, and that irritated her. If he was on Andrew's side, he'd have the answers she was looking for, but whether she could trust him was still an unknown.

She had done a little digging and found that his apartment was the penthouse on the left. There had been no movement, but there wasn't much to see if he wasn't on the balcony or standing at a front window. She planned to sit and watch the sun set and then go. No use wasting a great view.

She leaned the seat back a couple inches and stretched out. She had changed out of her fancy upmarket outfit and felt much more comfortable to be back in jeans and her favorite loose white top. The sun was setting and her view through to the ocean held her gaze.

The phone rang, breaking her reverie. It was Mick.

"What have you got for me?"

"Hi to you, too."

"Sorry, I'm on work time right now."

"Stake out?"

"How did you know that?"

"It was a lucky guess. So, I got the phone open and I've downloaded everything into a file for you. There are some photos that are odd though. A few pictures that appear to be crime scene photos but then there are also pictures of paintings. They seem innocent enough, but what would a grown man be doing with paintings of young girls?"

"Young girls?"

"Yeah. They're lovely paintings. It just doesn't fit why this guy would have a dozen paintings of these girls."

"Anything on there related to drugs?"

"Not that I can see."

Bristol processed that information. She trusted her gut, but she also knew not to jump to conclusions. "Well, part of my job is to delete whatever is on there so whether it's the dead girl or the paintings they don't want anyone to see, I'm not sure." Bristol banged her hand on the steering wheel. She was fed up with this whole thing. A knot formed in the pit of her stomach. She was in the middle of something and looking for the good side, but unsure if there even was one. Most of her jobs don't have a good side so she just chooses the side that pays, but the stakes were always clear. This was just a big muddy puddle.

"Bristol, you there?"

"Sorry, yeah, just thinking. Can you send me those photos now? I'll have a look."

"Are you okay? Do you know what you're getting into?"

"No, I don't, and that's the problem. I just want to have a quick look while I've got you on the phone."

The sun sank behind the horizon and Bristol looked up to see Cole standing on the balcony. He was unfortunately good looking, but good looking didn't mean you were one of the good guys. In fact, in her experience, it usually meant the opposite. It was too dark to tell if he had spotted her.

Her phone dinged as the photos came through and she changed the phone to speaker while she flipped through. The first couple showed a girl, probably in her early teens, dead on the pavement. The next few were just as Mick said, paintings of girls. They were all pretty, and even though the pictures weren't provocative, they were painted in a way that seemed out of place. She looked at the dead girl's face memorizing it, then scanned the paintings. None of them matched.

"Can you add those messages and phone calls to the other phone I gave you?" Bristol said.

"So I take it you are deviating from your original job?"

"It's looking that way. I'm not going to work for the bad guys on purpose. Not in this case anyway."

"And what if the bad guys come after you next?"

"That's the risk I take. And I'm good at hiding my tracks. But right now I need to get some answers. Then I'll know for sure."

"Do I dare ask where you get your answers from?"

"Do you ever?" She looked up and saw Cole was gone.

"Good point. Lila says hi and to keep safe."

"Give her a hug for me and tell her whatever you need to to make her smile."

"You don't have to keep putting yourself in harm's way you know."

"I've been in harm's way my whole life. I don't know how to do things differently. Besides, there is one girl dead and if these paintings are related, I want to make sure no one else ends up dead."

"How do you know they're even real people?"

"I don't, but I never have all the answers at once. That's the point of finding out more." Bristol spread her fingers on the photo to bring up the bottom corner. "There's a signature on the painting, but it's not clear, can you read it on your end?"

"Yeah, I spotted that too. The name is *E. Drake.*"

"You sure?"

"Yeah, I Googled him, although I can't find other

portraits he's done. His stuff is more political. At least that's what the website says. I'd call it disturbing."

"That's modern art for you. So nothing classic?"

"Not on his website."

"Did it say where he's based?"

"LA"

"Okay, I can look him up, maybe pay him a visit." Bristol looked back at Cole's place. A dark figure was scaling the wall. "Oh, shit … sorry."

"What is it?"

"Looks like Tanner already sent someone to clean up."

"Whose Tanner?"

"I've gotta go or else I'll miss out on my answers."

"Be safe."

"Whatever you have to tell yourself. Talk soon." She hung up the phone before he could say anymore.

She waited till the figure moved around the side before she got out of her car.

∞

Cole cracked open a mineral water and took it out onto the balcony to watch the remnants of the sun as it sank below the ocean. Out of the corner of his eye he spotted a red Corvette he hadn't seen on the street before. He kept his face pointed at the ocean, but he could make out the figure of a woman with long dark hair. The glowing of a phone lit up her face and confirmed his first guess. He didn't take her for a Corvette girl, but he had the very strong urge to join her in the car. He kept his feet firmly planted. Better to wait and see what her next move was.

It irked him a little that he was pleased to see her there. He became very aware of himself and took a sip of his drink, conscious that she might be watching. He began to dissect each move and how she would analyze it. It was disconcerting, but not enough to put him off. It had been a while since he'd had a proper challenge.

He moved back into the house. He should pour two drinks. That way, if she found her way in here, she'd see he was waiting for her. He frowned and sat down on a stool at the counter. This was ridiculous. Everything felt awkward and forced. Normally it flowed out of him, like at the bar. He had handled her in his usual way and had taken her by surprise, stealing her quarry, even though she got what she wanted in the end.

But now she was onto him. It wouldn't work the same way a second time. What he needed to do was persuade her to switch teams, or at the very least, drop the job on Andrew. Although, they'd just get someone else on him, and better the devil you know than the one you don't. He dropped his head. Now he was thinking in cliché.

He glanced over at the blueprints he had acquired of Lincoln Tower. He had been studying them further. There were several other issues he had noted but didn't add them into the report for Robert. He ran his finger over the corridor that led off the lobby. There was a room that was most likely used for the guards' break-room or maybe a conference room. There was another elevator back there he had considered using if things went pear-shaped.

He heard a car door shut. It wasn't slammed, and he almost missed it, which is probably what she was hoping for. He smiled then stood at the kitchen counter with his back to the balcony, still undecided about how to handle her. At least he knew she was coming. With all this second guessing, the best way to move forward would be with straight candor. That would probably throw her off anyway.

He moved back over to the balcony. He should make it easy for her. Save her trying to be too sly getting in. He quickly poured some of his drink into a cup, intending to catch her outside and offer her a drink. He stepped out and looked out onto the street. She wasn't there. He heard a rubbing sound and had started to turn when he saw arms come up over his head.

Instinctively he lifted his own arms, and his wrists caught the rope. The glass dropped to the floor and smashed. A force drove into the back of his legs and his knee smashed into the concrete. Pain ran up into his hip. He jerked hard on his arms but didn't have enough strength, and he was being pulled back. He hadn't expected Bristol to be this strong, but then he hadn't expected her to try to kill him either.

He struggled to breathe now as his knuckles pushed into his throat, and he realized he was holding back, not wanting to hurt her. Now his training kicked in, and he wrenched all of his strength to pull the hulking weight around to the side.

Getting a hand free, he smashed a fist into the figure that was now reachable. The sound that came out was not that of a woman, and the shape was all wrong. The face was covered with a balaclava, but it was definitely a man. He pushed the guy over the glass, knowing it wouldn't do any serious damage but might slow him down.

A knife gleamed, reflecting the moonlight, and Cole spotted it just in time to dive back inside as it was thrust at him.

He heard banging at the door and wondered if the neighbors had called the police yet or were there to complain.

The assailant jumped toward him with the knife, and Cole kicked out, knocking the guy back. Cole got to his feet as he saw the man move to kick him and started to block it, but his hand caught on the couch, and the kick got him in the side, sending him sprawling across the coffee table. If he made it out of here alive, he needed to rethink his interior decorating. If this became a regular thing, then there was way too much furniture in this room.

His head yanked back by his hair just at the sound of a crash behind him. He knew what was coming and lifted his arm to block the knife coming at his throat. Then the familiar sound of a gun with a silencer whispered into the room.

The weight of the man fell heavily on top of him and he was flattened to the floor, the knife landing in front of him. He reached out and grabbed it while twisting himself around trying to keep the, now-dead, man as a shield.

Bristol stood a few feet away, pointing the gun at his head.

Chapter 15

BRISTOL SAID NOTHING, just stood quietly, not ready to put the gun down yet.

"You okay in there?" A voice called from outside the apartment.

"Yeah, sorry for the disturbance. Just had a bit of an accident, but all fine. Thanks for checking," Cole said, watching Bristol.

The voice called out again. "I think your door might be broken." He sounded more confused than worried. This is not a place where people get attacked.

"Yeah, it probably is, but I'll get it fixed straight away so no issue. In fact, I've already called someone to come fix it."

"If you say so."

Bristol looked at Cole's hand holding the knife. She noticed a slight tremor. More likely from fatigue than from fear. His wrist was red and there was blood running down his face. They watched each other for a minute, then Cole set the knife on the coffee table and wrestled the dead guy off him. Blood covered the rug.

"Sorry about your rug," Bristol said, still holding the gun toward him.

"I didn't like the color anyway, so you did me a favor."

"Not to mention saving your life."

Cole pushed himself up off the floor and dropped onto a nearby chair. "You're still pointing the gun at me, so I'm holding off my thanks until I know I get to keep my life." He looked behind her toward the stairs that led down to his front door. "I think you might have wrecked my door."

She lowered her gun now. "But I saved your life."

"I don't know. Now that I think about it, I believe I could have taken him." He reached down and pulled the balaclava off the man, then looked at her. "Friend of yours?"

She had hoped it was Tanner but knew he would never get his hands dirty on something like this. "Nope."

"Would you like to sit?" Bristol looked at the couch then moved over to the kitchen counter and sat on a stool there. She still held the gun in her hand, and Cole was looking at it. "I'll be honest, when that guy first attacked me, I thought it was you."

"Why, because girls you meet want to see you dead?"

Cole smiled and shook his head. "The more I get to know you, the more I like you. But you have to work on your stalking skills. I saw you in your car."

"Thought you might."

"You did not."

"Did too." The side of her mouth crept up into a smile.

"We should go out sometime," Cole said, crossing his arms, unsure what exactly he was doing. Bristol lifted the gun again. "I'll take that as a maybe."

"It won't work this time, Cole."

"What won't?"

"That same old routine from the bar."

"Hey, I was nothing but completely honest. I told you from the start I wasn't hitting on you. You didn't belong there, and I was concerned for my friend. And quite frankly, I was right to be concerned, was I not?"

"Well, your *concern* meant I got slobbered on by Jabba the Hutt."

Cole laughed and put his hand on his throbbing ribs. "I had not intended that."

"Don't care. You are responsible for your actions. So now you owe me."

"I'm good with that."

"Do you know how to talk to a woman without flirting?"

"I can't help it if my natural charm comes across as flirtatious."

Bristol looked down at the dead man and realized how ridiculous the whole scenario was. "Okay, look. I just want some answers." She rested the gun in her lap.

"Don't you think the guy who was nearly killed should be the one asking questions."

"No, I think the one with the gun should be the one asking."

"Fair enough."

"Tell me about Andrew."

"Nothin' to tell."

Bristol lifted the gun again. "I could finish the job this guy started if you're no use to me."

"Go ahead. There's still not much to tell about Andrew. He's a good detective."

"What about husband?"

"What?"

"Does he beat his wife or anyone else for that matter?"

"Are we talking about the same man?"

Bristol sighed. "Hold on, I'll be right back."

She had the photos Tanner gave her in the car and swapped them for the gun. When she came back up the stairs, Cole was in the kitchen. "Hungry?"

She shook her head. "You've got a dead man in your living room and you're making dinner?"

"I've been in worse situations and had to get a meal together." He pulled vegetables out of the fridge and set a skillet on the gas burner. She held up the first photo that showed Andrew screaming into the face of a crying woman. He was holding both her wrists.

Cole looked at it then back down at the veggies. "Who gave you those?"

"Guy named Tanner."

Cole stopped chopping. "Tanner's the one who hired you?"

"Apparently I wasn't his first choice, so there's someone higher up pulling the strings, but he's my contact."

"I should have known."

"Yeah, he seemed to know you too."

Cole pointed at the dead man with his knife. He didn't say anything, just raised his eyebrows.

Bristol shrugged. "Sorry."

Cole put the knife down and ran his hand down his face. "So what exactly is it you do? And don't tell me makeovers."

"You could call it 'sleight of hand.'"

"So you're a magician?"

"More or less. I do the same things as a magician: distraction, manipulation of senses … "

"Deception? Murder?"

"Depends on the job. In this particular case, it's more of a smoke and mirrors thing."

"Frame the wrong guy for murder."

"What? No, for drugs."

"Drugs? So this doesn't have to do with the dead girl?"

"You mean the one on Andrew's phone."

"Yes, Andrew's phone. The one you need to give back."

"I'll get to it. Who's the dead girl?"

"I was hoping you could help with that."

"All I know about are the drugs."

"That's a good place to start. Tell me about the drugs."

"Tanner told me Internal Affairs was investigating, and he wanted to make sure their attention was on Andrew. He gave me some phone numbers and conversations that I assume are connected to known drug dealers."

"And you have no problem with framing Andrew and ruining his life?"

"Not when he deserves it."

"And you just take Tanner's word for it."

"He convinced me. Now I'm unconvinced. Something is going on. It's not right, and I'd like to stop it. I just don't know what or why yet."

Cole put the vegetables in the pan and started slicing up a sausage and haloumi. "That's not his wife," Cole said, nodding to the photo Bristol had laid on the counter.

"I didn't think so."

"She was a prostitute, high on something, who had lost it. Andrew was trying to talk her down. Ended up with his face scratched up because of it. Those pictures were taken a few years ago." He glanced at Bristol's arm and reached out, turning it over. "Looks like you've had a bit of scratching up."

"A friend's cat."

"For some reason I'm not surprised."

"I don't like cats, and I think they can tell."

Cole brushed the back of his hand on his face and smeared the blood. Bristol went around into the kitchen and wet a paper towel.

"Sorry, I'm a feeling a bit OCD," Bristol said as she patted the blood off his face. She lifted the hair off his temple to see where the blood came from. Cole swallowed but didn't comment, just let her do her thing.

"It's stopped bleeding."

She saw his face was red and nearly made a comment about him blushing but left it. They were both silent as Cole finished the meal. He served up two plates and set one before her, handing her a fork.

"Didn't I say I wasn't hungry?" The meal smelled amazing, and she hadn't eaten much today.

Cole shrugged. "Strictly a business meal, I promise."

She took the fork. Now that she had decided to eat, she dug in. "This is amazing. What is it? She said lifting the cheese with her fork."

"Haloumi."

"Never heard of it, but it's amazing."

"You've never heard of haloumi? Really?"

"I'm not as cultured as you are," she said, stuffing another forkful in.

"Maybe not, but you sure know how to eat."

"Are you making fun of me?"

"No," he laughed. "I'm impressed."

She finished before him, and he pushed his last piece of cheese up his plate for her.

"Thanks." She stabbed it with her fork. "You're a good cook. I can make the basics but never learned beyond that."

"You mean you weren't *interested* in learning."

"No," she said, pulling the fork away from her mouth. "I mean, we never had more than frozen meals at home so I couldn't even try."

Cole nodded. "Have you lived in LA all your life?"

"Yup. So tell me about the dead girl."

"You are great dinner company."

"You said it was a business dinner."

Cole paused, then said, "She was found dead, over-dose, on the side of the road. Andrew brought me in because he wasn't getting anywhere on it. So now I'm looking into it, but I don't know anything about her yet."

"Were you a detective when you were with the police?"

"How does everyone know about that?"

"I've got friends."

"I'm good at what I do, and Andrew needs help. Especially when guys like Tanner," he pointed at the dead guy, "are involved."

"Okay, so we don't know much about the drugs and we don't know much about the dead girl. What about the paintings?"

"Of the girls?"

"Yeah."

"Don't know."

Bristol threw her arms up in the air. "That was the whole reason I came in here. To get answers. I shouldn't have bothered."

"You did save my life though. That's worth some-thing. To me at least," he said sheepishly, but his grin was anything but sheepish.

"Okay, yeah, it's nice to save a life. Especially since it was partly my fault." She tapped her fork on her empty plate. "You don't have any information at all?"

"I'm working on it."

"Well, maybe we can work together ... I mean sepa-rately, but together ... share information ... we don't need to actually work *together*." She was flustered and tried to cover it. "You obviously have a particular skill set, although I'm not sure what it is yet."

"Do you know how to give a compliment without ruining it?" Cole chided.

"I wasn't trying to compliment you."

"Maybe you should. It might lighten you up."

"That's just how I am. Take it or leave it."

"I'll take it."

"It was a rhetorical comment."

Cole smiled and put the dishes in the dishwasher.

Bristol studied the dead man with her hands on her hips. "What do we do about him?"

"I can get rid of the body if you don't have a better use for him."

She tapped a finger on her lips. "Actually, I do have an idea if you're free tomorrow."

"Are you asking me out on a date?"

"No."

"Great, it's a date then."

Bristol clicked her tongue. "Can you transport the body?"

"Sure, but I thought we weren't working *together*."

"Should we forget about it then?"

"No, no, I'm happy to go along with your plan." He was trying hard not to smile.

"Okay, I've got to check it out, but I'll call you tomorrow."

"You need my number?"

"No, I don't."

"Ooh, I like it when a girl shows some initiative."

"Oh, good grief. You have got to stop doing that."

"Can't help it. You bring out the best in me. And by the way, I'm assuming this isn't a continuation of the job you were hired to do? We aren't still framing Andrew? I gotta look out for my buddy. He's got a baby on the way."

"It won't be the first time a client's decision to employ me has backfired on them."

She collected the photos and headed for the door.

"You have to leave so soon?"

"I'll be honest with you, Cole."

"Please do."

"I enjoyed this."

"Me too."

"But it's strictly business."

"Of course."

As she got into her car, she saw Cole leaning on the balcony watching her. It hadn't felt like business, and she had liked it too much. She shouldn't have arranged to work with him. She couldn't allow herself a slip-up. But she needed his help.

Cole bit his lip as he watched her drive off. He had never met anyone like her before. He touched the side of his face where she had wiped off the blood as he breathed in the night air.

His thoughts drifted to Tanner, and a shiver surged

through him. He was half the reason Cole left the police. Guys like that could get away with murder, literally. But when Cole went out of bounds to get some justice, he was booted. The last thing he wanted was Bristol in Tanner's sights.

Chapter 16

COLE DIDN'T SLEEP WELL, and it had nothing to do with the broken door or the dead man wrapped up in his living room. He'd seen a lot worse. He had dreamt about Bristol all night. In each dream she was in mortal danger, but he couldn't get to her in time to save her. She had died a dozen times in his dreams, so when he woke at 4:30, he was glad to see the last of his night, even though it was dark. Why a woman he barely knew had occupied his dreams so thoroughly, he couldn't understand.

He sipped a coffee as the sky began to lighten, his ears itching for the phone to ring. He'd be on edge until he had something he could do.

Throwing the dregs of the coffee down the sink, he decided to get the body into his trunk. That way he'd be ready to go.

The guy was solid, but once Cole had him over his shoulder, it was easy to get him into the trunk of his car.

He checked the clock when he got back inside and

winced. It was going to be a long morning if she didn't get back to him early.

When he headed to the kitchen to make another coffee, his phone rang. He raced back to the living room and grabbed the phone but dropped it twice before he could answer. He noticed it was a private number as he slid his finger across the screen.

"Cole here."

"Did you see the college girl on the news yesterday? Killed her professor?" The voice was smooth but unrecognizable.

"Who is this?" He wanted the phone to be clear for Bristol's call.

"You wanted information, and I have it."

Cole paused. "This is about Bristol."

"Very perceptive, Mr. Sullivan."

"Who is this?"

"We have a common acquaintance. Robert Carlson. He said you were looking for information and that I may be of assistance."

"That still doesn't tell me who you are."

The man laughed, his breath languid. "Silas Lincoln."

Cole's mouth dropped open, but he quickly closed it and said, "Mr. Lincoln. Thank you for taking the time to call me back on this matter. And it gives me the opportunity to say thank you for the job with Mr. Carlson."

"It's nothing, really. I thought he needed the help and you're the best." He paused for a couple seconds and Cole thought the phone had gone dead. He looked at it and saw it was still connected. "So did you see the girl on the news?"

"Oh … uh, yeah. Looked like the guy did a pretty good number on her."

"I know for a fact that man didn't lay a hand on her. Well, not that night anyway."

Cole looked out at the brightening sky over the ocean. "So Bristol's an assassin."

"Mmm, no, not anymore, unfortunately. You two have more in common than perhaps you realize. You both specialize in manipulating what's before you. Is that what this is about?"

"What?"

"Has she managed to manipulate you?" Cole heard the smile in Silas's voice. "I can't say I'd be surprised."

Cole leaned back. If he gave Silas what he wanted to hear, he might get more information. "She did get the better of me in the end, but not before I got her."

"Well, don't feel bad. She got the better of me once, a long time ago. But there is a reason I'm where I am today and that is because I let nothing go and I'm good at putting things back the way I want them."

Cole decided to keep his current acquaintance with Bristol to himself. "So who killed him then, the dad?"

Silas laughed again. "Bristol is good isn't she. No, it wasn't the father. That college girl is a cold-blooded killer, and Bristol made her look like Anne of Green Gables. And now everyone is in love with her."

"But the girl was injured. The police mentioned broken ribs. Where'd that come from?"

"Bristol is brutal, but she's efficient. She's a woman who does what's necessary to get the job done."

Cole was having trouble reconciling the woman in his apartment with someone who had no trouble hurting someone for the sake of appearances. "So she's got no conscience." His miscalculation could cost him more trouble than he needed. Had he underestimated her again? He had no way to know if she was sincere except for a gut feeling.

Silas interrupted his ruminating. "Oh yes, she certainly has a conscience. Her greatest weakness. But I suppose we all have our weaknesses."

"What's yours?"

"That I am too good at using people's weakness against them."

"This isn't a job interview, Mr. Lincoln. You don't need to make your strength sound like a weakness. Although I'd hesitate to call that a strength."

"Touché. And please, call me Silas. But I'm sure you understand why I will not divulge that information freely."

"I'm sure I can come up with something close to accurate."

"Perhaps," Silas said, his voice dropping half an octave. "But your weakness Cole is that you trust too easily. You see the good in people, and it makes you vulnerable. It will eventually be your undoing." His voice lightened again. "However, Bristol fascinates me. Watching her work is like observing an artist creating a masterpiece. That's why I recommend her to friends, so I can watch her work. I like to see what she creates, how she manipulates everything around her and uses everything to her advantage. It will all come crashing down on her someday. I just hope I'm there to see it."

If Silas had been standing in front of him, Cole would have had to suppress the urge to punch him in the face. Silas was a man who had more than likely ruined many lives, and the thought of him delighting in Bristol's downfall turned his stomach. But his comment about her using everything to her advantage set him on edge. "Do you know who her most recent employer is?"

Silas was quiet again. "No," he finally said. Cole knew that was a lie, but what reason did he have to hide it? "I hope I was helpful to you, Cole. If you need anything further, please do not hesitate to contact me."

"Thank you, Silas. I believe you've given me all the information I require." His voice was cold.

Silas chuckled.

"What."

"Nothing. You have a very nice day."

Bristol stopped at Mick's to pick up the two phones. He didn't say much, and after a quick tour of Lila's room and the special place she kept her most important dolls, Bristol was on her way. She followed her GPS to the address Tanner had given her. It was an abandoned commercial area, and the address was an old gas station with a large shed attached to it. She used bolt cutters on a chain on the door at the back and pushed her way inside. It had been a while since the place had been used, and she made some mental notes about how to change the look so it didn't appear set up. There were a few bits of equipment she would take full advantage of.

She rang Cole, who picked up on the second ring. "This is Cole."

"It's your favorite magician," she said before she could think better of it, but she heard his laugh and found she liked the sound of it. "I'll text you the address. I'm here now."

∞

Cole had walked to his car as soon as he heard her voice. Clenching and unclenching his fists, he was still unsure how to approach her.

The traffic wasn't terrible, and it only took forty-five minutes to arrive.

When he walked in the shed, he could see Bristol had done quite a bit of work on the place. She was sweeping the floor wearing a pair of large leather gloves. Her hair was tied up on top of her head and she was wearing ripped jeans and orange T-shirt tied in a knot at her waist. Cole had to swallow hard to get back his focus. He had a job to do.

"New fashion statement?" he said to get her attention.

"Hey." She kept sweeping without turning. She had known he was there. He found himself smiling.

She leaned the broom against the wall and ran her hand along one of the tables.

"What's with the gloves? I didn't think it was that cold."

"I've got something for you," she said, ignoring the question. She went to her bag and pulled out a phone and a plastic bag, pressing the gloves all over the phone, then slipped it into the bag. "Look what you found," she said, handing it to him. "And you won't believe who took it."

She pulled another package from the bag. He watched her, wondering what the next surprise would be. She ripped it open and pulled out a bag of white powder.

"Drugs?"

She pushed the fingers of the gloves onto the packet overtly and then dropped the packet behind one of the tables. "You bring the dead guy with you?"

"I did but I'm afraid to leave and miss any of the show." He didn't trust Silas, but the man was right about Bristol. Watching her work was mesmerizing. Every movement had purpose.

"I need the dead guy for my next trick."

"I guess I'm the magician's assistant then," he said and walked out of the building, wanting desperately to trust her.

He came back carrying the guy, wrapped in his rug, over his shoulder. "Where do you want him?"

She looked around and pointed at the corner. "They'll know he wasn't killed here," she said to herself. "Wait. Take him back out and drag him in."

"Why?"

"'Cause I said so."

Cole shook his head and walked back to the door. "From here?"

She clicked her tongue and walked over to him. "Do I have to orchestrate this whole thing on my own? I thought you were clever." She pushed past him and searched the ground outside. "There," she said, pointing to the corner of the gas station. "There are some old tire tracks there." She slowed her voice and exaggerated each syllable. "Pre-tend. you. are. parked. *there.* and. you. are. get-ting. the. dead. guy. out. of. your. tru—"

"—Got it."

"About time," she said, suppressing a smile. She watched Cole dragging the guy to make sure he did it right but found herself watching the muscles in his arms strain and looked away. She walked over to press her gloved hands into the countertop again.

When Cole had the guy in the corner, Bristol went over and ran her gloved hands all over him.

Cole stood back. "I'm feeling a bit jealous."

She looked up at him. "Tell you what. If I ever find you dead, I'll put my hands all over you too, okay?"

"What if I just pretend to be dead?"

"Don't be gross."

She took out more drugs, handled them, and stuffed them in the guy's pockets.

"I can see why he likes you," Cole said from the place he had leaned against the wall.

Bristol groaned. "Do you want to do it?"

"No," Cole laughed. "I mean, a guy who you did a job for a while back. He said he was impressed with your work."

Bristol shrugged. "I'm good at what I do."

Cole thought it was time to set things straight. "So you broke that girl's ribs on purpose?"

"Oh, you heard about that? No, I was only trying to bruise them. It's hard to get your force right. Especially in a confined space. Did you know it takes 4,000 newtons of force to break a bone?"

"Yes, actually, I did. How do you remain so detached from your work?"

"I told you, I'm good at what I do. Things don't go as well if you get emotionally involved."

"How'd you get into this line of work?"

"One thing led to another. It took me a while to figure out what I was best at. Now I try to get better, like by not breaking bones unnecessarily. But then I come across a job like this, and everything gets messy. Sometimes I wonder if I should stop caring and do what I'm paid to do instead of having standards. Oh, I almost forgot." She pulled open her bag.

"Never stop caring, Bristol. Standards are important."

Bristol pulled an old flip phone out of her bag and looked at Cole but said nothing. She tucked the phone into the dead guy's pants pocket.

Cole walked over to her. "You have a thing for phones?"

"They're such an easy way to plant evidence." She pulled off the gloves.

"You still haven't told me what's up with the gloves."

"Leather leaves its own fingerprint."

"Thanks for the forensics lesson, but is there a reason you're not telling me whose they are?"

"It's a surprise."

Cole looked at her for a long second. "Can I take you somewhere tonight?"

"Why?"

"Because."

She bit the inside of her lip. "Where?"

"It's a surprise."

"I don't go on dates."

"Then it won't be a date."

Bristol bit her lip again, then sighed. "I've got things to do."

Cole wanted to ask her what but knew it was pointless.

They were both awkwardly quiet for a minute, then Bristol said, "Who was it?"

"Who?"

"The guy I worked for a while back."

"Guy named Silas Lincoln. You've prob—" Cole watched the color drain out of her face. "You okay?"

"Yeah, I just didn't think I'd hear that name connected to me again."

"He said you got the better of him." Cole hadn't thought she could go any whiter, but she did.

"He knew — " Her hand went to her mouth.

Cole walked over and put a hand on her shoulder. "You're not okay."

"How well do you know Silas?"

"Not much, but enough to see you're afraid of him and I can understand why."

"I'm not afraid. I just." She was staring at the wall. "I've gotta go. I've got work to do."

"Wait."

"No, Cole. Listen. Everything is fine. That was a long time ago, and if he wanted to come after me, he already would have." She practically ran out of the building.

Chapter 17

BRISTOL SPENT a long time staring out her window. Silas knew. It shouldn't matter. It was a long time ago, but it rattled her. She changed for her visit to Drake's, pushing thoughts of Silas away so she could focus on the job she had to do.

Dressed in a blouse and skirt, she had made sure she looked the part of someone who could afford to buy art. Her heels clicked smartly at each step as she headed for her car.

After a few laps, Bristol found a parking space several blocks down from the warehouse that Edward Drake rented out to house his artwork.

The warehouse had a shop front with Drake's name printed across the door and a large window showcasing his work. Work that Bristol considered inappropriate for the general public. Mick was right. It was disturbing.

As soon as she set foot in the door, she got chills. The white walls and a high ceiling did nothing to ease the heaviness in the room. A space like this, so close to the city, must cost a fortune. She couldn't see his target market being very large, but then again, it was LA.

She had chosen her outfit to suit a wealthy woman ready to buy art on a whim, but she was well out of place here.

In the dead center of the room stood a sculpture of a woman who had been taken apart and put back together, like a butchered Picasso. Grotesque paintings filled the walls. If he was painting young girls on the side, then something was definitely wrong.

"Can I help you?"

Bristol turned to find herself shadowed by an oddly handsome-looking man who stood a good ten inches taller than her. His hair was parted in the middle and meticulously shaped, and his eyes were an unnerving deep green. He was thin but had a strong face. His clothes were completely black, but she noted they were stitched with gold thread.

He stood too close to her with his hands clasped behind his back and his head perched over her, a vulture on prey. She had the overwhelming urge to recoil but held her place.

"I'm looking for Mr. Drake."

He spread his long arms out to the side. "You've found him."

"Of course. I'm Bristol." She held out her hand. He took it limply and leaned down to kiss it. "Pleasure."

"Are all these pieces yours?"

"Mmm," he said, looking around the room.

"They're interesting," she said, her lips pursed. "But I'm looking for something a little more classic."

Drake smiled ironically. "I suppose you're in the wrong place."

Bristol grinned. "Yes, I see what you mean. But the reason I'm here is because I've seen your other work."

Drake's head tilted sideways, and his eyes squinted as he considered her from top to bottom. Her eyes glanced behind Drake to a painting of a woman tearing herself apart. There were similar paintings dotted around the room. She had the unsettling feeling he was attempting to paint her like that in his head.

She swallowed but kept her voice steady. "I've seen your portraits, the ones of the girls. They're beautiful, and I have a niece who I would love to hire you to paint."

The smile hadn't left his face, but it took on an amused tilt. "Yes." He picked at the gold thread on his sleeve. "Those paintings are for my exclusive clients only."

"And if I wanted to become an exclusive client? How would I go about doing that?"

He reached out and took a lock of her hair between his fingers running the length of it. Bristol held her ground.

"Would you allow me the pleasure of painting you first? That would certainly put you in my good graces. An excellent place to start."

Her eyes darted sideways at the paintings, then she laughed. "I don't even like to get my picture taken, let alone be painted … " She nodded toward the tortured woman. " … like that."

"That's too bad, because it's the only way you will get what you want. Those paintings come at a high price."

"I have money."

Drake chuckled. "When I say price, I don't necessarily mean monetary."

"Can I think about it?"

"Of course." Drake turned and walked toward a desk, took something off of it, and returned. He handed Bristol a postcard. It had elaborate swirls covering one side, and Bristol saw that it was an invitation.

"I'm having an art show tomorrow night. If you'd like to join me at the show, perhaps we can talk more. If you hand them that at the door, they'll allow you entry. It is an exclusive event."

Bristol glanced casually at the invitation and her breath caught. "The Broad Museum?"

"Yes, I have a wealthy benefactor who has connections and is very good to me."

The idea of his artwork in that building made her sick. She had been through the museum a few times, most recently to see the Infinity Mirrored Rooms. And while she didn't always understand modern art, and there were often pieces she didn't prefer, these pieces did not belong in a place like that.

"I'd love to come, thank you. You're kind to invite me."

"If you'll excuse me. I have a lot of work to do to prepare for tomorrow night."

"Certainly. Excuse me."

Bristol walked out the door and shuddered, as though shaking off the darkness of the place. For a moment, she had considered sitting for him. But playing by his rules would be a last resort, even if it would gain her information. And she'd bring Eli with her. After the way Drake had touched her, she felt she needed a bodyguard or, at the very least, a long, blisteringly hot shower.

◯◯

Drake put his phone to his ear. "We will have an extra guest tomorrow night. The young lady named Bristol you mentioned."

The voice on the other end laughed. "I don't think I could have planned it better myself. Except that I did plan it. I'll ring Tanner and tell him the good news."

"Oh, and Silas, if you could see to it, I'd like the opportunity to paint her."

Chapter 18

COLE STROLLED past the empty shops like he owned the place. A car backfired and could just as easily have been a gunshot. Two guys stood in a doorway with hoodies pulled down over their faces. One guy looked up at him as he walked by.

A homeless man was pushing a shopping cart full of his whole life, and mumbling to himself. But Cole kept his head up and kept moving like he was all business and would not get into anyone else's.

He arrived at a door and opened it. It used to lock but not anymore. He climbed up a flight of narrow stairs, each step an inch higher than it should be, and knocked on the first door on the left. No one answered, so he knocked harder.

"Whada ya wan?" came a drowsy voice.

"Is that you Marie?"

There was silence and then, "Marie's not here."

"Come on Marie, it's Cole. Open up."

"Cole! Why dinnit ya say so?"

The locks clicked and the chain rattled.

When the door opened, a long-legged blonde with last night's eye makeup smeared around her blue eyes was leaning provocatively against the wall. The drugs had whittled her away to a waif, and her tank top and shorts were stained.

"You've gone blonde," he said, ignoring the sultry stare. She twisted a strand of hair around her finger. The rest of it was heaped high on her head.

Cole wasn't sure whether the droop in her eyes was because she'd just gotten up or she was high on something. He suspected the latter.

"Hey Tash!" she yelled too loud for the space. She kept her eyes on Cole with a playful smile. "You won' believe who's here."

Another woman, shorter and the color of a caramel latte came from the back room and joined her friend. She wore a silky robe that was frayed and faded and hung off one shoulder.

She looked him over from his head to his toes. "Ain't you a sight for sore eyes, sugar."

"Tash," he said, and leaned in to kiss both women on the cheek.

"I can do better than that for ya," Tash said as she ran her fingernail down his arm.

Marie spoke up. "We'll give ya two for the price a one," she said, draping an arm over her friend.

"Ladies, I'll have to save it for another time."

Tash pouted. "That's what you always say. Ya never give us a chance to pay ya back." She shrugged her shoulder so the front of her robe opened to expose a dark red bra that left nothing to the imagination. Cole kept his eyes firmly on her face.

"I didn't do it to get anything back."

"That's what makes ya so desirable," said Marie. "Girls like us don' get anythin' for nothin'."

"Well, if you're desperate to pay me back, then today's your lucky day."

Marie laughed a low honky laugh and stepped toward him wrapping her arms around him. Cole peeled her off and pushed her back gently.

"Not like that. My way won't take up much of your time."

"Ya think our way would?" Tash said, "We could send ya into a tailspin before you knew what hit you."

"I have no doubt. But I'm looking for information."

Tash smiled her purple painted lips broadly. "Our way is more fun."

"Some other time."

"You always spoil everythin'." Tash huffed and walked back into a small living area, expecting him to follow.

"I know, and I'm afraid what I'm after isn't pleasant either."

Tash sighed and flopped onto the couch. "Make yourself at home," she said, resting her arm across the back of the couch and patting the seat next to her. Cole chose the armchair on the other side of the room, but Marie followed him over and sat on the arm of the chair, pushing a hip into his shoulder. Tash scowled at her.

Cole shifted forward on the seat and pulled a photo

of the dead girl out of his back pocket. He stayed sitting on the front edge of the chair to avoid Marie's hip.

He held it up saying nothing, just watching the faces of the two women who looked at each other and then back at him.

Tash shook her head and sighed. "If it was anyone but you Cole, I swear…"

"I'm out," said Marie. She put her hands up and took a few steps backward before grabbing a crumpled coat off the floor.

She called out as she left, "You know where to find me when you're ready for some fun."

Tash was sucking on the inside of her cheek. "No one wants ta talk about her."

"I know you're not a big fan of the police, but don't you want to find out what happened? Why the tight lips?" Tash grinned seductively and opened her mouth to make a crude comment, but Cole raised his eyebrows in warning, then said, "They found her OD'd on the side of the road. But nobody knows how she ended up there."

"A friend of a friend saw it happen. When he went over to see what was going on. They put a bullet in his head."

"A 'friend of a friend'?"

"Yeah."

"And where's this 'friend of a friend' now?"

"You mean where's the body?"

"Yeah."

"Prob'ly swimmin' with the fishies." Cole was silent. "What, ya don' believe me?"

"I know how stories can take on a life of their own."

"Fine." She crossed her arms and looked away from him like a spoiled kid.

"Can you prove any of it?"

Tash let out a high-pitched squeal of a laugh. "You of all people should know what a stupid question that is. *Can you prove any of it?* Yeah, sure. I'll go get ya the fingerprints I have stashed in my cupboard." She spit out a puff of air at the end.

"Sorry, you're right. I trust you, Tash. But can you give me any more details?"

Tash looked at him like she was deciding what to do. Cole knew he had her back on side, so he waited till she was ready. "For one thing, she wasn't a long-term drug user."

"How can you tell? Her arms said she was."

She looked at him like he was patronizing her. "You take a look at that photo and tell me she was a junkie," she said, pointing two fingers at the photo in his lap.

"Okay, anything else?"

"She got tossed out of a van."

Cole sat up straighter. "You're sure?"

"No, that friend of a friend got shot in the head 'cause he found some girl dead, on her own, on the side of the road." She finished off with an excessive eye roll.

"So she's not from around here?"

Tash shook her head but wouldn't look at him. She wanted him to know she was peeved.

Cole ignored her attitude and pulled out the photo of the two rings linked and held it up. "Ever seen this before?"

She barely glanced at it. "Nope."

"Come on."

She pointed an accusing finger. "I thought you looked out for us."

"Tash."

She sighed as though this was her biggest hassle all year. "I might know somethin', but it's gonna cost ya."

"I thought I already paid my dues."

"You got rid a' Mr. B, but that don' save me from whoever dumped that girl."

Cole pulled a twenty out of his wallet and handed it over.

She held it out between her index and middle fingers. "This is all my life is worth to you?" Cole shrugged, and she stuffed the bill into her bra.

She got up and moved to a bookshelf devoid of books. She grabbed a pack of cigarettes and an ashtray off a shelf and sat back down on the couch. After lighting a cigarette, she took a long drag and blew the smoke out toward the ceiling. Cole waited, letting her settle her nerves. She flicked ash into the tray and nodded. "I seen this before."

"The tattoo."

"Mmm. Last year a girl turns up. She's got a tattoo like that, but this one been on drugs a while. Said she was held against her will. Given drugs to keep her. But she escaped and now she's on the street lookin' for a hit."

"Held against her will?"

"Not everybody *chooses* to be a lady of the night." She ran her tongue along her bottom lip.

"You don't think she was making it up? Get sympathy so someone would give her something?"

"Wha', outta the goodness of their heart?" She hissed air through her teeth.

Cole looked down at the photo. "But she's just a girl."

Tash snorted. "So was I when I got started."

"So you think they're kidnapping girls and getting them addicted to drugs so they're stuck? And what, she accidentally OD's so they chuck her in the street?"

"I don' *think* anythin'. I don' *know* anythin'. If you ain't careful, you gonna get me killed," she said, leaning forward on the couch, agitated.

"What do you mean?"

She shrugged and took another drag. "You're the detective," she said while exhaling.

"Not anymore."

Tash chewed on one of her nails. "In this business when someone's done with ya, they throw ya out in the trash. That's all I know. But if ya wanna know more, talk to Marco. At the Red Moon. Marco took the first girl in for a bit.

"That's very generous of him," Cole said blandly.

"But don't tell him ya heard it from me."

"Naturally."

"He's not as bad as some."

Cole stood up and pulled out another twenty. Tash rested the cigarette in the ashtray as Cole approached. "Thanks, Tash. Take care of yourself," he said, stuffing the twenty down her top.

She bit her lip. "You sure you don't want to stick around and play a little?"

Cole smiled and leaned over to kiss her on the top of the head. Then got out of reach as she tried to cop a feel. "You're too special for that."

"You dog. You'll make someone a good husband one day. You go get yourself married. And then when you tire of her ya can visit your ol' friend Tash."

"I'll see you later, sweetheart," he said, turning.

"Don't be such a stranger. We could use more guys like you around here keepin' things safe."

He stopped and turned back again, holding up the photo. "That's what I'm trying to do."

$$\infty$$

The neon sign for the *Red Moon* was dark, but there was another one with dancing girls made of yellow neon still lit up. The girls' legs kicked every flash. Cole shook his head.

He pushed on the big front doors, but they were locked. He shaded his face with his hands and pressed up against the tinted glass. There was no one around, but through an archway to the bar in the back it looked like there was a light on.

He stepped back a couple of paces and looked right then left and saw what he was looking for — an alleyway two shops down.

The alley was in shadow and turned at the end to expose the back of the shops. He counted off as he walked past the first couple of doors to the one he was looking for. It had a black sign screwed to the door that read "RM." He tried the knob, but it was locked.

He knocked and waited. A large man opened the door a few inches. His bulk blocked any view of the inside. "Business or pleasure?" the man asked.

"I need to ask Marco a few questions."

"Marco doesn't get asked questions. He asks them." The man tried to slam the door, but Cole stuck his foot in at the last second.

"Business," Cole said, shaking his foot a little when the door opened again.

"Well, state your business."

Cole hoped he wouldn't regret this. "I've got a girl I think you'll be interested in. Long dark hair with legs to match."

"Can she dance?"

"The best I've seen."

The man grunted. "Marco's not here. Bring her back tonight."

"Is there any way we can discuss the details without the lady present?"

The man barked what sounded like a mix between a laugh and a threat: "Bring her back tonight." Then he slammed the door.

When Cole reached his car, he leaned against it, staring at his phone. He tried to imagine what Bristol's reaction would be. He turned and rested his elbows on the top of his car, then dialed.

"Yeah?"

"Hey, it's Cole."

"I know."

"Right. You busy tonight?"

"I thought we already discussed this."

"It's business. I need to talk to a guy at a place called the *Red Moon*."

"What does that have to do with me?"

"I can't get in without you. You're so much better at this than I am."

Bristol laughed. "You're not a very good liar."

"All right fine. I need you as collateral to get into the place."

"What kind of collateral?"

"Can you dress like a stripper?" He winced. He should have thought this through better, but it was too late now. He'd have to run with it.

"Do I need to hang up on you?"

"I'm serious. Make sure you look like you wouldn't mind havin' a dance on the table." Bristol was silent. "Don't tell me you've never done something like that to get the job done."

"I've never done that before."

"Then it will be a good experience for you. Learn something new. I'm helping you to expand your repertoire." Cole could feel Bristol's glare through the phone. "And it's business, I promise. It would help me out a lot."

"You're going to have to give me more information. I'm not dressing up for nothing."

"There was an incident that happened last year and might be connected to the dead girl."

"What kind of incident?"

"A girl turned up saying she had been a slave to

some guy who gave her drugs. This guy, Marco, looked after her for a while."

"Looked after her?"

"Yeah, well, I'm just going off what I was told. I want to see if he knows anything that might be connected."

"What's that have to do with the dead girl?"

"Maybe nothing, but the dead girl was seen being dumped in the same neighborhood. And the two girls may have had the same tattoo on their shoulder. Also, the dead girl wasn't a long-term drug user, and there was a witness who interfered and was killed. Well, according to a friend of a friend. It may be nothing, but it's the best lead I have." Cole let the silence hang on the phone. There was nothing more he could say to convince her.

"What time?" Bristol finally said.

"Meet at my place at seven and I'll drive us in."

Bristol was quiet again. "Is there a reason I can't drive myself?"

"Geez, you are touchy. It's not a great part of town."

"I can look after myself."

Cole tipped his head back and let out a breath. "Of course you can, but it would make me feel better." There was silence again.

"Okay, I'm in. See you at seven."

Chapter 19

BRISTOL WAS ALREADY HOME when Cole called. As he shared his new information, Bristol kept thinking of what she saw the other night at the boat. It could have been a girl being forced into that house across the water. The odds were almost nonexistent that it would be related, but she'd learned over the years not to ignore the small stuff. Besides, she had a few hours to kill, and it should be simple to cross that question off the list.

When she turned the corner onto the street she had previously seen only in the dark, there were news vans lined up on the side of the road.

The girl, whose name she remembered was Vanessa, had a yard full of people. Bristol pulled over where she could and walked toward the house. Deb stood on the top step addressing the crowd.

"Ladies and gentlemen, my client will make a short statement but will not be taking questions at this time." She ushered Vanessa forward to the horde of microphones. The girl had her head down. She took a deep breath and slowly looked up to face the crowd. Dressed in a light-colored turtleneck with a vest, a pencil skirt that was a little loose, and thick, dark tights, she looked several years younger than last time Bristol had seen her. The colors looked horrible on her and with no makeup and her hair pulled back into a low ponytail she looked plain and very innocent. Bristol was impressed.

"Thank you for coming." Vanessa began, reading off a card. "This has been a very traumatic time for me and my family, but your support has been overwhelming. It can be frightening for a young girl to stand up to abusers, and I will confess that it scared me to consider what I had become and the lengths I would go to protect myself. I am thankful for my psychologist, who has helped me to cope and to understand that I had every right to protect myself. The public has been incredible, and I would like to say thank you to all of those who have supported me and believed in me. My prayer is that those who are now victims would have the strength and courage to stick up for themselves and to seek help before they end up in the situation that I now face. Thank you."

This girl was a good actor. She paused in all the right places and added a tremble to her voice for emphasis. Deb must be having a field day. And maybe some good would come out of it after all. If Vanessa's brilliant performance meant that other girls who were actually being abused did something about it, perhaps Bristol had done something worthwhile. Maybe.

The crowd burst into questions, but Deb took charge and led the girl and her mom and dad back into the house.

The crowd began to disperse, and Bristol walked up to the front door. A few watched her, their eyes narrowed.

She knocked on the door and Deb answered it with her angry face on.

"Oh!" she said, immediately beaming. "What are you doing here? Do you want to come in?"

"Yes, please." Bristol considered turning and offering a self-satisfied smile to those who were watching but couldn't bring herself to do it.

"What is she doing here?" Vanessa said, hiding behind her dad, who was now standing with his arms crossed. He added his own thoughts. "I don't want her here," he said to Deb.

Bristol found it amusing they wouldn't address her directly.

"Oh, stop it. She's a professional. It's nothing personal. And besides you should kiss her feet for saving your daughter," Deb said, clicking her tongue. "Vanessa did a great job, didn't she?" she said, addressing Bristol. "Wouldn't have worked without your help." She turned and glared at the family behind her. "Now what can I do for you."

Bristol looked at the father, whose name she couldn't

remember. "I just have a quick question, then I'll be out of your way." She walked toward the back of the house. At the angle where she now stood it was hard to pick out which house it had been. But the boat that was moored at a large white one looked to be right. "That house," she said, pointing. "Do you know who lives there?" she asked Vanessa's dad.

"Why do you want to know?"

"Oh, just answer her question," Deb said in her aggressive way.

He looked at Deb and then back at Bristol. "That's Silas Lincoln's house." His chin rose slightly like he was proud to have such an important neighbor.

Bristol swallowed hard and kept her voice even. "Silas?"

"Yeah. I know the house is way below his status, but he doesn't use it much. I'm not actually sure why he's got it, but he's the one who told me about you. I rang him up that night because he told me once that if I ever needed help to get out of a difficult situation to let him know. I rang him to see if he could offer the name of a good lawyer, since I'm sure he's gotten himself out of some rough spots. He gave me your number."

"Thanks," Bristol said, then turned on her heel and walked toward the front of the house again.

"Is everything okay?" Deb said, catching up to her.

"Yeah, fine. I just have a lot to do."

"Okay, well, call me later if you need anything."

"Thanks." Bristol smiled her biggest, fakest smile as she opened the door and headed for her car. She wanted to run.

Silas was somehow keeping tabs on her. But if he knew she had betrayed him, why would he be encouraging others to hire her? She shivered despite the warm sun.

◯◯

Bristol went to the gym to blow off steam. Eli was busy training, so she didn't have to talk about it, which was good. He had a way of seeing right through her, and it would have been impossible to hide her anxiety.

Now she had to see Cole, which didn't help.

It was exactly 7:00 when Bristol arrived at his place. She reminded herself it was only business, but Cole had a way of making her feel off balance.

Taking a deep breath, she pushed her shoulders back against the car seat. She'd handled herself under worse circumstances; she could handle Cole for an hour or two.

When she gripped the door handle, her hand began to shake. She let go and wiped it down her pants. Maybe it wasn't too late to call it off.

A bang on the window sent a shock through her. She sprang for the gun in her bag, pointing it at Cole, who jumped back. She clenched her jaw, put the gun back, and got out of the car. The adrenaline surging through her was familiar and oddly reassuring.

"Sorry." Bristol grumbled at Cole's raised eyebrows. "Don't look at me like that. You should know better."

"You're right. It's my fault. I have this need to surprise you because I never seem to manage to do it."

"Well, congrats, you've managed. Happy?" Cole grinned. Bristol pointed a finger at him. "Don't start."

He looked at her car. "I thought you drove a Corvette."

"I was borrowing that car from a friend."

"Nice friend. But honestly, I think this car suits you better. Corvettes are too ostentatious for a classy girl like you."

"Thanks."

"Is it okay if I tell you you look good?" Cole said as he led her to his front door. She had opted for tight black leather pants instead of a skirt in case things went pear-shaped, and a blue halter camisole. She did look good, but she wasn't willing to go over the top to dress like a stripper. When they reached the door, he turned and stepped aside to let her in first. "Glad to see you dressed for action," he said, eying her pants.

"Thanks for noticing." Remembering they had a job to do helped Bristol refocus her energy, and the anxiety receded. She looked him up and down, not hiding her perusal. He had on dark chinos with a white button-down and his leather jacket.

Cole spread his arms and spun around. "Acceptable?"

"You think maybe a shinier shirt would help you fit in at the *Red Moon?*"

"Don't own one, unfortunately. And besides, I'm not the one they'll be looking at. Can I get you something to drink? Gin and tonic?" Cole said as he walked up the stairs.

"I don't drink gin and tonic."

"I know, I don't actually have gin or tonic." He turned to her at the top of the stairs. "I was trying to be funny."

She didn't smile until he turned back around. "What *do* you have?"

"Mineral water, tap water, orange juice … or I can make you a coffee."

"I don't drink coffee. That's all you have?"

"What is it you were hoping for?" he asked as he opened his fridge. "Oh, and I've got milk."

"Anything's fine." He pulled out a mineral water and showed it to her. She nodded. "So when you said you don't drink that time at the bar, you really don't drink at all?"

"Used to. It doesn't agree with me."

"Let me guess. It made you dark and moody."

Cole smiled sadly. "That's what it did to my dad. Another way for him to ignore me. But no, I always ended up in fights."

"Really? I wouldn't have guessed that about you." She watched Cole as he poured the water into two glasses. "Did he deserve it?"

"Did who deserve what?"

"Whoever it was you fought with that convinced you to give up alcohol."

"It was my best friend, and it was a fight over a girl he was in love with. I was convinced at the time that all women were in love with me, and I set out to prove it. Hit my best friend in the jaw and sent him to the ground. He nearly died."

Cole watched her for a reaction. She didn't give him one. "So you had to learn the hard way."

"Could have been worse I suppose. But I lost a good friend, even if he is still alive. I wasn't even interested in the girl."

Cole opening up like this made her uncomfortable. "Wow, you're kind of a jerk and a ladies' man," she said, lifting her eyebrows to lighten the mood.

Cole nodded. "When I drink, yeah." He lifted his water. "So I don't … ever."

"But hang on." Bristol crossed her arms and leaned a shoulder on the wall. "You weren't drinking at the bar the first night we met, and I'm pretty sure you were both a jerk and a ladies' man."

"I was just protecting a friend." He smiled but dropped his head, and when he lifted it again, the smile was gone. "You and I are a lot alike. We both use our looks to get what we want. But like you, it's just an act."

"How do you know mine's just an act?"

"Because I saw the recognition in your face at the bar when you tried it with me. You knew it wouldn't work and you haven't tried it again."

Bristol's stomach flipped. The real reason she wouldn't try it again was because she was afraid it was too close to the truth. The only safe way to be around Cole was to keep her guard up.

She absentmindedly flicked a strand of hair around her finger. Things were getting too serious again. "So what you're saying is, you're actually a really great guy?"

"Only when I'm not working."

"Okay, well, we're coworkers now. Does that mean you'll stop hitting on me?"

Cole opened his mouth and then closed it again, then finally said, "I really like you, Bristol."

"You barely know me."

"And you like me, and that's what is making this so uncomfortable for you."

She shifted on her feet. "Who said I was uncomfortable?" Cole let out a breath. "I don't date, Cole. I thought I made that clear."

"That seems to be a real issue with you."

"I don't want you to waste your time."

"What happened to you that you're so afraid of liking someone."

"What do you mean 'what happened'? It's just messy and makes things complicated."

"But not always in a bad way. Look at Andrew and his wife. Yeah, it's a bit messy 'cause things aren't good at work, but he has someone he loves and he's about to have a baby."

"Exactly my point. Things aren't just messy at work, their dangerous, and Andrew has inadvertently put his family in harm's way. What if something happens to him and they're left alone?"

"So it's the unknown. The possibility of something going wrong keeps you distant from people."

Bristol threw her hands up in the air and walked to the other side of the room. "Last time I checked, I was free to make my own decisions about my life."

Cole put his drink down on the counter too hard and the water splashed out. "Sorry. You're right."

"Can we just go now?" She stared at Cole and he stared back. Bristol refused to be the first one to look away. Finally, Cole looked down.

"Let's go," he said, his voice quiet.

Chapter 20

THEY DROVE IN SILENCE, but when Cole parked the car he said, "I've got to admit. I'm slightly out of my depth here."

"In what way."

"I'm used to working alone."

"That makes two of us."

They sat in silence again, Cole with his hand on the key still in the ignition. "I think it's the hair," he finally said.

"What?"

"You wondered how I knew you were uncomfortable. You play with your hair when you're nervous."

Bristol dropped her hand to her side mid-twist. "How do you know I don't always play with it?"

"Because you weren't at the bar."

They got out and walked a couple blocks to the club. The streets were busier now, although it was still early.

The building now read "Red Moon" in a garish red neon glow. Several people were milling about outside.

The doors were open with two oversize bouncers standing on either side with their feet planted and hands clasped behind their backs. Cole noted the earpieces the men wore. Flashing lights and techno music poured out the door. Bristol grabbed his hand and pulled him in. She seemed to know where she was going.

"You been here before?"

"Not this particular establishment, but I've been to a few. I just want to get this over with."

"You want a drink first?"

Bristol scrunched up her face. "Are you trying to be funny again?" Cole grinned like an idiot and she rolled her eyes.

Bristol headed for the bar, but Cole put a hand on her shoulder.

"You wait here. I'll let them know we're here."

Bristol stood to the side, out of the way, as people came and went.

Through an archway to the right, she could see a few girls already at work dancing for the patrons who had turned up.

A guy with a shaved head and a shiny shirt who looked like he was on steroids walked up to her, not hiding the fact that he was checking out every inch of her body. When he finally settled on her eyes, he licked his lips. Bristol raised an eyebrow and beat him to the punchline.

She took a step toward him and ran a finger down

the front of his shirt. "I don't think I've seen you around here before. You new?"

"Oh, babe. I am here every night and I don't know *how* I'd miss seeing an angel like you before." He reached up to put a hand on her waist. She grabbed it, twisting it around and pulling him close. He smelled like weed and his face contorted in pain. Fear filled his eyes. Good. Most guys with that much muscle don't know how to use it anyway.

She whispered into his ear, "When I let you go, you will turn around and walk away, never looking at me again. And maybe leave the other girls alone from now on too. You got that?"

The guy was shaking and managed a jerky nod. A sheen of sweat glistened on his top lip. Bristol shoved him away, and he took off out of the building.

"I really enjoyed that," Cole said from beside her.

"You weren't here to save the day, so I thought I'd take things into my own hands."

"If I had been here, things would have turned out exactly the same."

"Did you find him?"

"Yeah," Cole said but didn't move.

"What are we waiting for?" She put her hands on her hips.

He looked at her and bit his lip. "You couldn't look a little more…" She glared at him under her eyebrows like she was going to deck him. "Maybe I should say, a little less … like … you?"

Bristol sighed but then stood up straighter and put one foot slightly behind her in a model stance then winked at Cole and chomped her mouth like she was chewing gum. "How's this?"

Cole cleared his throat. "I'm actually worried about how good you are at that."

"Don't like it?" she said, chomping.

"You are a surprising woman." He headed back the way he came but turned to make sure Bristol was following him. She strutted after him, twirling her hair around her finger and chomping on her fake gum, and he tried hard not to laugh.

They approached the bar and the man behind it was rubbing the counter down in one spot while watching their approach. He had an eyebrow that stretched across his forehead. His shoulders hunched over his work, gave him a strong resemblance to a gorilla.

Cole sauntered up. "This is the girl I was telling you about."

He looked Bristol up and down. Bristol looked around the room like she was bored with the idea of an interview and more interested in the music. She moved her body to the techno music. She hated techno music.

"Wait here," he grunted. He walked over to the other guy at the bar, who was much smaller in stature, and nodded toward Cole and Bristol, then disappeared behind a beaded door.

When he came back out, he walked up to Bristol and grabbed her by the arm then turned to Cole. "You wait here."

"No way, man. I'm not letting her out of my sight."

The gorilla squared up to Cole.

"It's fine, baby," Bristol said with a smile, laying a

hand flat on his chest and leaning in to whisper. "I can handle myself, remember? I'll call you if I need you."

Cole crossed his arms. "Fine."

Gorilla led Bristol out the back. Cole didn't like the way the big guy put his hand on the small of her back to usher her through the door.

◯◯

Bristol was led into a small room that had a desk with a computer on one side and a couch on the other. The wallpaper was peeling from the corners of the room, and there were posters of naked girls pinned to the walls. Bristol had to work hard to keep the disgust off her face. She had known too many dirt bags in her life.

A man sat hunched over at the desk. He was writing something on a piece of paper, his hair falling in his face. The gorilla leaned over him and whispered in his ear. Bristol sat down in a small wooden folding chair, making sure to avoid the couch at all costs. She crossed her legs and bounced her foot up and down. Twisting her foot, she looked at her choice in footwear. Stilettos weren't easy to walk in, but they made a good weapon in a pinch.

The man hadn't looked at her yet but continued to lean over his paper as the gorilla walked out, closing the door behind him.

Finally, he turned. He was around forty with an Italian look and a receding hairline that was exposed when he pushed his hair back. He looked like he had bad acne as a kid.

"I'm Marco." He stood and walked over holding out his hand.

"Bristol."

"Wow, what a great name. We won't even need to change that." He held onto her finger when she let go of the handshake and took his time perusing her. Bristol really hoped things went wrong so she could put him on the ground.

"So where do you come from, *Bristol.*" He said her name like he was tasting it. She kept her voice light.

"Not far. You get many girls through here?"

"None as pretty as you," he said, dropping her finger.

"Oh, I bet you say that to all the girls."

He laughed low and rolled his desk chair over to sit across from her with his knee pushed in against her thigh.

"So what is it I can do for you. Or what is it you can do for me?"

"I've just gotten a bit cash-strapped and have an unfortunate habit that I need to take care of."

"Well, it just so happens I have a spot open, and you can get paid in different ways. What's your poison of choice?"

"Dollar bills are my first choice."

Marco nodded. "Good choice." She saw his jaw clench. "You have much experience dancing?"

"Not to get paid, but I've had my time up on tables entertaining the boys back home."

"That will do nicely to start with."

"What sort are the other girls you get in here?"

"Mostly like you. Need to get ahead. Have needs that need to be met."

Bristol licked her lips. This was going to take all night if she did it right. She didn't have the time, so she thought she'd go for it and clean up whatever mess she created.

"What's the strangest situation you ever came across?"

He sucked in his cheeks and looked at her for a couple seconds. Then his eyes drifted down her arms that were resting in her lap.

"I've seen my fair share."

"Any girls ever say they've been held captive?"

His reflexes were faster than she had expected. He grabbed her arm and twisted it around, wrestling her sideways and pinning her to the couch. "You a cop?" he spat in her ear. "You don't smell like a cop." He pushed his face into her hair breathing deeply as she struggled.

"Not a cop." She managed to get out. "Just clean up messes."

"Good, then I can teach you a lesson you'll never forget."

He grabbed both her wrists in one hand, and she knew what he was doing. She felt him tugging at his own pants and knew hers were next. Pain was shooting through one shoulder, but the other one had some strength and he would be distracted with his clothes right now, so she yanked one hand out of his grip and elbowed him somewhere in the ribs. It was enough for him to loosen his grip on her other hand and she spun around, shoved him off her, then kneed him in the crotch. He fell back, and she pushed him onto the floor and put her heel on his chest. "I only need to put a little downward pressure on here to punch a hole." Things had turned out quite well. She should have started with this approach. She'd remember that for next time.

He held one hand up in surrender with his other still between his legs.

"I want to know about a girl who came through here and said she had been held captive."

"Who, Lisa? That girl was a raving lunatic. She only told that story to get something for nothing. No one actually believed it."

"Did she mention anyone in particular?"

"I don't remember." Bristol pushed the heel of her shoe harder into his chest. "Okay, okay, she kept mentioning some guy named Robert. That's all I know. I swear."

"What happened to her?"

"She was dead within a month."

"Overdose?"

"Ran out in front of a truck." She pushed down again with her heel. "That's all I know, I swear."

She looked around the room but there was nothing to tie him up with, so she kicked him hard in the stomach to slow him down so she could escape. He would likely have a gun somewhere in the room, and she'd have better luck in a public place with Cole for back up.

She took off out the door and headed for the beads, ripping a few off as she came through. Cole read her body language without her having to waste time explaining. Gorilla, on the other hand, looked confused for half a second, which they took advantage of.

They ran for the door, but the two bouncers were waiting for them.

"The damn earpieces," Cole said. Marco hadn't wasted time getting people into place.

"If we don't get out of here now, we might not get out," Cole said as he kept moving forward, only slowing enough to read the scene.

"I'm ready if you are." Bristol smiled at him.

"You're enjoying this."

"I like playing this part better than the other."

"That's 'cause you aren't playing a part," Cole said as he kicked out at the first guy's knee.

Bristol twisted into a roundhouse kick and sent her guy back through the door. People scattered everywhere.

"Nice kick," Cole said as he turned to block gorilla's punch. Cole got in a hit to the kidneys that didn't seem to faze gorilla, who was coming in with a haymaker. Cole's arm shot up to block, and he was able to get in a one-two on the guy just as Marco joined the fight.

Marco was tough looking in the bully kind of way, but in a fair fight he didn't have the fighting skills. Bristol threw him off guard by going straight for him.

She punched him in the nose before he knew what was coming, and blood went everywhere. She turned to see Cole had gorilla on the ground but the bouncers where starting to make a move again.

She kicked at one again, but he got hold of her foot and flipped her to the ground. He was about to drop on her when Cole came flying through and tackled the guy to the ground. Bristol jumped up and saw that gorilla was coming to his senses. She dropped on him with her elbow.

Cole grabbed her arm to pull her up, and she nearly clocked him in the head. They had three guys on the ground and Marco took a step back, his face covered in blood and his hands up in surrender. Bristol and Cole climbed over the men on the ground and got out of the building.

"We gotta get out of here now before they get more firepower."

Bristol nodded, and they both sprinted for the car, Bristol slower than she would have liked. Maybe the shoes really were the wrong move.

Cole slid across the hood of the car, and they both jumped in.

"You did that just to show off." Bristol laughed as Cole slammed the car into drive and took off.

"Maybe," he said, revving the engine as they passed the *Red Moon.*

"You just had to do that didn't you." Bristol shook her head.

"What? It's like howling at the moon."

"Don't try to explain it to me. I'll never get the testosterone thing."

Chapter 21

BRISTOL LEANED HER SEAT BACK, catching her breath. "That was fun."

"It was, wasn't it?"

"You're not bad with your fist."

"Is that a compliment?"

Bristol tipped her head toward him and smiled. "Where'd you learn to fight like that? And don't tell me the police. That's not police training."

"I could ask you the same thing."

"I asked you first."

"It's a long story."

"Mine too."

"So … how'd Marco figure out you weren't a stripper … or did you give yourself away?"

"Subtle change of subject." She grinned. "I think he worked out I wasn't a drug user. And, if I'm honest, I wasn't trying very hard. I was tired of being looked at like someone's next meal."

"Don't blame you. It felt good taking those guys

down after the way they treated you. So did you find out anything?"

"Only that I don't make a believable pole dancer."

"No, you're right. You're too classy."

"All he said was that nobody believed her story and then she got flattened by a truck a month later."

"I thought you said you didn't get anything?"

"I didn't. It's a dead end. Said she mentioned a guy named Robert, but no last name." Cole sucked in a breath. "What is it?"

"Nothing. I mean, it wouldn't be. I just did a job for a guy named Robert."

"Robert is a pretty common name."

"That's why I said it's nothing, just caught me off guard is all. That's suspicious that she ended up dead though."

"Maybe, or maybe she was high and stepped out in front of the truck on accident. Or maybe she wanted to end it all. There's nothing conclusive to add. We still have very little information."

Cole winced and grabbed at his side. Bristol looked down. "You're bleeding." She pulled his hand back and saw the cut on his shirt. "Who had a knife? I didn't see one."

"I'm not sure, it's all one big ball of fists and kicking."

"Pull over."

"I'm fine."

Bristol smacked him on the arm. "Pull over."

Cole sighed dramatically and pulled over. Bristol

pulled up his shirt and saw the two-inch gash in his side. "This will need stitches."

"So should I pull in at the hospital then?" Cole said, knowing that was the last place they should go. Bristol slapped him on the arm again.

"You want me to drive? I know where we can get you stitched up."

"I can drive, just tell me where to go."

◯◯

They pulled up at the gym, and Bristol led Cole around the side to Eli's apartment.

She had to knock a few times before Eli came to the door rubbing sleep out of his eyes. Bristol glanced at Cole to see his reaction to the large man. People often took a step back when they first came into his presence. Cole just had a sheepish smile that said "Sorry to wake you."

When Eli saw the blood, he pulled the two of them inside quickly.

"What's happened?"

"We got into a fight. We're okay. Cole just needs a stitch-up."

Eli looked between the two of them, and when neither one of them offered further information, he led them to the kitchen and had Cole sit down.

"We just need to keep it down. Bethany has an early case tomorrow," Eli said as he brought in a first aid kit.

"I haven't seen Beth in ages. I nearly forgot you were married."

"No kidding. I forget sometimes too." Eli laughed. "Doesn't help that she hates to come into the gym."

"What does your wife do?" Cole asked.

"Social work. Long hours and little pay. Not to mention the stuff she sees."

"Just out of curiosity, why do you have everything needed for stitching? Seems a strange thing to have on hand," Cole asked, eyeing Eli.

Eli's smile was friendly. "I do a lot of stitching for the guys that come out of the boxing ring. Easier to do it here."

"Eli's also a doctor," Bristol offered. Eli looked at her only moving his eyes, then focused on Cole.

He lifted Cole's shirt to look at the cut. "Why don't you take your shirt off," he said as he spread out his tools on the table.

When Cole took his shirt off, Bristol fixed her eyes on a spot on the floor. Eli noticed. "So, Cole, how is it that you know Bristol. I hope it's not from the fight?"

"No, we're work colleagues," Bristol said, looking at the two men but then quickly back at the floor.

Cole clicked his tongue. "You're impossible."

"Sounds like you know her well," Eli snickered. "I like this guy Bristol. How come you haven't introduced us before? He's fit too. Have you seen these abs?"

Bristol's face reddened, so she threw her arms up and stepped away from them. "You two are the ones who are impossible. I'm going into the gym while you finish up," she said and headed for Eli's door to the gym.

"You're worse than I am," Cole said, laughing after she was gone.

"She deserved it. She makes things so difficult for herself. I wish she would lighten up," Eli said as he began stitching.

The two men were silent while Eli worked. When he finished, he set down his tools and looked at Cole. "You seem like a good guy, but I want you to know that if you hurt her, I will end you. I know that sounds cliché, but it's the way things are."

Cole leaned forward. "Eli, if I hurt her, I give you permission to end me. I know how special she is, and I have no intention of doing anything to harm her."

"Good, as long as we understand each other."

"I'm glad to know she has someone like you to look out for her. She needs that. I don't think she knows how to look after herself as well as she thinks."

"You *do* know her. Will there be any repercussions from the fight tonight?"

"No, the guys came out of it a lot worse than we did, and they know nothing about us."

"Good." Eli pressed a bandage over the stitches.

"Thanks for all your help."

"Anytime. You wait here. I'll get Bristol."

∞

Bristol was skipping rope barefoot when Eli came in. She stopped when she saw him. "All stitched up?"

"Yeah, he'll be fine. Shouldn't affect him too much. Bring him by in a couple weeks and I'll take the stitches out if he needs."

"I have a feeling he knows how to take out his own stitches."

"You're probably right."

Eli watched her as she put the jump rope away. She turned to him. "What?"

"Nothing."

"Stop it. There is nothing going on there and you know it."

"Did I say anything?"

"You didn't have to. I can see it on your face. Cole and I have been working together to try and help some people, and that is all."

"You should think about giving him a chance."

"Stop, Eli." She grabbed her shoes and walked back to the apartment. "Time to go, Cole," she said walking straight through to the front door. Cole looked at Eli, who shrugged.

"Can I come train at your gym sometime?" Cole said, following Bristol to the door.

"No!" Bristol called from outside.

"Of course you can. You're more than welcome."

"What's got into her?"

"Vulnerability. It's her kryptonite."

"I'll keep that in mind." Cole waved to Eli as he pulled the door closed.

"Why do I have the feeling you two were conspiring against me in there?" Bristol asked Cole when they got in the car.

"Because we were."

"Well, you can stay out of it. Eli is plenty."

"He is. I'm glad you've got him looking out for you."

"How's your cut?"

"Great. It's mostly numb at the moment, so I can barely tell it's there."

Bristol thrummed out the techno beat that had been playing at the Red Moon. Cole started the car and looked at her. "You'll have that music stuck in your head for days."

"Ew, you're right," Bristol fake whined.

"I can't leave you to such a horrible fate."

"Sure you can."

"No, I don't think so."

Bristol smacked him on his stitches, and Cole winced and laughed at the same time "Ow."

"I thought you said it was numb?"

"I said it was *mostly* numb."

"Huh, look at that. I finally managed to get my force right." She sneered playfully.

"I will not let you go home with that music in your head."

"Well then, what do you suggest?"

"I've got an idea." Bristol opened her mouth to protest but Cole spoke over her. "Stop it. Just let me fix this."

"Fine."

Chapter 22

TWENTY MINUTES LATER, Cole parked the car.

"Can I leave my shoes here? They're killin' me," Bristol said, holding up the heels she hadn't put back on.

"I won't tell if you won't."

When they got out of the car, Cole went to the trunk and pulled out a tee shirt. Bristol looked away while he changed.

They walked around the corner to a building that didn't look like much, but had a line of people waiting to get in. Jazz music was drifting out the door. Cole took Bristol's hand and walked up to the doorman.

The guy looked at Cole and smiled widely. "Cole, buddy, long time no see."

"I know. I've been going through withdrawals. We just had an encounter with a wall of techno music and need to clean the palate."

"Well, you've come to the right place, my friend." He stepped to the side to let them through and nodded at Bristol.

The atmosphere of the place was so different from the Red Moon, it was jarring. Like warm water on cold hands.

"So you're a jazz kind of guy."

"I like to think of myself as a well-rounded kind of guy. I don't listen to a lot of jazz, but I know enough to appreciate it. This place isn't strictly jazz either. It's more about the mood, a great place to unwind."

He led her through a maze of people to a spot near the back in a corner.

"Can I get you a drink?"

"A pinot would be nice."

"So we aren't working?"

She sighed. "No, you've broken me down. I'm having a night out with a friend." She emphasized the last word.

"I'll be right back."

Bristol leaned her elbows on the table and looked around at the crowd of people. A lot were talking, close to one another. Some were sipping their drinks and listening to the music that filled the room.

She stared at the floor trying to focus on the music but found it hard to follow. She closed her eyes and tried to find the focal point of the song, but it seemed to become more discordant the harder she listened.

There was a soft touch on her arm, and she opened her eyes. The glass of wine was set before her, and Cole was watching her. "Looks like I brought you to the right place."

"I've never listened to jazz much." She squinted.

"I'm having trouble following it. As soon as I think I've got where it's going, it changes."

"Your problem is, you're trying too hard."

"I didn't know there was such a thing."

"Here." Cole pulled a chair close. He grabbed her hands and shook them out.

"You just got weird."

"Come on, Bristol, trust me for once. Now close your eyes and relax." He kept hold of her hands and she closed her eyes and sat up straight, taking a deep breath. She listened and Cole shook her arms. They were stiff. "See?"

She opened her eyes and frowned. "Okay, let me try again." She closed her eyes and focused on relaxing her body. Cole shook her arms, and they were loose.

"Now, listen to the music and stay relaxed. Let the music move you instead of you trying to move with it."

She took a deep breath again and let her body go. Her head rocked with her shoulders and she found the beat of the music at her core, while the other notes came together in unusual ways. A few times she felt herself tighten up again, her brain getting in the way, so she'd shake her arms out and start again. By the end of the song she found her body tingling with the effect of the music. She opened her eyes. "I think this place might be my new favorite."

"Oh, great. Does that mean I'll keep running into you here? What a drag."

Bristol smiled and took a sip of her wine. "So."

"So."

"What now?"

"Well, I told you about my history of drinking. I think now it's your turn."

"For what?"

"I want to know something ugly about your past." Cole laughed. "I don't mean you have to spill your guts. I just wanna know something. Anything."

"Wow, no pressure. If I'd have known this would be a tit for tat, I might have kept my mouth shut."

A woman in a long sparkling red dress came on the stage. As she began to sing, her limbs swept through the air as if carried by the words.

"Hey, I know this song," Bristol said.

"*The Look of Love*, yeah. But I'm not letting you get out of giving me some gory details that easy. You can keep it simple. Tell me about the first time you killed someone."

Her eyes went wide. "That's simple?"

"Well, from what I understand you've killed a few, so I thought it would be something you've already processed, but we don't have to talk about it."

She considered him for a moment. "I don't like to think about it."

"Then tell me something else, something that doesn't bother you so much."

She looked up at the ceiling thinking. "Okay, but I've never told anyone this before. And you have to promise me you will never tell another soul."

Cole leaned forward his face serious. "Of course."

"Sometimes when I've had a rough day." She stopped and pressed her lips together. Cole sat frozen. "Sometimes I eat peanut butter straight out of the jar."

Her eyes were wide, but she was trying hard not to laugh, and it was starting to crack.

Cole huffed back against the wall. "Wow. Actually, you gave away more than you intended. Now I know you have a sense of humor. I never thought I'd see the day."

"What? That is a serious issue. I'm considering going to see a shrink about it."

The music changed to a faster tempo. "If you want to play that game then I've got a better idea," he said, grabbing her hand and pulling her toward the front of the room where people were dancing.

"Oh, nononono. I don't dance," Bristol said, resisting. "I only play the part."

"Sure you do." He got her to the floor and swung her around. Bristol resisted at first, then Cole stopped her and put a hand on each arm, staring into her eyes. "I know it doesn't come naturally to you, but if you let me lead and you just go with it, this will be a lot easier. Remember what we did at the table? Close your eyes and relax." Bristol looked at him warily. "Geez, you're hard work. I promise, I won't try to make out with you or grope you or anything."

Bristol closed her eyes, letting the music sweep through her body and they started to move. Even if she didn't like to admit it, she did feel safe with Cole. She even began to enjoy herself.

It was hard to resist the music. The beat was intoxicating once she stopped trying so hard. Cole had experience on the dance floor and spun her around until she was dizzy.

Then the music changed. The notes spread out and Cole pulled Bristol into him. When she pulled away, he said, "You're not going to get away that easy. This is one of my favorites, and you were having fun. Dancing slow is fun too. It doesn't have to be romantic."

She gave in but wasn't so sure. "What's the song?"

"It's called 'Broken,' by Madison Ryann Ward."

"Hmm. I like it." Her chin was near his shoulder and she was breathing in the scent of him. Her forehead brushed his cheek, and she was slow to move it away. It was hard to fight against everything all the time. His arm tightened on her back, pulling her incrementally closer, and she let him.

Her stomach started tingling and everything within her wanted to lean in all the way. To give in. Her head began to swim and her forehead moved back against his cheek. She took in his scent with a deep breath. Cole tipped his head into her hair. She leaned back and looked up at him. His eyes dropped to her lips and then back up, but he didn't move.

She saw him swallow, and she licked her lips then leaned forward. He matched her till they were close enough to breathe each other's air. Then the panic erupted at the bottom of her spine. It shot up into her throat and she found it hard to breathe.

She pushed him away, but he held her firmly.

She shook her head and ripped herself from his arms and bolted for the door.

Chapter 23

BRISTOL PLUNGED into the night and breathed in deeply through the cigarette smoke that hung in the air.

"Bristol, what's wrong?" Cole was right behind her.

She looked at him, unsure what to say, so instead she turned, walking fast down the sidewalk.

"Whoa, slow down."

"Can't. I can't do this."

"Do what?" Cole grabbed her arm lightly, but she shook it off. "Bristol, stop."

She stopped but didn't turn.

Cole stayed behind her, off to the side. He reached out and touched her shoulder and saw her stiffen. "Bristol, will you talk to me? I don't know what happened. I'm sorry. I don't know what I did."

"You didn't do anything." She choked up. "It's me. I just can't."

"Can't what? Have a friend?"

"You're not a friend, Cole," she said, turning to him. His head pulled back. "Bristol I — "

"No, I don't mean … It's me. It's too late for me."

Cole huffed out a laugh. "How old are you? You couldn't be thirty yet."

"Don't patronize me."

"I thought we were having a good time."

"We were. I had a great time tonight. I haven't had that much fun and been that relaxed in a long time, but it doesn't suit me. It terrifies me."

"Maybe you just have to get used to it. Give me a chance."

"No!"

Cole refused to back off. He would not give into her fears.

Bristol took a step toward him. "You asked me about my first kill." She looked down the street then back to him.

"Bristol — "

" — My mom had a boyfriend. One in a long line, but this one was a drug dealer. She'd do anything for another hit. Ronny would bring his mates over, and she'd *entertain* them. I was fourteen at the time, so it wasn't long before their eyes turned to me. Mom told them no at first, but then one night she was desperate." Cole opened his mouth like he was going to say something and put an arm out toward her. "No, Cole, I don't need your pity."

"Why do you think it's pity?"

She shook her head. "I was taking kickboxing lessons. Well, not lessons exactly, but I spent a lot of time at Eli's gym, and he taught me on the side. I watched and learned a lot. The first guy that came at me, I broke his nose. Then one of his buddies tried. They were all high, so it wasn't the same challenge had things been different. I took him down too." She began to shiver. "At that point, Ronny pulled out a gun, but said he had a better use for me. There was a guy who was interfering with his trade, and he wanted me to kill him. He said that if I got caught, I'd get off easy because I was a minor. I told him to do his own dirty work, so he cracked me over the head, and when I woke up … they were all over me." She rubbed her hands down her face. "My mom didn't want me to report it. I was going to take myself to the hospital, but…"

Cole closed his eyes. "Please tell me they were arrested."

"Ronny told my mom she'd never get her hands on drugs again if I pressed charges. He was good to his word. There wasn't a drug dealer in town that wanted to get on his bad side.

"It wasn't until she was writhing around on the floor and puking her guts out that I finally gave in. And that's when he had his control over me. He threatened to do it all over again. So I killed the guy for him.

"It was easier than I expected, and I was good at it. I was good at not getting caught too. Not only is no one going to think the fourteen-year-old did it, but I figured out how to make it look like an accident. He started hiring me out to his friends and even giving me a cut of the profit, but he was just a pimp with another name. I had no freedom, and one day he set me up with a client who wanted *him* dead. I thought I'd enjoy it, but I didn't.

"My mom got a lot worse after he was dead. She

knew I had done it. I don't know how. It messed her up, and it wasn't long before she overdosed, and I was on my own."

Bristol wrapped her arms around her shaking body.

"I'm so sorry," Cole said, still not moving, but wanting desperately to hold her.

"Not your fault."

"Bristol." He put a hand out to her again, but she shrank back.

"Cole, you don't understand. You get under my skin and all that does is open up all that garbage."

"Maybe that's a good thing."

"A good thing? You want to see me fall apart?" Her voice squeaked at the end. She was losing control, but she needed him to understand. She started walking for the car. "I will never let a man have control over me ever again."

"You think this is about control?"

"Not on purpose, but when my mind tells me to keep my distance from you, but every other part of me wants to give in, that isn't me being in control."

"Sure it is. It's letting your heart have a say in things."

"My hea—" A knot pushed up her throat, cutting off her words. She tried to swallow it, but it wouldn't budge.

She bent over putting her hands on her knees and shivered convulsively.

Cole couldn't take it anymore. He moved toward her quickly and wrapped his arms around her. She didn't have the strength to push him away. The knot came out in an agonizing groan from somewhere deep inside of her.

She shouldn't have talked about it. It had been safely locked away, but somehow it was now choking her. Cole had his arms around her and led her to where she could lean against the side of the car. No tears came, but she couldn't stop shaking. A few people walked by trying not to look.

After several deep breaths, the convulsions subsided, and she pushed away from him. "I'm so sorry. That was horrible. I don't know what that was."

"Don't apologize. I'm sorry for what happened to you."

"I need to go," she said, walking away from the car, looking down the street for a taxi.

"Please wait. I can take you home."

She continued walking, fast. Cole had to run to catch up. "Bristol, you don't have to feel embarrassed."

She stopped and turned to him. "I've just revealed my deepest secrets to someone I barely know. That's not normal." She started walking again.

Cole grabbed her arm. "You don't think we've gone beyond acquaintances? Look, I don't want to get all sentimental here, but I've never met anyone like you before." He brushed hair off her face. "I'm not going to let you just run away."

Bristol felt like her insides were tearing apart. She was desperate to run and hide, but a small part of her wanted to trust Cole too. He held her face in his hands. Everything in her wanted to lean forward but instead she batted his hands away. "No, Cole. I can't do this. You need to stay away from me."

"Why?" He walked with her but stayed a few feet behind to give her space.

She threw her arms up the air. "Pick a card, Cole." She held up one finger. "Because I'm a bad person." She put another finger up. "Because I can't be trusted." She put up a third finger. "Because everyone I care about gets taken away from me." She felt a choking sob building and swallowed it. "Just, please, Cole. Let me be. I can't do this."

She started walking again, and he followed quietly behind. He didn't want her to be alone in the city while she was like this.

He wasn't sure if she knew he was behind her the whole way, but he figured she did. A taxi pulled up, and she got in without looking at him. The taxi drove off, and Cole stood quietly for a few minutes, wondering what to do next. He ran his hands through his hair and turned to go. A man was standing there with a knife. "Give me your wallet."

"Not now. I'm not in the mood." He tried to walk by the guy, hoping he'd get the energy coming off Cole and recognize he was the wrong guy to mess with. The guy didn't get the hint and thrust the knife at him.

Cole grabbed his wrist, twisting it and dropping him to the ground. "Not now!" Cole shouted. He shoved the guy hard and the guy started making a weird grunting noise and pushing back on his feet like Cole was some sort of monster. Cole couldn't have cared less. He just needed to be anywhere but here.

Chapter 24

BRISTOL'S CAR was gone when Cole got home. He sat in his own for a while, drumming his fingers on the steering wheel. His job was to find solutions to problems, but right now he had nothing.

He finally got himself upstairs, and after a couple of fitful hours' sleep, he ended up on his porch watching the sky lighten. He could feel that adrenaline was still coursing through his body.

There was a knock at the door and Cole shot out of his seat and rushed down the stairs.

"I hoped you'd be up," Andrew said when Cole opened the door. "Oh man, you look as bad as I feel."

"Couldn't sleep? Jenny still keeping you up?"

"I feel bad saying it, but I've gotten used to it and sleep through most of the time. But she started getting pains a few hours ago. It was a false alarm, but you don't go back to sleep after something like that. Thought I'd come over and we could chat about the case."

Cole grunted then said, "Want a coffee?" He tipped his own cup up to Andrew.

"Yes, please."

The two men climbed the stairs. "I've got something for you," Cole said, pointing at the coffee table.

Andrew picked up the bag with his phone. "Well done. I was afraid to ask. You get her prints on it?"

"Not hers, but you'll still want to get it to forensics."

"Did you take care of her? Or do I need to keep an eye out."

Cole shook his head. "The things I've been through for you." Cole brewed another pot of coffee.

"Why do you still brew your coffee? I'd expect you of all people to have a proper coffee machine by now." Cole shrugged but didn't have the energy to get into a discussion about something so trivial.

Andrew turned his phone on through the plastic. "So that girl … what was her name?"

"Bristol," Cole said, staring at the coffee dripping from the machine.

"You going to fill me in?"

"You won't have to worry about her anymore."

"Oh."

"You sound disappointed."

"She wiped my phone clean. So now I have nothing."

"That's better than the alternative."

"Dammit." Cole turned. Andrew was looking intense with the bag hanging at his side. "I need those photos of the paintings, Cole. I've got something."

"Something to do with the case?"

"Yeah."

"I thought I told you to back off."

"I kept a low profile and contacted a friend at the NYPD. Asked him if he had ever seen the tattoo before or anything like it. I knew it was a long shot, but he got back to me about the tattoo."

"You're kidding. They've seen it?" Cole poured two coffees.

"A girl came into the police station over a year ago. Said she was kidnapped and abused. She had the tattoo. She didn't remember how it got there and was pretty messed up on drugs, but they investigated." Cole handed Andrew a coffee, and they sat down. "That's not all. They found a painting of the girl in the perp's house. Same type I found."

Cole took a deep breath and let it out slowly. "Did they find the guy?"

"Yeah."

"What did he have to say?"

"Nothing. He was dead. Hung himself. A suicide note said he was so remorseful for what he did that he couldn't live with himself."

Cole rubbed his hand across his mouth. "Before or after the girl escaped."

"After."

"Was it ruled a suicide?"

"He definitely wrote the note, and everything else pointed that way. Why?"

"If it was me, I'd want the guy dead before he talked. And I'd make sure it didn't raise more questions."

"At the time they thought it was only the one girl, so they didn't suspect foul play beyond this one guy."

"Did the girl give any details about her abduction?"

"She wasn't clear on a lot because of the drugs."

"Well, I found out some information from your crime scene too. There was another girl who turned up alive in the same area. Said she was held captive, but then she *accidentally* stepped in front of a truck. She had the same tattoo."

"Why haven't I got a record of that at the station?"

"She didn't go to the police. All she wanted was drugs."

"Those three girls will be the tip of an iceberg."

"That's what it sounds like."

"I need those photos, Cole. I need to run them through missing persons like I should have done in the first place. And I need to send them to New York."

"Bristol will have them," Cole said, setting his mug on the coffee table.

"Can you get them?"

"I don't know. It's complicated."

"Complicated?" He huffed about a breath and leaned back. "Wow."

"What's that supposed to mean?"

"You're serious. What's going on here, Cole? Has she gotten to you? Do you need me to step in here for you?"

"No, she's on our side now. She was misinformed. I explained the situation, and she got on board with us."

"So then what's the problem?" Andrew's tone was cautious.

"She's got a history that isn't pretty."

"I don't see what that has to do with getting the photos."

"I like her, Andrew. A lot."

"Okay. So, what? You tried to make a move, and she shot you down."

"She didn't want to."

Andrew laughed before he could stop himself. "I'm sorry, Cole. I'm just not following."

"Forget it."

"No, I'm sorry. But you're going to have to give me more than clipped answers."

Cole sighed, resigned. "She likes me, and I like her … god, this sounds like the school playground." Cole polished off his coffee then continued. "She's been hurt so badly in the past that she's not willing to open up. Except that she did and then freaked out, and I don't know where I stand with her now."

"You sure she's not toying with you? Putting on an act?" Cole grimaced. "Hey, I'm just looking out for you. I want to make sure she's as real in this as you are."

"It's definitely real."

"I'm sorry, man. But I'm glad you brought her over to our side." Andrew smirked. "I'd hate for someone you like to be an enemy of mine."

Cole ran his hand through his hair. "That reminds me. Tanner's the one on your case."

Andrew flopped back on the couch nearly slopping his coffee. "Of course he's caught up in this. At least now I know who to keep in view."

Cole sighed. "I can't think straight."

"You should go see her."

"Yeah, I know. I've got to get those paintings."

"Speaking as your friend, the paintings would make a great excuse to go see her and talk to her. If she's on our side — hell, if she's on the side of these girls, she's got to agree to see you."

Cole nodded. "You're a good friend, Andrew. I don't know how we lost touch over the last few years."

"That's how life goes sometimes. Once this is all sorted out — and I'm keeping a positive attitude about the possible outcome — we can make sure to catch up more."

Cole looked out at the ocean. "I'll get those paintings."

"Great. And don't forget to tell me how things go with your girl."

"She's not my girl."

"Not yet."

Cole looked back at Andrew. "You look after yourself. Tanner's not done with you yet."

"Now that I know which way the attack is coming from, I might be able to dig up a little dirt."

Cole shook his friend's hand, who pulled him in to a hug. They didn't say any more, but Cole felt more resigned in moving forward.

Chapter 25

BRISTOL WOKE up with a pounding headache. The night before was still wedged firmly in her waking thoughts. She groaned and rolled over, putting her hands on her face. Had she really told Cole everything? She never did that.

Ever.

Well, she wanted to get rid of him, so that should do the trick.

The taxi had dropped her at Cole's place, and part of her longed for him to turn up and stop her from leaving. The other part of her panicked, so she jumped in the car and raced home. As soon as she got home, she had fallen into bed and somehow slept like a log. Only now did she realize how sticky her feet were.

She rolled over and sat up, lifting her phone to read the time. 10:30. She didn't like getting up past 7:00. No wonder she felt so horrible.

She stretched and went for a shower first to wash the night off, but when she stood under the water, all she could see and feel was Cole holding her face. The shower used to be a refuge for her, but lately it forced her worst thoughts to mind. She needed to go to the gym.

After making a cup of tea, she couldn't do anything except stare at the wall. It was as if parts of herself had fallen out all over the place. She needed to get control back, and the place to start was with this damn job.

She grabbed her phone, punching in the number Tanner had given her: *I'm out. Keep your money. I don't care if you know where I live. I'm done.*

She had nothing to lose if they came after her. She hardened up, and a fragile peace returned. She put the tea in her travel mug and headed for the gym.

◯◯

Eli was working with one of his proteges, a sixteen-year-old freckle-faced kid with hair sticking out in all directions. She went straight to the bags and started punching. When a hand touched her back, she stopped.

"You're focusing your energy today," Eli said from behind her.

She took a deep breath and turned to him.

"Oh," he said, "I won't ask you any questions, I promise. Just tell me what you need."

She looked at him, shocked. The hardness she thought she had built back up around herself was a brittle shell to Eli's ability to see straight through her. She gritted her teeth hard, but the tears she hadn't cried last night started pouring down her face. She had to build those walls back up. Crying every time someone was kind to her wouldn't work. Why had she suddenly turned into this emotional wreck? Eli led her into his office and sat her down. She blew her nose and took the cup of tea he offered.

Eli sat quietly, waiting for her to make the first move.

"I don't know what's wrong with me."

"I can't say I'm surprised."

"You've never seen me cry before."

"Yeah, and that's not normal. Eventually it's going to spill."

She blew her nose again. "Why didn't I make different choices, Eli?"

He put a hand on her knee. "Our past choices don't define who we are now, you know." If her eyes weren't so puffy, she would have rolled them. "Mistakes don't make us bad people."

"What if we've got a pile of mistakes that lead us into making more mistakes?"

"Oh, that's right, because you're supposed to be perfect."

Bristol shook her head. "I'm a bad person, Eli, no matter what you say. I've made choices — I *make* choices, every day that make the world a worse place to live."

"*Make* different choices."

She groaned and leaned back on the couch. "It's not that simple."

"Why not?"

"Because I don't know what's right anymore."

Eli's laugh boomed through the room. "There's a sorry excuse if ever I heard one."

"How can you laugh at me when I'm sitting here with a puffy red face, dripping snot all over you?" she said, trying to laugh.

"You don't tell me a lot about what you do, but I've heard enough to know that you are conscious of the right choices and often make them under the very difficult circumstances you face."

"I don't even understand what you just said." She leaned on his bulging shoulder.

He put his arm around her. "You learned from a pro how to do the right thing under the wrong conditions."

"You can't be talking about you." Bristol sniffed.

"No, your mom."

Bristol sat up. "When did my mom ever do anything right?"

"She knew she had crossed a line she would never recover from. She loved you so much she brought you here and made me swear to keep an eye on you. I tried to help her see that there was still time to turn things around, but she couldn't see it. I will not let you make the same mistake."

"I think I handle myself better than my mom."

"You think so? You've got different problems, but they're leading you to the same place."

"I'm not going to take drugs, Eli."

"Self-destruction is more the word I was looking for. You keep everything inside and hold it so hard it's eating you from the inside out."

"My mom bottled nothing. She put everything out on the table and blamed everyone but herself."

"The real stuff, the stuff that she was most ashamed of, she never breathed to a soul. It would have killed her. She only told me right at the end."

"What stuff?"

"That's not for me to share. Except, I will say that she believed she was a bad mom. That she should have given you up for adoption instead of being selfish and wanting to have you herself. She loved you, Bristol. She just didn't know what to do with that love. In the end, the only way she knew how to keep the pain at bay was drugs."

"Well, I don't know what to do with love either, so it turns out we do have something in common. You and her, on the other hand, I don't know how you two ever became friends." Eli frowned and looked at the ground. "What?"

He considered her for a minute. "Your mom and I weren't ever really friends. I barely knew her."

Bristol stared at him. "That doesn't make any sense. Why would you take responsibility for me if you barely knew her?"

"She came into a free clinic I was working at one day, when you were little. You had a rash, and she was convinced it would kill you. I put her mind at ease and gave her some cream. Then she came back the next day, said you had a fever, which you didn't. After I checked you over, she asked me straight out if I'd take you and look after you." Eli shook his head. "I thought it was the drugs talking, but she looked at me so adamantly, and you were such a good little girl. Very curious and quiet. I told her to bring you by the gym sometime. When she dropped you off and then left, I thought I had made a huge mistake, but you fit right in and she did come back to get you, eventually. Then you just kinda grew on me."

"I don't know what to do with that information," Bristol said.

"You could try forgiving her."

"Forgive her? For what she did? For dumping me on you so she could go get high? But it wasn't okay."

Eli took Bristol's hand, enveloping it in his two massive ones. "Forgiveness has nothing to do with saying that what she did was okay. It's about letting it go. Breaking the hold it has over you so you can be free."

"I'll think about it."

"You do that."

Her phone buzzed in her bag, but she ignored it, terrified it was Cole.

She patted Eli on the leg. "Thanks for always being here, Eli. I don't know what I'd do without you."

"Why don't you go out and give Sam a run for his money? He's been getting cocky lately and needs to be put in his place."

"It would be my pleasure." She smiled as best she could. "I'll just run to the bathroom and wash my face first."

Bristol stepped into the ring and a familiar sense of her body relaxing and tensing up at the same time washed over her. This was just what she needed. She had taken the step to move away from the case and she was sure Cole would never speak to her again. Now she could let all that out and get back to the way things were. And if Tanner wanted to come after her, she had nothing left to lose, anyway. Maybe she could go away for a while or maybe for good. Although the idea of leaving Eli was a hard one to consider.

She went easy on Sam, but she could understand the potential Eli saw and made sure he knew he had a long way to go. By the time they finished, she was feeling much better.

When she got in her car, she remembered her phone buzzing and pulled it out to check who had called. There were five missed calls from Mick, she sighed. After losing his wife, he seemed to make it his duty to make sure Bristol was safe. It wasn't far to his place, so she decided she'd drive there and put his mind at ease.

◯◯

She turned the corner and spotted a police car first, and then what she guessed to be a detective's car.

She ran up to his door and could hear raised voices. Frowning, she knocked. The door swung open almost immediately and Mick was there looking hysterical. "Bristol!" He grabbed her and pulled her into a hug. She was about to push him back when he said, "They've taken her." Then he moved back and pointed at a man and a woman who stood in the living room. "And they're not doing a damn thing about it."

"Mr. Collins, please. We take child abductions very seriously."

"What?" Her stomach plummeted. "Where's Lila?"

"They've taken her," he said, grabbing her again.

She pushed him away. "Who, Mick?"

"I don't know. You know I've got — " He stopped and looked at the detectives.

Bristol looked at his desk. He had put his equipment away. He worked from home doing plenty of legal technical stuff, but he did plenty of illegal stuff too. Bristol's phone buzzed, and she immediately pulled it out. It was a private number: *You always did like to do things your own way. I'm curious…when your way threatens the lives of others, what will you choose? Will you do the job you were paid to do?*

If the police hadn't been there, she would have screamed. "I've gotta go, Mick." Her voice was low and hard.

"No, you can't go now." He followed her out.

"Let the police do what they have to, but I know who has her and I will go get her back."

"Bristol…"

"Trust me Mick. You do whatever the police ask. Don't give them a reason to look into you. I'll handle it."

◯◯

She slammed the car door and ripped out her phone to ring Tanner.

He answered after three rings. "This better be important."

"You son of a bitch. You better watch your back

'cause I am going to wrap my hands around your neck and squeeze the life out of you. And I'm going to enjoy every second of it."

"Whoa." Tanner laughed lightly. "To what do I owe the honor of such a violent phone call? I thought you weren't working for me anymore."

"You give her back now or I'll hunt you down. And if one finger is — "

" — Hang on a second. If someone important to you has been kidnapped, I had no part to play in that. That's not how I operate. Like you, I like a more hands-on approach when it comes to threats. But you have crossed the wrong man, and it's not me. I told him from the start I didn't think we should use you, but he insisted."

"Who."

"I'm not at liberty to divulge that information. But he'll do what he wants. I have no say in the matter."

Bristol hung up before she could scream into the phone. She threw it on the seat beside her hard enough that it bounced onto the floor and she rested her head on the steering wheel. "What am I gonna do?" She sobbed.

Chapter 26

BRISTOL DROVE DOWN THE ROAD, taking long deep breaths as she went, each one pushing her deeper into a void. Her tears had run out. Guilt and shame now clambered up her spine, and she embraced them, squeezing all her feelings into a thrumming numbness. Whoever it was pulling the strings didn't matter. She would sacrifice herself for Lila, to hell with everything and everyone else. She'd get Lila back and then disappear forever, whatever that meant.

Eli talked about making better choices, but when your only option is to ruin one person's life or ruin another, how do you decide? No matter what she chose it would be wrong, so what difference did it make? She chose Lila.

She pulled up in front of Andrew's house. There was still plenty of time to frame him. She would come back tonight and collect hair fibers from his house. She could get a shirt and put blood on it. It would be easy to finish the job she was hired to do.

The front door opened, and Bristol shrank down in her seat as Andrew's wife walked toward the road, rubbing one hand down the side of her giant belly. She went to the mailbox, put an envelope in, and lifted the flag. Oblivious to the fact that Bristol was about to ruin her life, she went about her normal life doing her normal things, assuming all was good in the world.

Bristol considered going in now to get it over with. She could knock on the door and make up some story about being a new neighbor on the block and wanting to get to know the area better. Then she could fawn over the interior decorating or the layout of the house and ask for a tour, pocketing whatever she might need as she went.

Bristol's phone dinged beside her. It was Mrs. Deacon: *CAT EMERGENCY!!!*

Bristol was beginning to regret teaching that woman how to text, but what would Mrs. D do if she didn't have Bristol to count on anymore? She couldn't think about that now.

Looking back up at the house, she made her decision. She'd wait until tonight. It was too risky to go in now. If Andrew's wife mentioned her visit, he might get suspicious. She could go home, save the stupid cat one more time, and then head back here tonight.

This baby will grow up without a dad so that Lila can grow up without a mom. It happens to people all the time. That's normal life, too.

◯◯

As Cole walked down the hallway to Bristol's place, he heard a strained murmur coming from the apartment next door. He could only just make out the word "please" spoken in a wispy, desperate tone. Maybe Bristol would know what was going on with the neighbor.

He knocked on Bristol's door and waited. Then knocked again.

"Sheeeebbbbaaa!" The woman's voice cried out from next door.

He looked from the neighbor's door back to Bristol's. If he hung around long enough, Bristol might eventually show. In the meantime, it was worth checking with the neighbor.

His hand was poised ready to knock on the neighbor's door, but then he dropped it. What is this woman going to think seeing a stranger standing at her door?

"Bristol will be here soon, is that what you want?" Cole heard through the door. That piqued Cole's interest enough to knock. He wrapped a knuckle on the door. "See, I told you," the woman said to whoever else was in there. "Come in! Come in!"

She would think he was Bristol, so he opened the door slowly. "Um, excuse me?" he said, with only his head across the threshold. The woman turned, startled. "Sorry, I'm a friend of Bristol's. I thought you sounded like you needed help."

The woman put her hand to her chest but didn't appear afraid. "You're a friend of Bristol?"

"Yes, I came over to see her, but she's not home."

"No, but I sent her a message and told her I need

her help, so I expect her to be here shortly," she said, walking toward him. "She's so good to me. Always looking out for me. So helpful. But I don't think Sheba likes her very much." She opened the door fully. "Would you like to come in? How are you with cats?"

"Cats?"

"Yes, mine is stuck out on the ledge."

"Ah, that's who you were talking to. I don't mind them. But I know enough to know he's probably not stuck. Cats tend to do what they want."

"*She,*" Mrs. Deacon said.

"Pardon?"

"Sheba is a girl. And she likes to think she's brave, but really I know she's scared."

"Right. What can I do to help?"

"Do you think you could get her back inside?"

Cole walked over to the window and leaned out. Sheba looked content right where she was. He turned and hopped up on the windowsill, so he was sitting on it and leaned out, holding the frame.

"Bristol used a can of tuna. Sheba likes tuna, but she doesn't like being tricked."

"I don't blame her."

"I think she felt betrayed." Cole peered back at the woman though the window. "Having someone dangle a treat in front of her and then pulling it back. It doesn't feel good. But you, you just go after what you want, don't you?" Cole pushed his lips together. His forehead creasing. She smiled, oblivious to the odd effect her words had on Cole.

He looked back out at the cat and laid his hand on

the ledge near her. Sheba sniffed his fingers. He scratched her on the ears, and she started to purr. He put his hand down on the ledge again and the cat moved closer, and he scratched her again. Then the cat moved into his hand, rubbing her face on his arm. He curled his arm around her and pulled her inside.

"Well, would you look at that? I think she might like you more than she likes me."

"I doubt that." Cole held that cat, continuing to scratch her behind the ears. He was out of his house too much to get a pet, but it was nice giving one a pat when you didn't have to take responsibility for it. "Would you like me to put a screen on that window for you? It would keep Sheba inside."

"Oh no. It blocks the breeze. Makes me feel caged."

"Right. You don't know when Bristol will be back by any chance?"

"Hmmm. Tough to say. I'm surprised she hasn't come already. Last time I told her I needed help she came much faster. But you're welcome to stay here while you wait."

"That's very kind of you, Mrs.?"

"Deacon." She giggled like a schoolgirl. "Are you two something of an item by any chance?"

"Ah, no," Cole said, moving to the door. "I might just have another quick check at her place." He moved through the door, still holding the cat.

"Pity. She's such a lovely girl and you're such a lovely man. I mean, you're not just handsome, but you saved my cat too, which means you must be a good sort. Not to mention that Sheba likes you."

Cole smiled. "It was lovely meeting y — "

" — Oh there you are, sweetie," Mrs. Deacon said, peering out past Cole. Cole turned to see Bristol looking like a deer in the headlights at the end of the hall. "This handsome young gentleman was looking for you and then he saved my cat. Wasn't that wonderful of him? He's my knight in shining armor." She squeezed Cole's cheek, and he handed the cat to her.

"I'll leave you two to your business," she said, winking at Bristol and shutting the door. Bristol hadn't moved. Cole could almost see her brain trying to decide if she should run.

"What are you doing here?"

"Look," Cole said, taking a step toward her. She took a step back. Cole put his hands up in front of him. "It's strictly business, I promise." Bristol stayed put. "We don't have to talk about last night, but those paintings that were on Andrew's phone, I need to have a look at them if you've still got them."

"Why?"

Cole scratched his head. "I'm not here to hurt you or to push you. I just need to see the paintings. It's important."

She made a fist then walked down the hall past him brushing his shoulder. It was an aggressive gesture, but it surprised Cole she was willing to touch him at all.

She opened her door and left it ajar as she moved inside. He took that as a yes.

When he walked into the apartment, she unlocked her phone and shoved it at him, then moved into what he figured was her bedroom. He looked around the place. It wasn't what he expected. It was very homey. She had a knitted blanket laying across a well-used couch that looked very comfortable. Bristol came out with a backpack and dropped it on the counter.

"Get what you needed? I've got things to do."

"Is something wrong? I mean besides last night. You just seem … "

"Get out of my head, Cole. You don't know what's going on, so just leave it."

He watched her. She didn't break eye contact with him at first, but then he saw something shift in her gaze and she looked away.

"What is it, Bristol? What's happened?"

She clenched her jaw and Cole saw her swallow. "I've got work to do, so if you're finished…" She reached out a hand for her phone.

Cole bit the inside of his cheek. "Your phone locked again. I haven't seen the photos." She unlocked the phone and handed it to him and crossed her arms while he slid his finger across the screen from one picture to the next. "I'll need to forward these to Andrew."

"Fine."

He looked at her, then back down at the phone. "Andrew found out more information." She didn't respond, but when he looked up again, he saw she was listening. "The NYPD had a girl turn up over a year ago with a similar tattoo."

"What?"

"Yeah, looks like we've got some sort of child-trafficking ring going on. Whoever hired you to frame Andrew, I mean above Tanner, he's trying to avoid more than a drugs charge. It looks like we may have a lot of girls in trouble."

"The paintings?"

"That's what we think. That's why I need these. We need to check them against missing persons."

"What makes you so sure the paintings are related?"

Cole saw a look of panic wash over her. He paused before answering. "They found a painting of the New York girl in the guy's house, but they couldn't question him because he had hung himself." Cole huffed. "He left a suicide note saying how bad he felt about it all. They didn't realize it was related to a larger ring, so the case was closed."

Bristol turned white, but Cole couldn't reach her before she hit the ground.

Chapter 27

BRISTOL BLINKED up at the ceiling. Cole hovered over her, pushing her hair out of her face. "You okay?"

She tried to sit up and was surprised to find she was lying on the couch. Cole pushed her back, but she fought against him.

"Just lie still a minute," he said as her head began to spin again.

She groaned and laid back, taking a few deep breaths. "What happened?"

"You fainted."

Bristol covered her face with her hands as the last conversation she had with Cole rushed back. "I can't believe this is happening. It never ends, Cole. I can't even ... "

"Bristol, please tell me what's going on."

She thought of Lila, locked up somewhere. "They took her." Her voice was high and choked.

"The girl in New York?"

Cole's mention of New York sent a convulsion through her body. "No, Lila."

"Who's Lila?"

It seemed as though every decision she made backfired on her. "I was going to frame him again. I just needed to get her back, but it will never end if I do that, will it?"

Cole took a deep breath and looked down. "They're threatening you." Cole's voice was full of gravel. "Who's Lila."

"My friend's little girl."

"You were going to frame Andrew to get her back."

Bristol nodded and reached for Cole's hand, squeezing it for emphasis. "You need to lock me up, Cole. I can't be trusted."

He knelt on the floor next to her and kept her hand in his. "Do you understand that you had a completely normal response to being threatened? You care about that little girl and you were willing to do whatever it took to get her back."

Bristol shook her head and closed her eyes. Her heart felt as though it was in a vice. A tear ran down her face and into her hair. Cole reached up and brushed the line it left with his thumb.

"I could have stopped it," Bristol said, scrunching up her eyes as another tear leaked out.

"No, Bristol, you couldn't have. You can't take responsibility for other people's evil actions."

"You don't understand," she moaned, pulling her hand away from his.

"Then help me to understand."

She looked at him and licked her lips. Her mouth felt like it was full of cotton. "That man in New York didn't commit suicide."

Cole was silent.

Bristol sat up slowly, resting her arms on her knees. Cole sat on the edge of the coffee table across from her. "Someone hired me. He said he was a relative of the girl. He told me what the guy had done to her and asked me to take care of it. I saw the painting of her at his house — " Her voice choked off for a second. "I had forgotten all about it until you mentioned it."

Cole stood up and started pacing.

Bristol continued, sure he would storm out at any moment, or worse, condemn her actions. At the time she had felt virtuous, making that monster suffer for what he had done. "First, I made sure the information I got about him was true."

"How'd you do that?"

"How do you think?" There was an edge to her voice and Cole's eyebrows shot up. "Sorry." She took a deep breath and softened her voice. "I didn't give him any option but to tell me the truth, and after I confirmed what he had done, I made him write that confession. Then I made it look like a suicide.

"He deserved everything he got, but I thought it was a one-person thing. It didn't occur to me it was bigger. Now I understand I wasn't hired for revenge. I was hired to silence him. I thought I was helping, but I only made things worse."

She stood up. Her eyes were full of a terrified innocence. "I'm so sorry, Cole. It's all my fault."

"It's not your fault. You did what you thought was right."

"Did I? Not once did I ask the guy if anyone else was involved. I could have stopped this way back then."

Her whole body trembled again like it did the night before.

She blinked, and suddenly Cole was right in front of her. He leaned over slightly so he was eye level with her. She looked down. "Bristol, I will not let you take the weight of this thing squarely on your own shoulders." He tilted his head. "Look at me."

She lifted her eyes to his as the tears fell freely down her face. Cole put a hand on her arm. "This isn't your fault. If it's anyone's fault, it's the guys who are doing this. All we can do is our best to stop it. And you don't have to do it alone."

She felt as though she was going to implode. Her consciousness ebbed, and she was afraid if she didn't grab hold of Cole now, she would slip away into nothing.

She reached out, wrapping her arms around his neck. He stiffened at first, but then put his arms around her and straightened, lifting her slightly off the ground. She let go of the pain she had been holding back and sobbed into his shoulder. They stayed that way for a while.

When she finally settled, he bent forward to put her feet back on the ground, and she pulled away, embarrassed.

"I'm sorry," she said, wiping her sleeve across her face.

"For what?"

"I just …" Then she saw the mess she left on his shoulder, and her mouth dropped open. "Oh no, I'm so sorry. I'll get something to clean that off," she said, turning quickly. The panic was returning.

He grabbed her arm. "It's fine."

"No, it's not." She wrenched her arm away but then stopped, shaking her head as the tears were brimming again. "I can't … " Cole led her to the couch and sat her down. "I'm so messed up." She wiped her face again. "I'm terrified for Lila, and I have no way to find her. My brain is muddled, and I can't think straight enough to figure out what to do. Not to mention that I've made so many mistakes in the past that have led right up to this moment. I'm afraid to get it wrong again.

"I've just got all this rage and fear surging through me. I mean look at me. I can't go a minute without falling apart. It's too much. I can't fix this. I'll just make it worse."

"Bristol, you need to stop blaming yourself. You've been manipulated in the past because you didn't know the truth. Now you know. Not to mention that you don't have to do it alone. You've got me and Andrew on your side. You might be a mess right now, but I know you can see this through. And I know you want to." He grabbed her arm and pulled gently until she got up. "You're going to go have a shower, and I'm going to get you a cup of whatever it is that will help you calm down, and we are going to figure this out. You and me.

"We will put an end to this because you're very good at what you do, and I'm very good at what I do, and we'll figure this out together."

Bristol sniffed. "Tea."

"What?"

"I like to drink tea."

He reached out his hand for her to take, then pulled her around and found the bathroom. He led her in.

"I'm not going to let you stay in here."

Cole laughed lightly. "I wasn't planning on it. Besides, I've got tea to make." He turned and moved out the door.

"Cole?"

"Yeah."

"Thank you. I don't know what I would have done if you hadn't turned up."

He just smiled and shut the door.

She lost track of time as she let the steaming water flow over her, and it was the first time in several days that she found the water soothing again.

Knowing that Cole was out there, on her side, was an odd feeling. She was so used to getting by on her own. Being able to share some of the responsibility and the burden allowed a little of the stress to dissipate.

That same panic still skirted around the edges of her mind, but she knew she needed Cole's help, so she pressed it back.

Wrapped in her fluffy bathrobe, she walked back to the living room. Cole stood at the window, looking out. He heard her enter and quickly moved back to the kitchen. "I boiled the water, but I'll just reheat it 'cause you had a really long shower."

"I needed it," she said, leaning her hip on the counter.

"Yes, you did. You have it weak or strong?"

"No point putting the tea in if you can't taste it."

"I wouldn't know. I don't drink tea," he said with a smirk.

"Well, not everyone can be as sophisticated as me."

"Glad to see you're feeling better." He handed her the mug, and they both moved to the living room. Bristol sat in the armchair and not on the couch, which Cole noted.

"Can you unlock your phone for me again? I still haven't managed to send the photos through to Andrew. We might get a lead off those."

Bristol punched in her number and leaned her head back against the chair. "Drake's the one who painted them. Maybe it's him? Although he doesn't strike me as a leader, but he's definitely creepy enough to be involved."

Cole scanned through the portrait photos and found that they were followed by a picture of the dead girl. "What are these?" Cole asked, turning the phone to show Bristol.

She shook her head. "That's everything Andrew had on his phone."

They were similar to the ones Andrew had shown

him the other night, but those were black and white and these were in color. One was a closeup of the girl's face, her green eyes staring into nothingness. A chill went through him. He knew those eyes. He flipped back through the paintings then back to the dead girl.

"I think I know who it is. Who's in charge."

"Who?" Bristol sat up.

"Drake might be involved, but your right, he's not at the top." Cole stood to pace the room again. "I think it might be Robert Carlson, the guy I did a job for, but I need to check it out to confirm. Also, maybe collect some evidence."

"This is the guy you mentioned before."

"Yeah. If we work together, I think we have a chance of saving Lila and these other girls."

"Do we know how many?"

Cole slid through the photos, counting. "Looks like ten at least."

Bristol jumped up. Talking about the case brought her strength back and gave her something to focus her energy on. "Okay. Well, I've got an invite to Drake's art show tonight."

"I'm impressed. How'd you manage that?"

"I'm charming." She shot him her sweetest smile then went serious again. "While you're checking on Robert, I'll head there and keep an eye on Drake and see who else shows up."

"Maybe I should come with you."

"No, I can't be seen with you. That'll put Lila at greater risk. If they think I might be doing the work I was hired for, I can buy us more time. Besides, there will be lots of people there. I'll be safe."

"Okay." Cole didn't look convinced. "You get ready for your party. I'll head out now and check on Robert. We'll get Lila back, I promise."

Bristol blinked at him a couple times. "You can't make a promise like that, Cole. Don't ever make a promise like that. You don't know what the outcome will be. I know that better than anyone."

"Sorry, you're right. But we will do everything we can. You just focus on working your magic and exposing the illusion from your end, and I'll see what I can find on mine."

She walked him to the door. He turned and ran a hand down her arm. "You okay?"

"Yeah, I will be." She stood on her toes and leaned in, kissing him lightly on the lips. Then stepped back. "Thank you … again."

He fisted a handful of her robe but then let it go. His voice was deep. "Anytime."

It took all his self-control to walk out, and Bristol closed the door gently behind him. He leaned against the wall pushing his lips together. He closed his eyes and put his hand to his mouth then pushed off the wall and bounded down the hall. He'd tuck that away for later.

Chapter 28

COLE WALKED through the door of the Lincoln Tower and waved at the guard, who now stood at attention. The man nearly smiled but caught himself at the last second. He watched Cole walk past without moving his head.

Robert must have dealt with his guards already. That could pose a problem.

Cole approached the desk, noting the door behind. An image of the ground floor blueprint sprang to mind. He hadn't told Robert everything.

When he reached the desk, he rested his hand on the counter. "I need to see Mr. Carlson please. You can tell him it's Cole Sullivan."

The guard lifted his chin as though sizing him up. "I'm sorry sir, he's not in the building at the moment."

Cole resisted a sigh and cast a glance over to the elevators. "Of course he isn't," he said to himself, then looked back at the guard. "That's fine. I'll visit another colleague while I'm here. Thanks."

Ron and Kyle watched him approach. He had his story ready.

"Hey, fellas." He walked through the detectors like he owned the place. "Got nothin' with me today." The smile on his face was charming and casual.

Kyle held a hand up. "I'm sorry sir, but I'll need to see your ID, and we'll need to call ahead."

"Kyle, what's this all about? You know who I am."

"You're the breakfast guy and it's not breakfast."

Cole leaned in toward Kyle as though he was confiding. "Okay, it's actually a girl I'm here to see. I met her while delivering breakfast. I've been out of town these last couple days, and I wanted to surprise her and be all charming and see if I can take her out for a nice meal."

"Sorry, sir."

Cole took a few steps back. They must have been raked over the coals for letting him get through before. There was no way to talk his way in this time, but that was fine because there were other ways.

He leaned his weight back for a second and then plowed through toward the elevator, palming Kyle, who nearly fell flat on his back. Cole mentally apologized, but knew Kyle would be telling this story to the girls at the bar, so it was beneficial to all involved.

He reached the elevator and pressed the button just for effect as Kyle tackled him, wrenching his arms behind his back. Cole smiled. *God, I love a loophole.*

The guard at the counter helped Kyle escort Cole to the room he already knew was out the back. It was painted hospital white and looked like they used it as a temporary office space or, in this instance, a temporary jail cell. It had a desk and chair, and the courtesy of a water cooler in the corner.

Kyle pointed at the chair. The rapid flexing of his jaw gave away the adrenaline coursing through his veins. He was looking cockier than usual.

"I'd rather stand, thanks," Cole said.

Kyle pulled out a phone and stepped out of the room to make his call to the police. He locked the door behind him.

Cole's arms were long, and he easily brought his cuffed hands from his back to his front. Reaching awkwardly into his pocket, he pulled out his own phone and rang Bristol.

"Cole, what is it? Did you find something?"

"Working on it. Just had a few minutes spare and thought I'd see how you were feeling."

"I'm fine. Just finished getting ready."

"Whatcha wearing?" There was silence on the other side. "You always misunderstand me. It was a genuine question."

"It's black tie. I dressed appropriately."

"Can you send me a photo?"

The phone disconnected, and Cole snickered to himself. She was feeling better.

There was a knock at the door, which Cole found amusing, and Kyle peeked his head in. "The police have been called. They'll be here shortly."

Cole gave him two thumbs up.

Kyle shook his head and left the room, locking the door again. Cole looked at the ceiling and sighed, then moved over to the desk. There was a bright blue plastic desk caddy in a drawer that had all the usual things; pens, pencils, paperclips, and lint. He had a paperclip in his pocket for this very thing but enjoyed it more when he could use what he found in his environment. He grabbed a metal ruler, also in the drawer, and used it to bend the paperclip the way he needed, then stuck one end into a hole in the cuffs, releasing the ratchet.

Cole's phone dinged. He pulled it out while dropping the cuffs into the drawer. Bristol had taken a picture of herself in a long black dress that looked like was poured over her. It was sophisticated, elegant, and damn sexy. She was flipping him off into the mirror.

He ran a hand through his hair. "I think I'm in love."

If he wasn't careful, that woman would drive him to distraction. He had to get this job done so he could get back to her. He wasn't happy about her being at the art show on her own.

He stuffed the phone back into his pocket and grabbed another paper clip to go with the one he had and unfolded it while he walked to the door.

Cole knew how to pick just about every lock that was pickable. He looked at the clock above the desk to time himself for the fun of it.

… Twelve seconds.

He was a little rusty. That type of lock should have taken him less than ten.

He ducked his head out quickly and saw it was clear, so moved down to the corner, pausing to check the next hallway. According to the blueprints, the service elevator would be just around the next corner.

This particular elevator only went to the parking level, and he was unsure what the point of it was, but on that level he would have access to the other elevators. And because they checked vehicles before entering, there would be no guards to deal with.

He swiped Kyle's key card, which he had pinched back at the metal detectors, and headed down.

The only disaster now would be that Kyle's card wouldn't give him access to Robert's floor. He didn't have the lid from the breakfast container he had used the first time to ratchet the doors open.

After changing elevators, he swiped the card again and pushed the button for the executive level. The door closed, and the elevator began to climb. Cole leaned against the wall in relief.

When the door opened, he raced to where he knew the painting would be. Except it wasn't. That was one thing Cole hadn't counted on. He smashed his hand on the wall. He could see those green eyes and was certain it was the same girl, but without the evidence it didn't make much difference.

"Can I help you?" Came a voice from behind.

Cole spun into a defensive stance. "Oh, it's you," he said, dropping his arms.

Robert's secretary stood several steps away from him with her arms crossed. "Robert isn't here and wasn't expecting you."

"Yes, I know. Sorry, I was just doing some follow up. The painting that was here. The girl with the green eyes. Robert said that was his daughter."

"Daughter?"

"Yes."

"Robert doesn't have a daughter. He doesn't have any children. He removed that painting earlier today. He said he was purchasing another one that he would put up tomorrow." Cole clenched his teeth. "Do I need to call security?"

"No, it's fine, they already know I'm here. Can I make a suggestion?"

"If you're brief. I have things to do."

"You seem like a decent woman. And you must be good at your job to work for someone like Robert, but I would suggest you find someone else to work for. Robert's a monster."

"You need to go." Her voice was firm, but he saw something in her face. She knew he was right.

He made his way back down to the parking garage. He'd have to hot-wire the worst-looking car to avoid a car alarm and any further trouble.

An older model Ford Escort was his best bet. There were no blinking red lights on the interior, so he gave it a shot and got lucky.

He drove up and out without a hitch and parked the stolen car around the corner, calling it in to the police station as he walked a couple blocks to his own car. He pulled out his phone and looked at Bristol's photo again, then rang her.

"I've got work to do, and you keep interrupting." Bristol's voice held the hint of a smile.

"Yeah, but I've got to say — and this is meant to be taken completely as a come on — you look incredible."

"I thought you would say hot. That's more your style."

"I'm offended. I thought you knew me better by now. Besides, 'hot' is not the right adjective for that dress. And I liked your accessory."

"I'm not wearing any accessories."

"The bird." Bristol laughed. It was light and relaxed, and Cole liked the sound of it. A lot. "And thank you for not hanging up on me because I'm calling you for another reason that *is* business related. I just had to get that out of the way."

"Good, I'm glad we can get back to business."

"There was a painting of a girl with green eyes that I saw last time I was in Robert's building. I'm sure it's the dead girl."

"So you got it?"

"No, it's gone. His secretary said he removed it this morning in preparation for purchasing a new one."

"Son of a bitch."

"Yeah."

"I Googled a picture of him, so I know who to keep an eye out for, although it will be hard not to strangle him if I see him. I'll text you if he's here."

"You're there now?"

"Yeah. About to head into the parking garage."

"Don't engage him. Just give me a call. I'll deal with him." The phone was silent. "Bristol?"

"Yeah. Okay. I've gotta go."

"Talk soon. Make sure you call me if you think there will be trouble. I'll be headed that way shortly."

"Remember what I said. I can't be seen with you."

"What if it's an emergency?"

"It won't be."

"But what if it is?"

"Okay, fine. If it's an emergency. But I'll let you know. You need to promise you'll wait for my word."

Now Cole was silent.

"Please, Cole. I can't mess this one up."

"Fine. I'm going to go see Andrew and fill him in. Make sure he's ready if we have to move quickly."

"Okay, I've gotta go."

Chapter 29

BRISTOL PULLED into the underground parking at the museum and scanned the cars and other patrons who had already arrived. She was late, fashionably, and it appeared as though most were already upstairs.

Near the entrance, she spotted a car she had hoped to see. Tanner's Mercedes. She grinned. It made sense that he was connected to Drake. It would give her an opportunity she had been waiting for. Getting the gloves off Tanner was easy. It was getting them back to him before he noticed they were gone that she had been most concerned about, but she just got lucky.

She parked her aging sedan in a far corner of the garage so it wouldn't stand out among the other cars, which all looked to be worth around fifty grand or more. In the back, hers would be ignored as a car that had been abandoned earlier in the day.

She turned to the back seat and grabbed the leather gloves, dropping them on the gauzy wrap that lay across the front passenger seat. When she got out of the car and saw the long walk to the entrance, she changed her mind and pulled the wrap and the gloves out, stashing them closer to Tanner's car.

The reception area of the museum was nearly empty. One other attendee didn't waste time and eagerly ascended the stairs. There were two men who stood to the side with a clear view of everyone entering. Their hands were clasped behind their backs, and they had earpieces. She was sure they were armed.

They watched her when she walked in. One of the men couldn't hide his surprise at her entry, which caused a flutter in her stomach. Why would he be surprised to see her? She didn't recognize him but resisted the temptation to study his face to see if she could place him. If she was conspicuous already, that would only make things worse. She didn't want to give him any more time to consider his astonishment at her presence, so she turned and headed up the stairs through *the vault*, a seemingly handcrafted tunnel that opened up into a white room with a honeycomb ceiling. The first time she came here, she felt like a bee entering its hive.

An attendant with white gloves waited at the top, and after she showed him her invitation, he ushered her through with a sweep of the hand.

The affair had a glamorous appeal that she might have enjoyed more if her heart wasn't beating so hard, and if the artwork displayed weren't Drake's. She still couldn't fathom why anyone would agree to display his artwork, no matter how much he was willing to pay.

The space held about forty people and they were virtually silent. While she had never been to an art show, she figured there should be more conversation. She pretended to study the art while noting faces. She had yet to see Tanner or Robert.

"Well, well, well," said a voice behind her.

She turned abruptly. "Tanner? I didn't expect to see you here. You don't strike me as an art aficionado type."

"I don't mind rubbing elbows with these guys. Besides, these paintings are more interesting than your typical vase and fruit bowl." He leaned toward her. "So have you cooled off since your little outburst?"

She matched his lean and lifted her chin close to his face. "Tanner, even if you haven't laid a hand on Lila, you still better watch your back. Guys like you always get it in the end."

He put a hand on her chin. "Only in the movies, sweetheart."

"Don't bet on it." She pushed away from him then looked around her. "It's suddenly a bit chilly in here, and I forgot my wrap." She gave him a cold look and headed back down the stairs.

"Forgot my wrap," she called out to the white-gloved man but with her head facing down the stairs so the security at the bottom would hear her and not get suspicious when she left and reappeared again.

◯◯

Back in the show-room-floor of a parking garage, she pulled her loot from its hiding place, wrapped the gauze around her shoulders, and carried the gloves to Tanner's car. She unlocked it with his key fob, which she had just robbed him of, and tucked the gloves under the seat in the back. He wouldn't find them straight away. Not until he went looking.

Back upstairs she smiled shyly at white-gloves when she topped the stairs, and he bowed his head and smiled back.

Tanner wasn't far away, and he faced the other direction, making it easy to bump into him from the back. "Oops," she said, dropping the keys into his pocket. "Like I said, watch your back."

The night had started off well. She drifted toward the other end of the hall where there was a concentration of men.

Men.

It suddenly occurred to her why the guard had looked surprised at her attendance. She was the only woman in the room.

Without changing her stride, she gazed listlessly around the room. Almost no one spoke to one another. Some of the men looked like they were afraid to be caught with their hand in the cookie jar, especially when they saw her. Others were arrogant, as though untouchable.

A waiter with a tray of wines and champagnes

stopped near her and she put a hand up. "Thank you, but I'm not drinking tonight."

"Would you like a juice or something else?"

"No, thank you."

He moved on to the other guests.

The paintings on the far end had been obscured by so many crowded around them, but now they came into view. She recognized them from her phone. The art show was a ruse. All these men were here to buy girls.

One man in particular stood in front of a painting running a finger down the frame.

"We're not supposed to touch them," came a weaseling voice from a shortish man with beady eyes. He was one with the "cookie jar" look.

"I've already purchased this one. I can do what I like," said the taller man. He was a good-looking man in his fifties, and she recognized him as Robert Carlson. He frowned at the beady-eyed man as though he'd just stepped in dog crap. The beady-eyed man pawed off his comment and moved away to drool over the other paintings.

She couldn't risk taking a picture, but she knew this girl with short brown hair and green eyes. The girl stood out to her among the other paintings when she first looked at them on her phone. She noticed this girl because she looked like she had some fight in her. Bristol hoped the girl would fight till her dying breath. That's what she would do.

Cole's words to *not* engage Robert rang in her ears. She didn't like to break her word, but she was confident he wouldn't do anything here, and she couldn't pass up the opportunity simply because Cole was overprotective.

She sidled up beside him. "Lovely painting," she said, leaning in. Robert was surprised at her presence but hid it quickly. "I'm sorry, I couldn't help but overhear you say you've already purchased it. You have good taste."

His smile made it clear he was used to hearing compliments and had convinced himself that people really meant them. He was a man who didn't care *why* someone complimented him. He just wanted to hear it.

"She does have a certain quality about her," he drawled, while his eyes raked over the painting. "I had another, but it was recently destroyed."

She could have scratched his eyes out right then and there, but she played the game instead. "Fire?"

"Mmmm," he said, noncommittally. "I get to take her home tonight." He said nodding at the painting.

The thing she loved about arrogance is that men like Robert always expected they were winning. It meant that while they thought they was being clever, Bristol was getting the information she wanted.

"Do they let you take the paintings straight off the wall tonight?" She placed her hand on her chest as though in astonishment.

He thought she was impressed. "When they have a customer as respected as myself, they provide certain accommodations. However, there is a touch of preparation that goes into it."

"Gentleman!" came a voice from the side of the room. It was Drake, standing on a small stage. "Thank you for coming tonight. All of the works of art you see displayed here tonight are for sale. Of course I know you're here for my masterpieces." He waved a hand across to the paintings and spotted Bristol. He nodded to her almost imperceptibly. "Some of you have already made your purchase, but please understand we are on a schedule and if you want to take your paintings with you tonight, you will need to wrap things up shortly. Thank you."

She was running out of time. Drake stepped off the stage, and she turned her attention back to Robert. "Do you take it straight from the museum, or do they have a warehouse?" In her haste she hadn't controlled her voice, and she caught an urgency in it she should have hidden.

A hint of suspicion flash in Robert's eyes. He had heard it too. "The paintings are here. Why would they move them to a warehouse?" She shrugged and feigned innocence. "If you'll excuse me." He eyed her and walked off.

In frustration she made a fist, pushing her fingernails into her palm. She still knew nothing.

Moving back across the room, she stayed close to the wall. If the girls were being held here, she'd need to move fast. It was time to get Cole's help. He could get Andrew to bring in the police, and they'd have the manpower to search.

She scanned the room for Robert. She didn't want him to see her making a call. It might raise his suspicion too much. But then she decided it was time to get out of there. She'd be more help on the outside. Her presence here was too obvious.

A cold hand rested on her shoulder. She grimaced before she put on a smile. She didn't have time to fob people off. She turned, ready to excuse herself, but the man standing before her sent a shiver of terror through her. She stood frozen.

Chapter 30

TO GIVE Bristol more time at the museum on her own, Cole headed to the police department to fill Andrew in on what was happening. There wasn't enough evidence for Andrew to get a warrant on Robert's place, but they still had Bristol's reconnaissance mission and maybe the NYPD had a lead.

He hadn't been into the building since the day they escorted him out. Most of the other officers had gotten on pretty well with him though, so turning up, as long as Tanner or one of his lackeys wasn't there, shouldn't be any trouble. He sent Andrew a text to let him know he was there.

The officer at the desk monitored him while he paced back and forth. Cole kept his eyes down and crossed his arms, looking as suspicious as he could to give the guy something to make his evening more interesting.

It wasn't long before Andrew turned up.

"Hey, come through," he said to Cole, then nodded

to the officer. The officer tipped his chin up at Andrew, but Cole thought he looked disappointed. It'll be a long night at the desk.

"Boy, it's been a while since I've seen these walls," Cole said, looking around the office.

"Hey, Sullivan." One of Cole's old colleagues came up and patted him on the back. "Long time, no see. How ya been?"

"Hey, Neeks. Good, thanks."

"I hear you're doing okay for yourself out there."

"Couldn't be better." Cole glanced at Andrew. He didn't know who Andrew had confided in but was smart enough to keep his mouth shut, especially around Neeks. He wasn't a bad guy, but he had a big mouth.

"What brings you back in here?"

"Just visiting an old friend." Cole nodded toward Andrew.

"Well, it's good to see ya. Andrew, you should bring him out for drinks some time."

"I'll do that."

There was an awkward silence and Neeks got the picture. "See you around, Cole." He hiked up his pants and moved back to his own desk.

Andrew crumpled up a piece of paper and tossed it at Cole who batted it into a nearby bin, a game they used to play when they both felt like their eyeballs would fall out from grunt work.

"I got the photos you sent through. Thanks," Andrew said as he leaned back in his chair with his arms behind his head. "You gonna tell me how your lady friend is?"

"Better. This very moment she is attending one of Edward Drake's art shows."

"Our artist?"

"Yeah."

"How'd she manage to get in there?"

"She's Bristol."

"Maybe I should put her on the payroll."

"I have the feeling she wouldn't be interested, but she is helping us out on this case so that's definitely a plus."

"Boy, we lucked out with that one. I'd say I'm a very lucky man that she backed off me. I think I would have been screwed."

"Probably, but listen, I've got more information about your dead girl. I know for a fact that Robert Carlson is involved, and he's most likely your killer. I just can't prove it."

Andrew sat upright in his chair. "*The* Robert Carlson?"

"The one and only."

"Damn. Why can't we prove it?"

"When I was in his building, I saw a painting, like the other ones. But this one was of your dead girl."

"You're sure?"

"Positive."

"If you know it's there, I will find a way to go in and get it." Andrew was ready to leap from his chair.

"I already tried that. He's taken it down so he can replace it."

Andrew fell back into his seat and ran a hand down

his face. "If he's replacing her, at least we know where one of the girls will be."

"I'm hoping Bristol will get something solid. You haven't found anything with missing persons?"

"Not yet. I've sent the pictures out to a few more PD's. The girls might not be locals, or they may have been chosen because they wouldn't be missed."

"That's a possibility." Cole slouched in his chair. "I guess there isn't much more we can do now but wait. This case is driving me crazy. Every time we seem to get a lead, it dead-ends."

"Bristol will find something."

"I just hope she doesn't put herself in danger to do it."

◯◯

"Bristol, my love. You don't know how pleased I am to see you." Silas had sidled up beside her. His smile was controlled and deadly. It was the kind of smile you'd expect a monster to have before eating its prey.

Seeing him there began to solidify her idea that he was involved somehow, but buying a girl for himself seemed a bit beneath him.

Bristol struggled to maintain her own control. "Silas." Her head swam, but her determination to win gave her a boost. "It's been a long time."

"Not as long for me."

"I don't follow." She swallowed and saw Silas's glance down at her throat.

He leaned in and whispered in her ear. "No, but I've

been following you." His breath across her face brought goosebumps to her skin. She was sure he would notice.

He moved back and spoke more casually. "Ever since you worked for me, I've been following you and recommending you to friends. In fact, you did a job for my neighbor just the other night. The dead professor?"

"So I heard."

Silas smiled. "You knew?"

"I found out. I don't expect you were trying to keep it a secret."

"Well, I had hoped to be the one to surprise you with the news. But I should know better. You are too clever. I can't expect much to slip by you. But it doesn't keep me from trying.

"That lawyer friend of yours sure does a good job."

Bristol leaned against the wall and looked out across the room, trying to appear indifferent to his presence, but it was really because she didn't have the guts to look him in the eyes. "Yes, well, thanks for referrals. I wondered why business had been so good lately."

"But I am a tad discouraged."

"Why is that?"

"Because while you do such a brilliant job for my acquaintances, you never seem to do the jobs I hire you for." He paused. "By the way, my wife says hello."

It was a good thing she was leaning on the wall, otherwise she would have fallen.

"Well, she did before I killed her."

Bristol had to take short, shallow breaths. "How'd you find her?"

"It wasn't easy." He laughed. "You are very good at

your job. Unfortunately, it wasn't the one I hired you to do. But lucky for me I always double-check other people's work, and yours didn't quite add up. I can't say I'm surprised. There was always something about you that said you aren't as hardhearted as you pretend to be. It's what makes you so interesting." He ran a finger down her arm. "It worked out for me in the end, like most things. Everyone thought she was dead already, so it made things so much more fun. I got to be the one to end her life, and I could take my time."

"You're a monster."

Silas tsked. "Such harsh words, Bristol. Very unbecoming of a lady such as yourself."

She took a deep breath and lifted her head, pushing the fear from her mind. "So it sounds like you got everything you wanted in the end. You can leave me alone now. I don't need your charity."

"But you see, I couldn't resist the opportunity to work with you again."

The lights blinked off and then back on a couple of times. Bristol looked up at the ceiling.

"Almost time to finish up," Silas said, taking her arm gently.

"I'll never work for you again. You're going to have to find someone else." She was ready to rip her arm out of his grasp and storm out, but at her words, Silas smiled with his mouth open and his eyes closed. He was relishing the moment, and she didn't know why, which scared her more than anything. She tried to pull her arm away from him, but his grip tightened and his eyes sprang open. "So I do get to surprise you after all." His eyes were wide. "Your friend Lila is quite a lovely little girl with that red hair of hers."

She tried to punch him in the face with her free arm, but he was expecting it, and she ended up with both her arms in his grip.

"I think I've left you on too long of a leash up to this point. I'll keep you much closer from now on."

He was strong, but she was skilled and could easily break his hold. But she looked around the room and it was clear she was outnumbered. Tanner was watching from the other side of the room, half his mouth hitched in a grin.

She'd need to use another tactic and stood as dignified as she could with her arms restrained. "If you'll excuse me. I need to visit the ladies' room before we finish up here."

"Of course." He snapped his fingers up in the air toward Tanner, who approached. "Tanner will escort you. Make sure you don't get lost." Tanner strolled over, a big smile on his face. "Take her to the lavatories. Afterward, we will escort her to the *special* sitting room."

Tanner grabbed her roughly by the arm. "I told Silas we should have gotten rid of you the moment I smelled trouble. But as always, he knows better. It's way more fun this way." He sneered, half dragging her toward the bathrooms.

She knew before she entered that there would be no way out.

∞

Cole's phone buzzed in his hand. He had been checking it every couple of minutes, waiting for Bristol to call, but when she finally did, he nearly dropped the phone. "Bristol, how's it going." Cole flicked his hand in the air to get Andrew's attention. When he saw Cole, he sat on the edge of his chair, his full attention focused now on the phone call.

Bristol's voice was shaky. "I'm in trouble. And don't say *I told you so*."

She tried to make light of it, but Cole knew if it was bad enough for her to admit she was in trouble, then it must be bad.

"Where are you?"

"The bathroom at the museum."

"Is Robert there?"

"He is, but — "

"Did you stay away from him like I asked?"

"Of course I didn't, but Cole — "

"I knew he would be trouble."

"Cole, stop. It's not Robert. I mean, he's here, and he's already bought a painting."

"A girl."

"Yes, a girl. But that's it. He's just a buyer. He's not the one in charge, Silas Lincoln is."

"Silas Lincoln?" Cole looked at Andrew. Andrew mouthed the name back then dropped his head into his hands.

"Yes, he's the one who hired me. Remember I did a job for him a while back?"

"Yeah."

"And remember how I screwed him over."

"Kind of, but you never told me the story."

"He hired me to kill his wife. Then I found out how horrible he was to her and that he wanted her dead just because he's a bastard, so I faked her death and helped her escape."

"He found out."

"Yeah, and then found her and killed her anyway."

"Oh man, Bristol I'm so sorry."

"I think he's been following me since then. I found out the other day that he has been giving my number out to people. He lives across the harbor from the last guy I did a job for."

"The girl with the professor?"

"Yeah. When I was there, I saw what looked like someone being forced to go into what I only recently found out was Silas's house. But it wasn't clear enough to tell for certain that someone was in trouble. Now that I know more, I'd say that was one of the girls."

"Okay, we can look into that, but what about right now. Can you get out?"

" … I don't know. He's got Tanner on me, and their intention is to keep me with them."

Cole clenched his fist but kept his voice even. He wanted to run out of there right now and storm the museum so he could smash a few heads, but losing his cool like that would only put her at more risk. He had to keep his mind sharp. "Do you know if Silas has the girls there with him?"

"He might. They've announced that final purchases need to be made so they can make delivery. I tried to get more information out of Robert, but I ran out of time."

"Okay, you stay as safe as you can, and I'll be there soon. I'm just a few blocks away. I can't promise I won't blow your cover, but if the girls are there, then Lila probably is too."

"It doesn't matter, my cover is blown. We haven't got much time, so get moving."

"On it." He flicked the phone off. "We need to get police over to the museum now. They're wrapping it up, and we need to get there before they move the girls."

"Bristol can confirm they're there?"

"No, but it's our best bet right now."

"If I go tearing in there without probable cause, there will be hell to pay. Especially with a guy like Silas Lincoln involved."

"Bristol is definitely in trouble, and she's called for help. Doesn't that give you probable cause?"

Andrew leaned back and wiped the sheen of sweat off his forehead that had been building up. "You haven't told me how Silas fits into all of this."

"Oh yeah, I need to you find out where that girl shot her teacher."

"What?"

"That girl who was assaulted by her teacher, and she shot him on her yacht."

"Oh, yeah, her. Why?"

"Bristol said Silas lives across the water and she thinks she saw a girl being forced into the house."

"*Thinks?* Cole, this sort of stuff is what got you in trouble in the first place."

"Andrew."

"We've got a file on him about a mile long, but

nothing sticks. He's got contracts with the government and a lot of dirt on a lot of people, so they aren't eager to give him a reason to trade freedom for information. We'll have an easier time pinning it all on Tanner than we will getting Silas."

"It's a good thing I'm not a cop then."

"Alright, I'll get you that address. It might take some time though."

"I'm going over to the museum now. Can you get a few guys to back me up or not?"

Andrew threw his hands in the air. "Why not?"

Both men jumped into action. Cole went straight for the door. "I'll see you over there."

Chapter 31

TANNER HADN'T MOVED from his post when Bristol came out of the bathroom. She walked past him like she was ignoring him and headed for the stairs even though she knew he wouldn't let her go.

The room had emptied somewhat. Possibly those who didn't make a purchase were the first to leave. The rest may just be waiting to collect the girls. Cole wouldn't be far, but she didn't know if she could keep herself safe until he arrived.

She sensed Tanner's approach behind her. If she timed it right, she could get in a kick and make a run for it. Thank goodness her dress had a slit.

"Hang on, I have something for you." His voice came from directly behind her. He had reached her quicker than she expected. He grabbed her arm, so she improvised, bringing her other arm around intending to smash him in the nose.

Just as her elbow made contact, she felt a sharp sting in her neck, and everything went black.

Cole sprinted for his car. Every second felt like an eternity. When he reached it, he noted the traffic and decided it would be faster to run. He was a good runner, and it was only a few blocks to the museum. He slammed his hand on top of the car and took off through the traffic. A few horns beeped at him as he zigzagged across the street, then he had to dodge pedestrians as he raced down the sidewalk.

He reached the reception area of the museum and stopped long enough to register the two armed men who approached, reaching for their weapons. He turned, sweeping his foot around and kicked one of the men in the chest then continued his momentum and got the other with a punch to the jaw.

He knocked the second guy out cold, but the first guy was getting up, so Cole kicked him again, sending him sprawling. He could tell they were trained men and would recover quickly, but he didn't have the time to finish them off. Hopefully Andrew wasn't too far behind.

He ran up the stairs, taking them two at a time and emerged into the main room breathing hard and ready for a fight. There were a few men in tuxes milling around who turned to stare at him. One guy looked terrified and skulked his way out of view.

"Can I help you with something, Cole? This is a private party and I don't believe you were invited."

Cole spun around and found himself standing toe to toe with Robert.

∞

When the darkness receded, Bristol tried to move but found she couldn't. She kicked out in response as she lay on her side.

"God dammit!" A gruff voice shouted out. She must have made contact. She got a kick in the ribs for her trouble. "Give me another needle will ya? I don't have time for this." She tried to fight, but it was no use.

Before they stuck her again, she became aware of movement and a rumbling, and it occurred to her, just before she blacked out, that she was in a vehicle.

∞

"Robert. Just the man I was looking for," Cole said, jutting his chin out.

Robert looked past him down the stairs.

"Nobody's coming to help you. In fact, the police will be here soon."

Robert smiled and stepped back. "Good, they'll be able to remove you from the premises."

"Where's Bristol?"

"I don't have the faintest idea who you're talking about."

One big step and Cole had Robert by the collar. "Don't mess with me Robert. Tell me where they've taken her."

Robert pushed him away and brushed down the front of his tux to straighten it. "Cole, I thought you were a reasonable man. You're intelligent and clever, but I'm afraid you've grown a bit delusional."

"I know about the girls."

Robert raised his eyebrows in innocence. "The girls?"

"The paintings. Like the one you had hanging at your office. The one you said was your daughter."

Robert lifted his shoulders. "Your point being?"

"You don't have a daughter."

"You're the one who suggested it was my daughter. It was easier to go along with that than try to explain. I had a busy day ahead of me."

"Yes, I suppose that is simpler than the truth. The truth that you bought that girl and then killed her and threw her on the side of the road. And now you're here collecting another one."

Robert's face went dark. "That's quite an accusation, Mr. Sullivan. I hope you have something to back that up."

"It's only a matter of time till we find the girls. If you cooperate now, they might go easy on you."

"They?"

"The police."

"Oh yes, those police you said are right behind you. Do you play poker, Mr. Sullivan? Because if you do, you should work on your poker face. It doesn't take a genius to figure out you're bluffing."

"You think I'm bluffing?" Cole stepped forward but didn't grab Robert this time. He was walking a fine line, and Robert knew it. He had nothing. Everything hinged on the girls being here, and the way Robert was behaving gave the impression they weren't. "Tell me where the girls are."

"How about I just show you," Robert said, walking past Cole toward the far end of the room.

Cole knew he was playing games and restrained himself, but he felt like a caged bull as he followed Robert.

A man in white gloves was wrapping a painting on a table that had been placed in the middle of the area. "It's ready, sir. Would you like me to have it delivered to your car?"

"Yes, thank you." He turned to Cole and gestured at the remaining paintings. "They're lovely, aren't they? Perhaps next time we can add a painting of this person 'Bristol' that you're looking for." He was smug and Cole snapped. He pulled his arm back intending to break Robert's nose. He'd worry about the consequences later and feel a lot better now. Robert's eyes flicked behind him, and as Cole was about to release his fist, he was grabbed from behind. The guards had recovered.

"Feel free to take him away and do whatever you like." Robert snapped his hand in the air to dismiss them.

If Andrew didn't turn up soon, this was going to get ugly. Cole twisted as the two men muscled him back toward the stairs. He stomped on a foot. The guy flinched but didn't let go. Instead, he punched Cole in the stomach, winding him.

When Cole got his breath back, he stayed folded

over, pretending he was still struggling for breath. Then he twisted around and slid out of his jacket, wrapped it around the neck of one of the guards, yanking him around to use as a human shield, and pulled the guy's gun.

Andrew's head emerged from the stairs, and when he saw Cole, he raced the rest of the way up shouting "Whoa, whoa, whoa." Then he saw the other guard with a gun and pulled his own. "I'm with the LAPD. Everyone put your guns down."

Cole unwound his jacket from the guard's neck and shoved him away. He held up both hands with the gun hanging from his finger. "I was only defending myself."

Andrew motioned to one of the police officers who stood waiting for a command. "Take those guns, will ya?" He pointed to another one. "You — take your team and fan out. Check everywhere." He turned to Cole then. "You don't make things easy for me, do you."

Robert walked up to Andrew. "I assume you're the one in charge here?"

"I am. Detective Turough."

"Then can you please have this man arrested?" he said, indicating to Cole. "He's trespassing and disturbing the peace. He'll be lucky if I don't have him charged with assault. The guards were simply doing their jobs and trying to escort Mr. Sullivan out of the building."

"Robert Carlson?" Andrew said. "Cole is a concerned citizen who has gotten a little overzealous. If you want to pursue his arrest, you will need to file charges down at the station. What I'm here about, right now, is that we have reason to believe there are people being held here against their will."

Robert looked shocked. "That's terrible. By all means, search the grounds. I hope you find whoever is responsible."

Andrew looked pissed, and Cole knew he wanted to punch Robert as much as he did, but Andrew kept himself controlled better than Cole.

"Is Edward Drake here?" Andrew asked Robert.

"Not that I'm aware."

Cole spoke up. "What about Silas Lincoln?"

"No, sorry, you just missed him." Robert curled his lip and Cole tried to grab him again, but Andrew was the one to stop him this time. "See what I mean?" Robert said to Andrew. "If you're not careful, you'll have to put your little guard dog down. Now, if you'll excuse me, my business here is finished." Robert brushed past Cole, clipping him in the shoulder as he went.

Cole was about to follow when Andrew grabbed his arm. "Cole," he whispered. "If you're not careful, I will have to lock you up. If we are going to get to the bottom of this, I need you to be in complete control. And when I'm around, don't hit anyone."

Cole had his jaw clenched but nodded. He knew Andrew was right.

Andrew looked around at the paintings that remained and shook his head.

Cole pulled out his phone and called Bristol. A recorded message said the phone was off or out of service. He didn't expect her to answer, but hearing that message caused another surge of adrenaline. He would need to do something soon, or he'd explode.

Another man, short and stocky, inched past them and took his painting that was now wrapped. "Would you like us to deliver it to your car?" the white-gloved man asked.

"No," he said, eyeballing the police. "I'll take it myself." He inched past them again and headed for the stairs.

"We can't just let them walk out. Can't you find a reason to arrest them?"

Andrew spoke under his breath. "Arrest them for what? Buying artwork?" Andrew put a hand on his forehead. "Have you forgotten everything from your time with us?"

"Bristol's in trouble. They probably have her where they have the girls, but if you let these guys go, we might never get them back."

"What kind of cop do you think I am? I've got surveillance on these guys. I've got someone collecting plate numbers and another guy taking photos of everyone who exits. It's the best we can do under the circumstances. We can follow them up later."

Cole's face went hard. "Later might be too late for Bristol. But you're right. I know you're doing everything you can."

Andrew got a phone call. "Turough here." He listened. "Great, can you text it through to me?" Then he hung up. He was about to say something to Cole when an officer signaled to Andrew as he walked over.

"There's no one here besides these guys."

Cole kicked the wall.

Andrew nodded. "I'll finish up here, thanks." He waited for the man to walk away, then he turned to Cole, whose head was hanging. "I got Silas's address." That got Cole's attention. "I'll text it through to you, but you have *got* to be careful. I don't want to have to arrest you, or worse, put you in a body bag. I have to stay here and clean up this mess, but you obviously don't have to." Andrew sent the text. "Be careful. I'll try to get over there if I can, but I'm not sure if I'll be able to bring backup."

Cole's phone dinged as the address came through. "Thanks." He slapped Andrew on the shoulder and took off.

One of the police officers walked over to Andrew. "You think it's a good idea to let him go?"

Andrew took a deep breath and turned to the officer. "Right now, it's my best option, but that doesn't mean it's a good one."

Chapter 32

VERY SLOWLY, reality came back to Bristol. It started with a metallic taste in her mouth, then came the sounds of muffled talking and something rustling. Light began to seep through her eyelids, and she felt a pain in her neck. She tried to bring her arm up to rub it but couldn't move. She groaned, trying to remember what had happened. Finally, she pried her eyes open by sheer will and blinked against the light. Shifting her body she felt the cold floor beneath her. She was lying on her side, her face pressed into the cold floor.

A figure crouched down in front of her. She could only make out an outline. "You're mine now, Bristol," Silas whispered in her ear. "Let's make it official, shall we?" He brushed the hair off her face, and she tried to spit on him but her mouth was too dry. "I knew it was always meant to be this way, but I had to wait for the right time. You're the kind of woman that is just begging to be owned."

Bristol thrashed around, trying to catch him with her knees, but Silas stood and moved back. "That's good, Bristol. I hope you never fully lose that fighting spirit."

"I'll never stop fighting you, Silas." Her voice was raspy, and she had to work hard to get her words out. "I'd expect you to know me well enough by now to know I would never let you control me."

Silas clasped his hands in front of him and stepped back, that same monstrous smile on his face.

A man she didn't recognize carried over some sort of stick. It looked like a screwdriver, but she couldn't focus her eyes properly. The word *torture* entered her mind, and she struggled to bring her arms up again but it was hopeless. The man grabbed her shoulder and shoved her forward. He pressed a knee into her back, pushing her hard against the floor, then an explosion of pain ripped across her shoulder and she blacked out again.

◯◯

It was the raggedness of her breathing that she noticed first this time. All she could think was to sit still and work out a plan. Her memory of recent events was foggy, but she knew she was in trouble. She breathed slowly trying to keep calm and determine if anyone else was near.

She was sitting now. With her head down, she risked opening her eyes to get a look at her surroundings. Rope bound her hands to the arm of the chair she sat on. She closed her eyes again and focused her energy on listening. There was the sound of light scratching, but she didn't know what to attribute it to. Rats?

She gently flexed her arms and legs against her restraints.

"Careful, or you'll hurt yourself." Came a soft voice across the room. She kept her head down and heard a rustle, then black shoes on the carpeted floor appeared in her line of vision. A hand reached out and rested on her knee. Gold thread was woven through the hem of the sleeve. "This will work better if you'd look up for me."

Bristol didn't move, but the hand on her knee did. Drake lifted her chin with his warm fingers. "You think you could hold it there?" She yanked her head away. "Touchy. Doesn't matter. I always get my way in the end, and Silas has been kind enough to orchestrate the opportunity for me to paint you while he takes care of other business. He's already offered me a lot of money for this painting, but I'm not sure yet whether I'll sell it. I'm becoming more attached to it with each stroke."

Bristol's head was fuzzy, and she still struggled to focus. She pushed against the restraints because she couldn't get her mouth to work.

"Actually, I can work with this," Drake said, hurrying back behind an easel. "By all means keep struggling. I will interpret it into my painting. It's brilliant."

Bristol stopped and finally got her tongue off the roof of her mouth but was at a loss for what to say. A snarky comment came to mind, but he'd just toy with her. She could threaten him, but it wouldn't do much good under the circumstance. So instead, she groaned and dropped her head like it was too heavy for her. She had already given a bit away by struggling but maybe she could salvage it. She lolled her head around as though trying to lift it. Her senses were slow to return, but they were coming back.

There was a knock at the door, and Bristol twisted her head enough to see that it was Tanner who entered. "The boss wants to know if you'll be finished with her shortly." Drake let out a long, loud sigh. "No point sighing for my benefit. I couldn't care less. If it were up to me, I would have shot her and thrown her in a ditch."

"But it's not up to you is it? Why waste a completely good specimen when you can create something wonderful? Not that I expect you to understand."

With her head tipped forward, she allowed herself a roll of the eyes. If Tanner would leave, she could feign a seizure or something and maybe Drake would release her.

Tanner moved out of her vision toward Drake. "How much does something like this cost?"

"You couldn't afford it," Drake said dryly.

Tanner snickered and then walked over to Bristol. She kept her head down and groaned lightly. He jerked forward like he was going to punch her in the stomach, and she flinched. He snickered again. "Thought so. Don't trust her, Drake. She's smarter than you. You've got fifteen more minutes."

He left, and the room and was silent except for Drake's breathing and the scratching of pencil on paper.

"You wouldn't try anything with me, would you Bristol? I could tell by looking at you that you appreciated my art. You act like is disgusts you, but I know it fascinates you. You have a tortured soul that calls out to it and understands it isn't grotesque, it's reality."

Bristol lifted her head. "You don't know me as well as you think you do."

"Oh, no? Silas has told me stories about you. I know all about your deviant behavior."

"Deviant isn't the word for it."

Drake laughed. "Does that help you sleep better at night?"

"Is the fifteen minutes up yet?"

"You were uncomfortable with the idea of my painting you. Wait till Silas gets hold of you. You'll think I'm a saint."

Bristol gave up the pretense of being woozy and took the opportunity to look around the room. There was a heavy drape hanging on one wall, probably hiding a window. It felt like a bedroom, and she wondered if this was Silas's house on the water. If it was, she was glad she had told Cole about it.

She tried to stretch as best as she could. She wasn't sure how long she had been tied up, but it had to be at least several hours. Her muscles weren't going to like it if she got the opportunity to escape.

Pulling one shoulder forward, a spasm of pain shot across her back and she couldn't hold back a gasp.

Drake looked up at her. "That's good. Do more of that."

She glared at him then remembered the screwdriver. She twisted her neck around to see what they had done.

Her skin was red and there was a raw area in the middle. It wasn't a screwdriver. It was a branding iron. There was a raised welt of two circles, connected.

"If it was me, I wouldn't have messed with your flawless skin, but Silas likes to put labels on his possessions."

Bristol wretched and then closed her eyes, breathing slowly to settle her stomach. With her eyes closed, she felt that same dark dream return. But this time she couldn't wake up to escape it. If Cole didn't find her soon, she'd be lost in the nightmare forever.

Before she was ready for it, the fifteen minutes were up. Tanner came back into the room with his gun out. Bristol hadn't gotten a look at his face last time, and she now saw that her elbow had connected with his face back at the museum. His left eye was swollen and bruised. It was a small victory.

"Cut her loose," he said, waving the gun between Drake and Bristol.

"I'm not your lap dog, Tanner," Drake said, folding his arms.

"That may be, but you are Silas's, and I have a gun, so cut her loose before I just go ahead and shoot the both of you.

"Honestly, the things I go through for a cut of the action."

Tanner kept the gun aimed at Bristol's head as Drake removed the rope. When he finished, he jerked away, unsure of what she might do. If her life wasn't in danger, she would have found it amusing and probably would have jumped on him and rearranged his limbs so that they resembled those of his paintings.

"Silas wants you," Tanner said to Drake, then flicked the gun up a couple times at Bristol who rose slowly as Drake left the room. Her muscles were tight and sore. She thought she had her strength back, but the room began to spin, and she had to lean back on the arm of the chair.

"I thought we had already been through this before. Now let's go." Tanner grabbed her arm and pulled her toward the door.

Bristol would have glared at him, but she didn't want to waste her energy. Instead, she focused on moving as best as she could. Her feet were bare, and she was grateful she didn't need to attempt walking in heels. It wouldn't have ended well the way her head was spinning.

It was dark when they entered the hallway, and looking to the right, she saw what appeared to be a living room, and through a large set of glass doors, light reflected off the harbor.

Her head spun then, and she threw her arm up to catch the wall and slipped down it.

Tanner grabbed her and wrenched her up so her shoulder felt like it was being pulled from its socket. "I haven't got time for this," he said as he dragged her along the floor. She tried to gather her feet under her, but he wouldn't give her the chance.

At the top of a flight of stairs he threw her against

the wall and pointed the gun to her head. "You can walk down yourself or I can throw you. Your choice."

She pulled herself up using the railing for support and stumbled down the stairs with the gun pushed into her back. The lights were on down here and they were bright. She followed a wide hallway around a corner to a metal door at the end. Tanner unlocked it and shoved her in, slamming it behind her.

Chapter 33

COLE PUT HIS FOOT DOWN. It was over an hour's drive to Huntington Harbor and that was too long.

His knuckles were white on the steering wheel, and he had to remind himself to breathe, but when the red and blue lights flashed in his rearview mirror, he held his breath to keep from blowing out a string of expletives. Instead, he pulled over and rang Andrew.

Andrew answered immediately. "What's happening? Everything okay?"

"I just got pulled over. I need you to talk to the police officer and tell him to let me go."

Andrew groaned. "I understand you're in a hurry, but you'd probably get there faster if you didn't break the law."

"Come on, Andrew. I don't have time for this."

The officer knocked on his window. Cole buzzed it down and lifted the phone. "It's for you."

"I pulled you over because you were speeding, but

it's also illegal to talk on the phone while you're driving."

"I called after I pulled over. It's Detective Andrew Turough, LAPD."

"Sir, you need to hang up the phone and give me your license and registration."

Cole put the phone up to his ear. "Andrew, you'll have to call it in from your end."

"Now." The officer leaned closer and rested his hand on the gun at his hip for emphasis.

Cole clicked the phone off and put it aside. He gave the cop what he wanted and replaced his hands on the steering wheel to keep things from escalating unnecessarily.

"Stay here. I'll be right back." The cop went back to his car, and Cole rested his head on the steering wheel, banging it a couple of times, then leaned back and let out a long slow breath.

It felt like a lifetime before the cop came back.

"I've been asked to let you go. But I can't give you an escort, so unless you want to get pulled over again, I suggest you drive within the speed limits."

"Thank you, sir."

"And Detective Turough wanted me to tell you that if you get pulled over again, don't call him."

"Fine. Thank you. Have a good night."

Cole took off as soon as the officer was back at his car. It was hard not to speed, but he knew he was pushing his limits with Andrew, who was doing everything he could, so Cole made sure he didn't get pulled over again.

The room was very dimly lit, and after the bright lights of the hallway, Bristol couldn't see. She leaned against the door and listened.

"Bishy?" came a quiet voice from the corner.

"Lila? Oh my god, Lila, is that you? I'm sorry baby, I can't see. Where are you?" She heard movement, and the girl grabbed Bristol firmly around the legs and started crying. Bristol pulled her away lightly then squatted down and pulled her in, hugging her fiercely. Lila pushed against her, and they both fell back against the wall awkwardly, holding each other. Lila sobbed, drawing in sharp bubbly breaths, and Bristol found it hard to hold back her own tears.

"It's okay, sweetheart. I'm here now. I won't let anything happen to you."

She remembered Cole's promise about finding Lila. She had rebuked him, but now she understood how badly she wanted Lila to feel safe and knew that's what Cole had tried to do for her.

Once Lila got her breath back, Bristol scooted more comfortably up against the wall and held Lila in her lap. Her eyes were adjusting, and she moved her hands over Lila's body. "Have they hurt you at all? Are you okay? Did they burn you with anything?" Bristol touched the girl's shoulders gently.

"No. They're mean sometimes, and they have guns that are scary, but they haven't done anything to me but make me eat gross food sometimes, but mostly it's McDonald's."

"So it's not all bad." Bristol smiled, trying to push the fear back for Lila as much as possible. She ran her hand down the side of Lila's face. "I'm so glad you're okay."

"Can we go now?"

"Not yet, sweetheart. They don't want me to go either, but I'm smarter than them and I'm going to get us out of here."

"Okay," Lila said, leaning back against her. Bristol's heart nearly broke at the complete trust Lila gave to her, and she hoped she'd be able to back up her words. Now that Silas had *her*, she hoped, at the very least, he'd let Lila go, but she wasn't convinced that was his plan. And she still didn't know where all the other girls were.

"Hey Lila, have there been any other girls in here with you?"

"Just Gemma."

"Gemma? Where is she now, do you know?"

Lila sat up and pointed across the room. Bristol hadn't even bothered looking at anything but Lila, but now that her eyes had adjusted, across the room she could see a girl huddled in the corner. Her knees were up under her chin and she watched them, not moving.

"When did they put her in here?"

"She was here first."

"Were there more girls here when you arrived?"

"No, just Gemma. She's really sick."

Bristol set Lila aside and stood up. The girl across the room shrank back farther into the corner. "I'm not going to hurt you, Gemma. I'm here to help."

"She is," Lila said, walking over to the other girl and

touching her arm. The girl wasn't afraid of Lila. "She's my friend."

Bristol walked over slowly, and the girl unfolded her arms, linking one into Lila's and leaning into her. It was obvious she had trouble holding up under her own weight.

"Lila, do you know if they've hurt her?"

"I think so. She's sick all the time. Sometimes they take her out alone, and when she gets back, she has trouble sitting up."

Bristol sat down with the girls and took Gemma's arm gently, holding it out so she could look at it. She ran a hand down the inside of her forearm.

"They've been giving you needles?"

The girl dipped her head and looked like she struggled to lift it back up.

"What about your shoulder," Bristol said, reaching up her arm.

The girl flinched. "It hurts," she croaked. Bristol pulled her hand back.

"Were there other girls in here with you before Lila came?"

Gemma shook her head and leaned it back onto the wall.

Bristol couldn't understand why only one girl would be here. They had all the paintings on the wall at the museum, and it would make sense that at one point they would have all been together, even if some of them had been sold off already.

"Gemma, do you know how many days you've been

in here?" Gemma rolled her head side to side on the wall.

"Did they bring you here on a boat at night?"

Gemma thought for a second, then nodded.

"I thought so." If she had acted that night, she may have been able to stop all this. She felt the tremors beginning again and closed her eyes, breathing deeply. She remembered Cole grabbing hold of her when she nearly fell apart, and somehow that settled her nerves. She had to believe he'd come, and she couldn't let these girls down by falling apart now.

"Twice," Gemma said.

Bristol was startled by the sound of the girl's voice, but it helped bring her out of her fear. "Twice what?"

"The boat."

"What do you mean?"

"I came here … " She stopped and swallowed. " … later, they took me out again."

"To where?"

Gemma shook her head. "Just out … then back."

"They didn't do anything to you?"

"No, but four guards. First time … was two."

Bristol closed her eyes, picturing the other night when the boat had passed. The way the scene had played out, it was obvious they weren't trying to hide. It was as if they had wanted her to see it. But that made no sense.

There was a clank at the door, and Bristol jumped up in front of the girls. The door opened, and the light that spilled into the room hurt her eyes.

"Bathroom break," the man at the door said. Bristol shaded her face and tried to get a look out the door at how many guards there were. It looked like three, all armed, which was overkill, but obviously Silas knew enough to take extra precautions with her around.

She stepped forward, and the guy at the front pointed a gun at her. "Just the girls."

Bristol looked at Gemma and Lila, who got up slowly. Lila was helping Gemma, who found it difficult to stand. Bristol wrapped her arm around her and helped her up. "They do this once or twice a day," Lila whispered to Bristol. "We just go to the bathroom and come back."

Bristol put a hand on Gemma's back and rubbed it gently, avoiding her shoulder. As they moved to the door, Gemma's face came into the light and, despite the effect of the drugs they were giving her, Bristol got her first proper look at the girl. She recognized her from the painting at the museum that Robert had bought. She was a beautiful girl, around thirteen, with striking green eyes and honey hair.

"Get moving," the man at the front said, grabbing Gemma roughly by the arm and pushing her out the door. She stumbled and nearly fell but the next guard pulled her up and leaned her against the wall.

Bristol was desperate not to let the girls out of her sight, but this was not the time to make a move. Asserting herself now would work against her.

Lila hesitated to leave Bristol's side, so Bristol touched her lightly on the shoulder. "It's okay, Lila. Better to go to the toilet than have to go here in the corner." She smiled and Lila nodded.

Bristol took a step forward and to the side, memorizing everything about the hallway and the men.

"You can move to the back wall," the guard closest said.

Bristol hesitated, and he grabbed Lila and put his gun to her head. Lila squealed and tried to pull away. Bristol put her hands up and retreated backward until she bumped the wall. "Sorry Lila. Everything's okay."

"Let's go," he said, moving the girls down the hall. The third guard pulled the door shut.

Bristol leaned against the wall for a minute to slow her heart rate. Seeing the gun pointed at Lila had been hard. Especially when it was because of her own stubbornness.

She pushed off the wall and stepped over to the door. Leaning against the wall next to it, she ran a hand down the crease where the door would open.

It would be too dark for the guards to see inside when they opened it. There was no way for them to know where she was. If she waited there when the girls came through, she might be able to swing around and surprise one of them, even with her own eyes impeded by the sudden light. But she knew now what she was dealing with, and once she got ahold of one, she could use him as a shield against the other two. The hardest part would be to get it all done without alerting the rest of the house. It would put them all at risk, especially if they checked the room before sending the girls in, she might need to be a quick shot. She closed her eyes and pictured the drills she had gone through, disarming a man and then shooting. It was far from ideal, but if she didn't do something now, it would soon be too late. Bristol flexed her hands and took a deep calming breath. She was ready.

Chapter 34

COLE ARRIVED at the address Andrew gave him and parked down the block between streetlights in the only bit of shadow he could find. He flexed his hands as he walked to the back of the car and opened the trunk. It was stocked with most things he might need on a job. There were a couple of weapon options. He took what he needed and tucked his gun into the holster at his side.

He jogged the block to Silas's house as though he was just some guy out for a run. In the dark, people shouldn't notice he wasn't dressed for it.

He slowed down as he approached the house, and just as he passed, he bent over pretending to be out of breath.

The house was mostly garage at the front, probably three cars worth, with no windows. A solid wall fence, over twelve feet high, kept him from seeing what was on the other side.

It was a nice-looking house, but not to the standard he would expect from Silas. He felt a shrill of panic pass through him at the possibility that this was the wrong address. And even if it was Silas's place, Bristol might not be here. He pushed the thought from his mind and refocused, turning his head and rubbing it along his arm like he was wiping off sweat to get a good look around at the neighbors. It was quiet.

He jogged back and tucked in behind a hedge to stand out of sight and assess the fence. He had added parkour to his training a few years ago to add variety to his exercise routine, and scaling walls was one of his favorite workouts. But at this height, he'd need a running start.

He took one more look around, then ran away from the wall, turned, and took five leaping steps back over and planted a foot, pushing himself up. His other foot found its mark and propelled him up the rest of the way until he could grab the top of the wall. It was flat on top, and as he hefted himself up, his intention was to sit at the top and see what he could before jumping down. But as he leaned over the top, he saw the head of a guard who was lifting his face to the noise above. Cole let his momentum carry him over onto the guy who had spotted him too late. Cole grabbed him around the neck as he fell and twisted.

The two men lay tangled on the ground, but only Cole got up.

He crept over to a dark window, but found it was covered by a curtain. He moved along the side of the wall toward the back and could hear a boat coming down the harbor. When he reached the corner of the house, he got a clear view of the dock that was lit by the moon that had risen full. There were several men there, armed. One he was sure was Silas.

The boat moored at the dock, and Cole recognized Robert as he jumped from it. He was running out of time.

He scanned the yard for any cover it offered, which was minimal. The moon was great for seeing what was happening, but it meant he couldn't get any farther that way. He moved back to the window and pulled his picks out of his pocket with shaking hands. The shot of adrenaline he had gotten from taking out the first guard was good for action, but not for steady hands. He took a deep breath, confident now that Bristol would be there, although what condition she was in, he couldn't let himself consider. He was doing this for the other girls as well, but he'd be lying to himself if he didn't admit she was the main reason he was there.

He pushed a flat pick into the window jam to jimmy the lock. He was betting on the probability that an alarm wouldn't be armed while people were coming and going.When it clicked open, he paused, but no alarm sounded.

He pushed the window up and climbed through a heavy curtain. The room was empty except for a chair with a rope draped over it, and an easel. He swallowed hard and walked over to the easel, biting his cheek as he came around to face the canvas. The figure on the page was twisted in agony with one arm wrapped around her belly and the other twisting at the wrong angle. Even with the face distorted in pain, he recognized it. Rage coiled in his stomach. Bristol was here, and she had better still be alive.

He pulled a knife out of his boot and slashed the painting, shredding it from existence to the point where he found himself sweating when he was done. He ran the back of his hand across his forehead as he surveyed his destruction, then tucked the knife back in his boot and moved to the door, opening it a crack. He still had work to do.

"One at a time, and if you try anything, remember, we'll kill you first and then her," a voice said.

Cole tipped his head out and saw two girls, one quite young, moving through an adjacent hallway. He pulled his head back just as the man at the back crossed the hall. When they had passed, he moved out into the hall and peered back the way they had come. There was an open door that led down from where the girls must have come from.

Bingo.

He crept down the stairs with his gun ready.

There was a door along the wall, and he opened it to find a closet. He closed it and slid around the corner and saw the large metal door at the end of the hall. He walked up and pulled at the handle, then put a hand to it.

He knocked softly. "Hello? Bristol, you in there?"

There was a small bang on the door. "Cole?"

Cole let out a loud sigh close to a groan. "Thank god. Are you okay?"

"Yeah, mostly … You found me."

He pressed his open hand on the door. "Have they done anything to you?"

"No … well, nothing that can't be fixed."

"I saw the painting and I … I was worried. I destroyed it. The painting."

Bristol was quiet for a second. "Thank you, Cole."

"I'm gonna get you out."

"The guards could be back any minute."

"Yeah, I saw them upstairs. Do you know where they're taking the girls?"

"Toilet break, but Cole. Lila's here and only one other girl."

"You found Lila. That's great."

"No, Cole, I mean yes, but I don't know where all the other girls are. There is only one girl here besides Lila."

"We'll sort that out later. Right now we need to get you out of there. What do you think about this door, think I can break it down? It seems pretty solid."

"No, don't try to break it down, it is solid. You'll have to let them open it for you."

"That's a much better idea. I'll ask them when they come back down."

"You'll ask them," Bristol said dully.

"Isn't that how you do it? But I'll make sure to be polite. Just make sure you're ready."

"I'm ready."

Cole moved back to the closet down the hall and opened it. It was full of shelves with supplies. He looked up the hall and sighed. He hadn't taken notice of the contents the first time he opened it and would have to move quickly. He shoved some sheets to the side and moved some other bits and pieces onto other shelves. There were voices at the top of the stairs.

He folded himself up onto a lower shelf and felt it give way slightly. *Please don't break.* He reached out for the door and pulled it shut nearly all the way using his fingers pressed into the inside to pull it a little farther just as they came around the corner. The shelf cracked under his weight, and he held his breath as though that would make him lighter. Nobody stopped, so he let himself breathe a little. He could feel the shelf sagging further, but he could still hear movement on the other side of the door. He reached up with his other hand and pulled on the shelf above to take some weight off.

When the sounds moved farther down the hall, Cole pushed the door open slightly. Unfortunately, it opened toward the stairs, so he couldn't tell whether anyone was just on the other side, but he didn't have time to waste, and he still had the element of surprise. He sprang out only to find the hallway clear.

He checked quickly around the corner and saw the three guards with the door open and the two girls walking through. This was as good a time as any. All the guards were facing the room, so he stepped out behind them.

"Now!" Cole yelled when he grabbed the guy closest to him. He caught sight of the guard next to the door getting a punch in the face with a nice right hook. He shouldn't have been looking. The guy he was fighting swung his fist into Cole's side. Cole spun around and elbowed the third guard who had come over, obviously thinking Cole was the bigger threat, although Cole wasn't so sure. Then he twisted around and chopped the other guy in the neck.

Bristol pushed the girls into the room to get them out of the way and grabbed the gun off the guard she had just sent to the ground. She stood up in time to see Cole hit one of them in the neck. The guy at her feet started to move, so she kicked him again. The extra guard on Cole grabbed him from behind and Bristol considered helping him, but then he leaned back into the guard, kicking out at the other guy and sending him down the hall, then he flipped the extra guard over his back and slammed him into the ground.

"Not bad," she said. The guard down the hall was out cold. The one at Cole's feet scrambled to get up and have another go. Cole kicked him in the ribs then the head. "You're learning to fight better in small quarters. Good thing you had a little practice at your place." She crossed her arms and smiled.

"This time I wasn't going easy on them thinking it was you," Cole said, walking over and looking her over. She had said she was okay, but Cole wouldn't be satisfied until he knew for sure. She still had on the black dress but had lost her shoes. "You know, if those girls weren't standing there watching, I think I'd be tempted to kiss you about now."

"I thought this was strictly business."

Cole shrugged.

Someone down the hall started clapping, and Cole spun around.

"You are good, aren't you?"

Cole wasted no time pointing his gun at Silas before he had finished his sentence.

Chapter 35

SILAS STOOD with his arms folded as two men, their guns ready, came around the corner.

Bristol turned to the girls. "Lila, Gemma, go back inside the room, up against the side wall." They obeyed, and Bristol shut the door almost all the way.

"You could shoot me," Silas said, "but not fast enough to keep you both from dying before I hit the ground. And then who would protect the girls?"

Cole leaned over to put his gun on the floor.

"Kick it over, please," Silas said.

Bristol was still holding the guard's gun, and she leaned down to put hers on the ground as Cole kicked his away.

"No, not you Bristol. Just hang on to that for now."

She was still leaning over and looked at Cole then back at Silas. "Why?"

"You'll find out soon enough."

She stood back up straight and looked at Cole again. Her arm hung limp at her side, her hand barely holding the grip. She started taking shallow breaths. This wasn't good.

Silas took a step forward. "You got here early, Cole. You keep on impressing me."

"Early?"

"Yes. It shouldn't be too long before the police arrive as well."

Cole's eyes narrowed. Bristol's finger slid to the trigger. She knew that look on Silas's face. She had seen it before on her mom's boyfriend when he realized that he could use Bristol. She wanted desperately to shoot the grin off Silas's face. She would have done it if she were the only one there. Her own death would have been a small price to pay to rid the world of that monster.

"And you think you're going to get off scot-free when the police turn up?"

"Appearances can be deceiving."

"That depends on what they find."

"What the police will find is that I had been visiting my friend across the water — You remember him, Bristol? He's very thankful for what you did for his daughter and would hate for the truth to come out."

"He's your alibi," Bristol said.

"I always keep people close who have a lot to lose. They come in handy." He let that hang in the air for a second before he continued. "Anyway, what the police will find is that while I was visiting him, I saw a commotion over here at my place. I came over with my entourage and asked my *friend* to call the police. When I arrived, I was shocked by what I found." Silas clasped his hands behind his back and rocked forward and then back on his feet. "Are you curious about what I found?"

"We aren't interested in your games," Cole said.

He smiled. "I know. That's what makes this so much fun for me. You've been a part of my plan the whole time and didn't even know it."

"You're bluffing. Making up for your screw up." Bristol nearly spat at him.

"Am I? Where are all the girls you were expecting to find?"

"You've moved them somewhere else."

Silas frowned. "I'm very disappointed in you Bristol. I thought you knew me better. You really think I'm that dull?"

Cole turned and looked at Bristol. She looked defiant but he could see uncertainty clipping at her eyes. He sighed loudly. "So you're saying there never was a child-trafficking ring?"

"Oh no, there definitely was. I made quite a bit of money too. It was a very lucrative business, but part of being a good businessman is knowing when a venture needs to end. And that's why the police will find that when I arrived here tonight, I discovered that two of my associates, Robert Carlson and Edward Drake, have been running a child-trafficking ring. Can you imagine my horror when I discovered what had been going on under my own roof?"

"So your great plan is to frame a couple of guys for your crime? That's not very creative or interesting," Cole said, hoping to buy time. He believed Silas that the police were coming, but the gun in Bristol's hand had him unnerved, and he could see by her fidgeting fingers that she was agitated by it as well.

Silas put his hands on his hips and looked at Cole with mock annoyance.

Bristol spoke up then in clipped tones. "What does that have to do with us?"

"Ah yes, thank you, Bristol. Now we are getting to the good part. Cole, I have been monitoring you for a little while. I was impressed with your work and always thought to use you as a resource someday. Then when Robert accidentally killed his girl and disposed of her in the same place another of his girls had ended up … " Silas pinched the bridge of his nose and sighed. "Honestly, Bristol, at that point I wished I could have hired you to take care of things, but you are a delicate creature that I have to handle with a little more care." He took a deep breath and continued his story. "Detective Turough began investigating the girl, so I looked into him and found the connection with you, Cole. That's when I insisted Robert hire you. I needed someone to lay eyes on that painting in his building, and I knew your police buddy would never get in there. Once I found out about your connection to Andrew, it was a simple matter of getting Tanner to mention you and, I'll be honest, that came together easier than I expected."

"Then why did you try to have Cole killed?" Bristol said.

"Oh, that. That's what happens when you don't give your employees the full story. Tanner went out on his own initiative. I was lucky you were there to keep Cole safe."

Cole started laughing. "You're making this up."

Silas smiled but continued. "Again I will ask, why do you think there is only the one girl? I mean besides Lila. There's only one girl because it was only to frame Robert and Drake. Drake, I've grown tired of, and he's becoming more and more demanding. It was always my intention to set him up. I don't like to leave loose ends. That's why I arranged for him to work here, but when Robert became a problem, I added him into the game. After all, he's the one who made this mess in the first place. He's upstairs now, unknowingly preparing for his own demise.

"All I had to do was pick out a girl I knew he'd go for, and Drake helped me — the idiot — by painting a bunch more and setting himself up in the process. The rest of the men at the art show I just bluffed. But my plan was simpler in the beginning. I only intended on you, Cole, making the connection with the painting and passing the information on to Andrew, but then my neighbor rang for help the other day and a wonderful opportunity unfolded before me. One well-timed boat ride past you that night, Bristol, and you just couldn't let it go."

"But why hire me to set up Andrew?"

"Come on Bristol. You can't figure that out? You are terribly predictable. I knew you'd look into Andrew and find out what a good guy he was." Silas made a face like he smelled something rotting. "It was easier to tell you to frame him so you could pick his side and think it was your idea. I knew if given the right cause, you would inevitably join the other side. Just like you did with my wife. "

"I still don't understand. You make it sound very impressive, if in fact you are the one behind it all, but I can't see why," Bristol said, trying to remain calm. It was a question she was terrified he'd have an answer for.

"I don't do things by halves. It would be no fun to simply bow out gracefully. And besides, I've grown bored with so much money and power. Making a game out of this whole event has been a wonderful challenge."

Bristol rolled her eyes. "You'll never get away with it. You're too embroiled in the whole thing. It's at your own house for crying out loud."

"That was the whole point of having this house. I don't use it at all, but Drake does. This is where he does his portraits. There will be plenty of evidence in the house that I so trustingly let him use. And I have a neighbor who will say whatever I need him to."

One of the guards behind Silas put a hand over his earpiece and listened, then he whispered in Silas's ear.

Silas nodded, then his eyes focused on Bristol. "Just one more thing before we wrap up here. I need you to do something for me, Bristol. We were always meant to work together, you and I, but there were always these issues in the way, so I found a way for you to give in to me fully." He looked past Bristol at the door behind her. "Ask Gemma to come out, please."

She didn't move, and the guards lifted their guns. "I could kill you all right now." He lifted his eyebrows, but then his face softened as if he cared. "Don't worry. I won't hurt her."

Bristol still wouldn't move, so Silas nodded at one of the guards who pushed his way past her while the other guard kept his gun trained on her. Gemma was pulled out and over to Silas. She fell to the ground and huddled against the wall. "I would have picked the little one, but there would be no sport in that because I already know the answer. So, who dies? Cole or the girl? Simple." He nodded down to the gun in her hand.

Bristol looked at it then back up at him. "Are you kidding me?"

"You shoot Cole or the girl, or I shoot them both."

"And what does that accomplish?"

"You've never been able to follow through on anything I ask you to do if you aren't comfortable with it. Now, you will do as I say and forever be mine. Or you all die, and I explain to the police how you were involved and that we had to kill you in self-defense." Silas scoffed. "I can't believe you are making me explain it."

Bristol looked at Cole. He didn't remove his eyes from hers. "You know what you need to do."

There was shouting upstairs. Silas looked at his watch. "Not bad. Come on, hurry it up. I haven't got long because as it will turn out, I only got here as you shot ... whomever. Tragic."

"And you think they'll believe you over me."

"Yes. Because I came in here to find Cole had broken in and you shot him to help me. Or you shot the girl because you were trying to destroy evidence. Either way, I own you."

There were shouts at the top of the stairs. Bristol wondered if there was a way to delay it long enough.

"Now!" Silas yelled at Bristol.

"Bristol, you know what to do," Cole said, staring at her hard. "Just not the face. I'm kind of partial to it."

"Cole, I…"

Silas grabbed the gun from the guard and pointed it at the girl's head. "Three, two…"

Bristol aimed, closed her eyes, and pulled the trigger, shooting Cole in the chest. The sound of the shot blasted through the hall, and Bristol's whole body jolted. She opened her eyes to see Cole collapsed on the ground. With her ears muffled, her head felt as though it were packed with cotton. Gemma was screaming, and police poured into the hall taking guns off everyone, including her.

Bristol just stared at Cole.

Silas gushed his thanks for their quick arrival. "I think he was part of it," Silas said of Cole. A police officer was talking to Bristol, but she couldn't hear him.

Gemma was still screaming and started clawing at Silas as two police officers pulled her off.

"Be gentle with her," Silas said. "I think they've pumped her full of drugs." Then he nodded at Bristol. "She saved my life." He said as the officers checked her for more weapons. Another police officer moved past into the room and found Lila.

Bristol pulled her gaze from Cole and saw that Silas and his men were standing quietly with a police officer who took notes. No hands behind their backs.

"He's got a pulse," said an officer who was checking

Cole. Bristol sucked in a breath too quickly and hiccupped. He couldn't have a pulse. Her shot would have killed him instantly.

A disembodied voice began to speak.

"All I had to do was pick out a girl I knew he'd go for, and Drake helped me — the idiot — by painting a bunch more and setting himself up in the process. The rest of the men at the art show I just bluffed. But it was simpler…"

Everyone froze and looked down at Cole, who groaned as he pushed himself over. He looked up at Bristol and pulled his shirt up showing the vest he had been wearing. Bristol choked out a laugh.

"I only intended on you, Cole, making the connection with the painting and passing the information on."

Cole held up his phone and tapped it to stop. "Officer, I think everything you will need is on here."

Bristol was sure Silas had gone a shade paler, but his face was stoic, and he didn't speak.

Cole pushed himself up off the ground and held his phone up to Bristol. "I'm starting to get what you see in these things. They really are handy, aren't they?"

He handed his phone to the officer in charge, who took it and said, "I think we'll bring everyone down to the station and get this sorted out down there."

"Of course," Cole said, moving over to Bristol. He walked up close to her and put a hand on either side of her face, "You okay?"

She smiled and leaned her head on his chest. "Thank you, Cole. You have no idea … "

Chapter 36

BRISTOL'S ARMS were folded on the metal table in the interview room, and her head rested on her arms. She was weary, but the events of the night meant her leg jiggled rapidly under the table.

Someone had brought her a jacket during her interview with the detective in charge, so she was warm enough. But even though she would be free to go shortly, the process was tiring.

She had altered her explanation of events that led up to the night and was unsure how things would pan out from there but was too tired to care. The most important thing was that everyone else was safe. She assumed they were, but every time she had asked a question, they just said they'd have to find out.

She had been alone in the room for about ten minutes when the door opened. She lifted her head. Andrew was there with a smile on his face. This was her first time seeing him since that night at the grocery store.

He walked over and rested a hand on her shoulder. Bristol winced. "You okay?"

She forced a smile. "I'm hanging in there."

"By the way, my wife says thanks for the ice cream."

"Does that mean I'm forgiven for stealing your phone?"

"It was for a good cause, wasn't it?"

"Not originally."

"From what I understand, I owe you one."

"You don't owe me anything."

Andrew drummed his fingers on the table. "Have they told you anything?"

Bristol shook her head.

"Feel free to ask me," he said as he moved around to sit in a chair opposite.

"Really?"

"Fire away."

She leaned back trying to decide which answers she needed first. "Is Lila back with her dad?"

"Yes. She's at the hospital for observation, but Mick is with her."

"And Gemma?"

"She's also in the hospital, recovering. She doesn't remember much, and she's got a long road ahead of her but she's in good hands."

"Silas hasn't wormed his way out yet?"

"Not a chance. That recording Cole got was priceless. He's got his lawyer, but I don't see him getting away with anything."

"I suppose they have Drake and Robert in custody now too?"

"Not exactly. They were both shot dead."

Bristol shook her head. "I can't say I'm sorry or surprised."

"Word is that Detective Tanner arrived just in time to see Robert shoot Drake. Robert then threatened him, so he shot Robert. If it wasn't for the recording, it would have been easy to frame them."

Bristol shook her head again. "Well, don't worry. Tanner will get what's coming to him."

"I've seen too many guys like him get away with their crimes. I'm not holding my breath. But no point dwelling on that now."

"And … Cole? How's he doing?"

"You can see him if you want."

"Now?"

"Yeah, you want to get out of here?"

"Oh, yes, please." Bristol was on her way to the door before she finished speaking.

"You lost your shoes," Andrew said, getting up from the table.

Bristol looked down at her feet. No one had noticed, and she hadn't mentioned it.

"I didn't really want to wear someone else's old sneakers."

"Good call."

When they reached the front door, he opened it and put a hand on her back as she walked out. It was still dark, but it couldn't have been far off sunrise. "You can hang on to that jacket for now. Just get it back here when you can."

"Thanks."

"You two have a good night." Andrew nodded at Cole, who was leaning against the wall. Bristol hadn't seen him until that moment. They had been separated when they were brought in. She had been eager to see him, but now that he was there, she felt awkward. Andrew waved at the two and went back inside.

Cole pushed himself off the wall and walked over. "How you holding up?"

"I'm all right," she said, fidgeting with the hem of the jacket. "How's your chest?"

"Bruised," Cole said, rubbing the spot. "You warm enough?"

Bristol pulled the jacket tighter around her. "I'll be fine. Just need to find some shoes."

"I still have yours from the other night at the Red Moon in my car."

"Oh, right. I think I'd prefer bare feet to those things." She tried to laugh, but it turned into a shaky sigh.

Cole put a hand on her shoulder. "You're not all right."

"No, I am. It's just … Things could have turned out very different tonight."

"Don't think about that. Everything turned out okay."

"It did, but that doesn't change the fact that I shot you. I mean, what if I had shot you in the face or something?"

"I knew you wouldn't."

"How?"

"You like it too much."

She laughed. "You never give up do you."

"What can I say?"

Bristol frowned. "Cole, when I shot you … when I thought you were dead on the floor, something inside of me shattered."

He put a hand on her face. "I told you to trust me."

She took his hand off her face and shook her head. "Then when I saw you were alive … " She dropped her head for a second then looked up and grabbed the front of his shirt. "Don't do that again."

"What, die?"

"Yeah."

The door opened behind them. "Well, hello there you two."

Cole looked up and groaned. Bristol didn't need to look. "Tanner," she turned, "so good to see you."

"You're both looking well. Cole, it was lucky you had that vest on. That would have been terrible if you had died."

Cole opened his mouth to say something, but Bristol cut him off. "From what I hear you were a bit of a hero, turning up when you did. You probably saved us all." She turned to Cole. "Isn't that right?"

Cole looked at her and cocked his head but said nothing.

She nodded to him as a cool breeze ruffled her hair. "It's getting cold tonight," Bristol said as she wrapped her arms around herself and shivered. "I should have brought a hat."

Tanner huffed out a laugh and pulled a pair of

gloves out of his pocket. "Always be prepared, eh Bristol?"

"Nice gloves," Bristol said, keeping her face deadpan.

"You like these? They were a gift. It's nice when the weather changes and you can pull these things out."

Cole eyed the gloves and bit down hard on the inside of his cheeks.

Tanner wiggled his fingers into his gloves. "Well, I should get going. I've got a lot to do, being a hero and all." He winked and turned on his heel.

"See you around, Tanner," Bristol said when he turned.

Tanner lifted a gloved hand and waved as he walked out of view.

Cole grabbed Bristol's shoulders and turned her fully toward him. "Are you kidding me?"

Bristol shrugged. "I do what I can. It's the small wins, really."

"So those are the gloves. From the drug lab."

"Surprise." She said splaying her fingers out to the side in mock celebration.

"You are the most incredible woman I have ever met in my entire life."

"Careful, I might get a big head. How about I buy you a coffee to keep me humble."

"You mean like a date?"

"Why does it have to be a date?"

"'Cause I like driving you crazy."

"I thought maybe after the gloves thing, you'd be nice to me."A smile slid up Cole's face, and he looked at her under his eyebrows. "Oh, stop it," Bristol said, slapping him on the arm. "Fine, you can call it a date."

"Can I put my arm around you?"

Bristol's eyes slitted. "Don't you think you're pushing it a little?"

"You did shoot me."

"You're impossible." She sighed and looked at him like she was considering it. "Maybe just this once."

He smiled and grabbed her by the waist, lifting her and half carrying her down the stairs. "That's very generous of you."

She laughed like she hadn't laughed in a long time and put an arm around him as they headed down the sidewalk.

◯◯

The End

Enjoy the book?

Book reviews are the most powerful tool I have as an author to grow my readership. If I had the sway of a New York publisher, perhaps it would be easier to gain attention, but a simple reader review is way better than what any top publisher can offer…

Readers like yourself are what make the biggest difference to an author, and if you've enjoyed this book and wouldn't mind spending a few minutes leaving a review, it would help me out immensely.

Also by V F Streets

SMOKE AND MIRRORS (Bristol Kelley Book Two)

Bristol thought she was free when she watched Silas walk
away in handcuffs. But when an important piece of evidence
is thrown out on a technicality, she discovers Silas isn't the
only one who wants to manipulate her.

OUT ON A LIMB (Erin Hart Book One)

For Erin Hart, burglary is a means to an end. She also
happens to be very good at it. But when her brother is
sentenced to decades in prison for a crime he didn't commit,
she risks everything to give him back the life that was stolen.

About the Author

V F Streets is the author of the Vigilante Justice Series. You can find her on www.pgturners.com or feel free to contact her by email at vfstreets@pgturners.com. Otherwise you can connect with her here -

Acknowledgments

Thanks to God for being who He says He is. To mum and dad - you are always so excited about my writing. To Matt and the kids for being interested even if you aren't going to read my books. To Jenni Fry for your proofreading skills and a bit extra. And to many friends who have been encouraging to me on this journey. You've kept my spirits up when I was tired of the whole thing and made sure I didn't give up.